The ,

The Anniversary

Andy Austin's family are killed in a road accident. With a sense of injustice, he becomes obsessed on seeking revenge on the car driver and his three passengers by making each of them suffer as he has. This obsession drives him to kill a relative of each of the men on the anniversary of the accident. As the police and others get closer to catching him the truth begins to emerge, and it becomes clear that not everyone is without a guilty secret.

Also by this Author:

Jack's Lottery Plan

This is the funny and moving story of Jack Burns, just a normal bloke with a simple dream to get a flat with his girlfriend, Hannah, and help her become the great actress he knows she really is. One day he finds out that a friend has secretly won the lottery and is going to share the winnings with his ten best friends. Jack embarks on a clandestine plan to become one of those ten so that he can get the money to help achieve his, and Hannah's, dreams. But his plan goes hopelessly wrong impacting Jack and his friends in ways he would never have imagined.

www.ianandersonhome.wixsite.com/ianandersonauthor

The Anniversary

The Anniversary

By

Ian Anderson

www.ianandersonhome.wixsite.com/ianandersonauthor

August 2020

The Anniversary

Chapter 1
15th December, one year earlier

It had been a fun night out. A good laugh. In many ways, a normal Friday night for the four young men. A few drinks, maybe chat up some girls…or at least try to… and then home via McDonald's for a burger and chips. Or occasionally, if it was the end of the month and they'd been paid, they might splash out on a curry.

The four of them had been lifelong friends and were now all in their early twenties. They'd gone to school and grown up together, and they knew almost everything there was to know about each other. On this particular Friday night, they were all now in Jack's car and he was driving them home. Jack was twenty three and often thought of himself as the leader of the group. It was usually him that did the organising or made the decisions on what they were going to do. Dan was sat beside him in the passenger seat and Chris and Jason were in the back. Dan was a year older at twenty four and quieter than the other two who were both the same age as Jack.

As usual they were having a laugh with each other. A bit of banter. In the last pub they'd visited, Chris had started chatting to a girl and bought her a drink, but just when he thought he was getting somewhere, she'd disappeared. Chris had short blonde hair and he was the joker in the pack, always coming out with some funny comment. His friends were giving him no sympathy tonight though and Chris accepted that this time he was going to be the brunt of their jokes.

Jack had the radio turned up and the music was booming out making the car vibrate like a mobile disco. As was always the case at this time of year it was a Christmas song. Jack was getting a bit bored with them by now, they seemed to play the same ones over and over like you were stuck in some sort of time warp. He was still singing along to it though - it was the Wizard song, *I wish it could be Christmas Every Day.* Jack wondered how much money they had made from that one song – didn't you get some sort of royalty payment every time it was played on the radio? If that was the case then someone must have made a mint. That one and the Slade record – they never seemed to be off the radio.

As Jack was the one driving tonight he'd only had a couple of soft drinks but the other three had all been drinking pints of lager and were in varying degrees of being a bit drunk.

As Christmas was coming up they were all a little short of money and so they'd agreed that it would have to be a McDonald's burger stop on the way home and that's where Jack was now heading. It was a fine, cold night. It had rained earlier but everything had pretty much dried up since then.

Jack knew the road like the back of his hand, so much so he sometimes felt he was driving on autopilot. He came this way to work and a similar route for most of his social activities – which were mainly football and pubs. He'd pass a shop or turn a corner without even realising he was doing it. As he neared the town centre he glanced down at his speedometer to ensure that he wasn't driving above the speed limit. There were so many cameras and unmarked police cars around nowadays that you could get caught anytime, but Jack was always careful and he hadn't been stopped so far. Although it was mid-December the winter had been fairly mild and tonight was no different. The roads were bone dry and there was no sign of any frost.

Chris and Jason were messing around in the back of the car and Jack glanced at them in his rear view mirror, admiring his own newly grown beard as he did so. Chris wasn't looking happy but Jason's face was flushed red, merging in with his ginger hair, and he was laughing hysterically. Jack felt a bump in the lower part of the back of his seat as the two friends grappled over a mobile phone. He laughed and looked in his mirror again. He saw the phone being thrown from one side of the car to the

7

other above Chris's flailing hands and felt another bump in the back of his seat as his two mates wrestled over the phone.

Jack glanced across at Dan. He was sitting silently in the passenger seat apparently lost in his own thoughts and oblivious to what was going on behind him. Dan wore glasses and also had a beard but it was much bushier than Jack's who liked to keep his closely trimmed.

Up ahead Jack noticed a group of people walking along the pavement and he drew level with them as he slowed down, approaching a red traffic light. The group walked past the car and Jack squinted out of his side window into the darkness to get a look at them. There were five people in the group, what looked like an older couple and three men, maybe about the same age as Jack and his mates in the car. They were all wrapped up wearing jackets in a variety of styles and colours and Jack noticed the face of the man nearest to him as it lit up under the glow from the traffic light. He also had a close cropped beard and he was grinning.

A minute later, the lights changed to green and Jack accelerated away. The group were still walking along the pavement about fifty metres ahead, but one of them had stopped and was bending down to tie his shoe lace. He was wearing a red jacket and Jack knew it was the same man who he had noticed a minute or so earlier.

Jack saw him begin to stand up as he got nearer and suddenly the car veered to the side and

8

there was another bump, but this time it wasn't in the back of Jack's seat, it seemed to come from lower down by his feet. He saw some bright colours flying across his windscreen. They were vivid, like fireworks flashing against a dark sky. A red then a blue. He saw them clearly. He was aware of Dan moving forward, his hand reaching out to his left as if he was trying to grab something, his mouth open, as if frozen, and then there were more bumps and a strange high pitched, screeching noise coming from somewhere outside the car.

And then everything went black.

Chapter 2
15th December, one year later

Pete was feeling pleased with himself. He'd done almost all of his Christmas shopping in one go. It felt like he'd done it in record time too and now he was already on his way home. He only had his Mum's present to get but he knew that she would tell him exactly what she wanted - and where he should get it from, probably some sort of perfume, so that wouldn't be a problem. And there were still eleven days until Christmas. Pete loved Christmas, but he hated Christmas shopping and he hadn't been looking forward to today so he was feeling chuffed it was almost over.

He'd got off the bus a few minutes earlier, at what had now become his usual stop. It was the 461, his regular bus for the last few months, taking him in and out of town, back and forward to work. He realised he'd begun to start recognising some of the other passengers, giving them a cursory nod as he walked passed them to his seat, although he'd never actually talked to any of them yet. There were a couple of people that talked to each other but most people just sat silently, doing something on their phones or listening to music through a set of white, spidery earphones. He always sat in the same seat if it was free. Fourth back on the left hand side. On the few times it was already occupied he'd sat in the one behind it. He wasn't sure why but it had become *his* part of the bus.

He was walking the last half mile or so back to his house. It was the house he'd been born and grew up in. A proper family home. The Wilson family home. Four bedrooms, semi-detached. Nice sized garden at the rear where he'd spent many an hour playing with his brothers and sisters. Mainly his two brothers. Lots of football and during the summer they'd switch to cricket. Made a real mess of his dad's lawn, but he didn't seem to care and often joined in with them like the big kid that he often was, He couldn't imagine not living there but knew at some point he'd have to get his own place, get married and all that stuff. It would be nice to have his own place, but not just yet. There was plenty of time for all that. He smiled to himself, still feeling a bit smug at having completed his Christmas shopping.

He began to feel a chill in the air as he walked along the path, but at least it was dry and the path wasn't too muddy. Not bad for December. It was starting to turn dark and the two heavy bags full of presents were beginning to pull on his arms, but he knew it would only be a few minutes until he was home and sitting comfortably in a nice warm house. Feet up in front of the telly with a nice hot cup of coffee his mum would have brought him. The bags of presents lying by the chair.

'I'll put them away in a bit mum, just give me a minute to relax please!'

His thoughts turned to his family as he got nearer home. He wished his brother Jack could have come and picked him up to save him this final walk, especially with all this Christmas shopping. That would have been handy. But he knew that wasn't possible as Jack was still only half way through his driving ban. Pete had found it a real pain not being able to use his younger brother as a taxi service like he used to do. On the positive side, at least it was giving him some exercise and he had actually lost some weight over the last few months. However he also knew Jack missed driving and the family were planning to surprise him with a new car when the time came. Well not new, new. Second hand, but at least something different, maybe something a bit more sporty. A new car would be a fresh start for Jack and the family all knew that could only be good for him. They could all do with something good this Christmas.

Pete turned down a gravel pathway that led to the cut through to the canal. From there he could walk along the towpath until he finally reached the right of way that went up to Leadenhall Drive and his house. Number ten.

Pete was twenty five years old and he lived there with his Mum and Dad, Jack and their young sister Maisy. They had been a bigger family but his older brother, Tom, had left home a couple of years earlier when he'd finally managed to get a job, and his other sister Sarah had passed away just over a year ago. He knew that he should really be looking for somewhere else to live, he was getting too old to still be living with his parents, and he resolved to start saving some money in the New Year.

As he walked along the towpath he glanced back and saw a figure about fifty metres behind him. From what he could see it looked like a man, something about the way he walked, but other than that he couldn't make out any of his features. He thought about waiting to see if it was someone he knew. Not many people used this path unless they were local, and as Pete had lived here all of his life he knew most of them. But as he was carrying two heavy bags, he wanted to get home as quickly as possible and so he decided to just keep on walking. The man might catch up with him at some point anyway.

He turned a bend in the path and looked back again. The man was much closer now. It was definitely a man. He was obviously walking faster than Pete but he still couldn't recognise who it was and so he kept going. At this rate, the man would soon catch up with Pete anyhow. All Pete could make out was someone with a dark hooded jacket, hands in pockets, quite tall but with his head facing

13

downwards, obviously intent on getting home, just like Pete was. It was getting cold.

Pete was about twenty metres from the turning into the right of way when he sensed the man was close behind him, although he couldn't hear him, there was just a feeling that he was there. Suddenly he felt something hit the back of his legs and he fell forward on to his face. It felt like he was falling in slow motion but he was unable to stop himself as his hands were full with the bags of Christmas presents. He hit the ground with a bang, face first, splitting his lip, and the bags spilled out their contents in front of him. He saw the toy rabbit he'd got for Maisy tumble out and land in a muddy puddle a few feet away, a brown stain already beginning to creep across its white fur - and he cried out in anger and despair. At the same time he felt himself being dragged backwards by his legs off the path into the withered grass and bushes that ran alongside it. A pair of hands grabbed him around his middle and rolled him onto his side. He let go of his bags and then he felt a sharp pain in his midriff as he was kicked in the stomach by a heavy boot. As he gasped, he felt another kick, this time to his groin. He tried to cry out but couldn't get any breath. His mind was racing, he couldn't understand what was going on. This wasn't right. What was happening? He was almost home. This *was* his home. Another kick came, this time to his face and he heard a cracking noise as his nose broke and blood ran down into his mouth. Instinctively he threw his hands up to cover his face from another kick and he coughed as the blood in his mouth started to choke him.

He started to try and get up but a hand pushed his face back down into the grass and dirt and he couldn't see anything again. He couldn't breathe. He felt the man's hot breath on his ear as he leaned in close to him and then, for the first time, he heard the man speak.

'Do you know what today's date is Pete?' the man asked - but he didn't wait for a reply and carried on talking, still pressing Pete's face into the ground. Pete was trying to swallow but his mouth was full of blood and dirt.

'It's the fifteenth of December. Remember that date. Jack and the rest of your family will. They'll never forget it. Neither will I,' he said grinding out the last three words as if to emphasise their importance.

Who is this guy, thought Pete, what does he want and how does he know Jack? Lots of questions were shooting around in his head, all in a split second. None of it made sense. He tried to push his head up so he could speak. He needed to ask some of the questions. He wanted to see who this man was. The man pulled his hair sharply, forcing his head up and backwards allowing him to take a gulp of air but before Pete could say anything he briefly saw something bright and silvery flash across his face and then there was a sharp pain in his throat, like he'd been stung.

His eyes were locked on Maisy's toy rabbit and he could see it getting darker and darker as the muddy water seeped through its fur. And then the water began to turn from brown to red. He felt desperate. He tried to reach out for the rabbit, he had to rescue it for Maisy, but his arm wouldn't move. He felt like he was drowning - but there was no water. He tried to gulp and cough, but he'd lost control and nothing happened.

Chapter 3

His name was John Davies although everyone who knew him called him Junkie John. Not many people *really* knew him though. Not many people knew the real person who'd been born John Albert Davies the one who'd had a life before it had been taken over by drugs. Heroin mostly but sometimes anything would do.

John Davies was twenty seven years old but he looked a lot older than that. His face was sunken and grey. His hair straggly, unkempt and thinning. His loose fitting clothes hanging from his ravaged body. But somehow, despite it all, despite all the drugs, he had survived.

He hadn't always looked like this though, in fact the first twenty years of his life had been pretty normal, if there was such a thing nowadays. Along with his brother Jamie, he'd been brought up by his mum after his dad had left them when he was born. His mum said they were better off without him and as John had never known him he didn't really care that his dad wasn't there. John had left school and got himself a decent job working for a plumbing

17

firm where he was learning the trade and would soon be a fully qualified plumber. Then not long after he'd turned twenty, his dad reappeared. He just turned up at the house one day, twenty years after he'd gone, as if he'd just popped out for a newspaper. John had been the only one in the house when he'd arrived and his dad had turned on the charm and persuaded him to go out for a drink with him where he said he would explain why he left and what he'd been doing since.

Over a few pints he told John how proud he was of him and how he'd been keeping track of everything he'd been doing over the years as he grew up. He told John a few stories of what he'd been doing – most of which seemed to involve him working in various places overseas. After a few more pints he'd asked John if he had any spare cash on him as he'd left his wallet at home. It was only then that John realised he'd bought all the drinks so far but he was happy to show his dad that he still had fifty pounds in his wallet. His dad smiled, drained his pint and stood up telling John that there was someone he had to meet and John should come along too. "*I want to introduce my boy.*" John remembered were his exact words and John couldn't remember when he last felt so happy. They'd walked a short distance from the pub, John's dad leading the way down several side streets until he stopped outside a house with a ramshackle wooden gate. John had asked him where they were and his dad had said a friend lived there. John remembered thinking the garden needed a bit of tidying up as his dad led him to the front door. He knocked on it once and pushed it open, walking into a dimly lit hallway. He beckoned John to follow him and as he did so John stumbled slightly catching his foot on the doorstep. Oops, he thought, maybe I shouldn't have had that last pint but he kept on going following his dad through a door into a room on the right of the hallway.

This room was dimly lit too and the curtains were closed and there was a strange, dusky smell. As John's eyes adjusted to the lack of light he could see that there were three men sitting on a collection of mismatched sofas and armchairs all of them smoking and drinking from cans of lager. John remembered noticing that they all had straggly beards. They'd all greeted John's dad like an old friend and one of them handed him a can which he opened and greedily took a long drink before passing it back to John. John took a gulp of the lager and they both sat down on an empty sofa. One of the men passed a cigarette to John's dad and he inhaled it deeply, blowing it out slowly. He did the same again and then passed it to John.

Looking back John knew that it was weed, even though he'd never smoked it before, and he copied his dad taking a long draw on the cigarette. It tickled his throat and made him want to cough but he managed to supress it and took a second smoke before passing it back to his dad. He felt good. It was great just hanging out with his dad.

19

Later that night his dad introduced him to another friend. He was called Heroin and after that John's life was never the same again.

Now he was walking along the towpath, not going anywhere in particular. Just walking. It was a path he used quite often. It was quiet and it was somewhere you could just sit and have a smoke without anyone disturbing you. Today though, he wasn't here for that. He was skint and didn't have anything to smoke. He was just walking to take his mind off things. To take his mind off how he was going to get his next hit. He was walking slowly with his hands buried deep in his pockets, shivering, when he noticed something by the side of the pathway up ahead. As he got nearer he realised it was a man. Probably a junkie or an alkie sleeping it off, he thought. As he drew level with the man he saw that he was lying there with a couple of bags of stuff spilled out beside him. He noticed a brown toy rabbit lying in front of the man's head. He looked young but his face was muddy and red. He nudged the man with his foot but he didn't move. He looked around but there was no-one else in sight. It was dark now and he knew not many people came down here at night. He crouched down and felt in the man's pockets and pulled out a wallet. He quickly looked inside and saw that there were some notes and a couple of cards. He stood up again and slipped the wallet into his own pocket before turning and walking quickly back the way he had come.

Chapter 4

'Who found the body?' asked Detective Inspector Strong, standing on the path looking around taking in the scene. He stretched his back, extending out his six foot frame. Strong was in his late forties, rapidly approaching fifty, but he had kept himself pretty fit. He had always been slim, one of those people whose metabolism seemingly allowed him to eat whatever he wanted without putting on any weight. He had been an active sportsman in his younger years but a combination of his age and his workload had limited that now to maybe a few games of tennis a year.

It was a bright day and the sun was dipping down towards the horizon, soon to disappear. Strong was thinking how peaceful the canal was and how he'd always imagined living somewhere by a river, or perhaps the sea. Getting up in the morning and going for a walk along a quiet beach with just the sound of the waves to accompany him. Maybe he would do that when he retired, if that day ever came.

'A woman out walking her dog, lives on the same estate, Leadenhall, she recognised him. She's pretty shocked,' his assistant and trusted right hand man, DS Campbell replied. Campbell was a few years younger than Strong and they had been working together for the last four and a half years. Strong liked him, he could be a bit impetuous at times but he was never afraid to voice his ideas or opinions and that was what Strong wanted from his team. Strong had taken it on himself to develop Campbell, help hone his natural instincts and support him in the path to promotion to a Detective Inspector role at some point. But not just yet, Strong hoped, he needed him now.

Strong could imagine the woman being shocked at finding the corpse. He had seen a few dead bodies himself over the last few years and knew the immediate horror and confusion of finding a lifeless human being. The body was often apparently whole, the same features, seemingly all there, but unmoving, like a perfect waxwork model. The feeling of seeing a dead body never went away. The first couple of times he felt that he could just reach down, give them a shake and they'd wake up, it looked like they would. But now he knew differently.

'Do we have a name yet?' Strong asked his colleague.

'Yes, his name is Peter Wilson, lives on the…' Campbell started before Strong interrupted him.

'Did you say Wilson?' he asked, '*Peter* Wilson?' emphasising the first name.

'Yes that's correct,' Campbell replied glancing down at his notebook to reassure himself that he hadn't got it wrong.

Campbell told Strong what they currently knew. The man had been identified as Peter Wilson, twenty-four years old, single and lived with his family nearby. He worked for a local Insurance company as an Administrative Assistant and had no previous police record. The Police forensic team, or SOCOs, as they were more commonly known in the police, were working on the crime scene. It had been carefully taped off with a couple of iron spikes and some blue and white police tape to stop any unauthorised persons entering the area and possibly spoiling any evidence they might find. It didn't look like too many people came this way anyhow, maybe a few dog walkers or joggers, thought Strong.

The SOCOs initial, *don't hold me to it*, estimate was that the victim had been killed the day before, probably late afternoon and had lain overnight, partly obscured by the long, wintry grass and a couple of thorny bushes, until the lady with the dog had come across the two bags and then, unfortunately for her, the lifeless body of her neighbour Peter Wilson.

'Had he been reported missing?' Strong asked his colleague.

'Not to us,' Campbell replied, 'the family were concerned he hadn't come home last night but with him being a single lad and all that they just thought he'd hooked up with some mates or a girl

23

for the night and that he'd reappear sometime today.'

'Unfortunately not,' Strong replied, kicking a round stone into the canal and watching the ripples expand out across the dark water to the far side and rebound back from the opposite bank, colliding mid-stream and destroying the peaceful symmetry of the water. He looked up again and imagined himself sitting on the opposite side of the canal with a fishing rod in hand and a flask of coffee at his side. Maybe one day, he thought to himself.

The two policemen walked a few metres further along the side of the canal and Campbell filled Strong in on the rest of the detail as far as they knew at this point. It looked like the victim had been attacked from behind, beaten up, he had bruising on his face and body, and then he had his throat cut with a sharp blade, probably a knife, but no weapon had been found yet. The likelihood was that it had been dumped in the canal, which would have largely destroyed any forensic evidence there might have been. If they found it.

The motive wasn't clear either. It could have been a straightforward mugging but the victim's Christmas shopping was still lying beside the body and his keys and other personal possessions had been found in his trouser and jacket pockets. He'd also been wearing a watch and ring neither of which had been taken. The only thing they hadn't found was a wallet, which considering he had been Christmas shopping, they'd expected he would have had.

'Strange that,' Campbell said, 'why just take the wallet and why kill him, not your usual type of mugging.'

'Anyone have any ideas yet on why someone would want to kill him?' asked Strong, looking around at the team of police assembled there. He had a strange feeling about this one. Was it the start of something?

'Not really, we haven't found anyone that saw either Wilson or his killer yet. He'd got off a bus and was walking along here on his way home, been doing his Christmas shopping,' and they both looked across to the two bags of presents still lying where they fell.

'We've had an initial discussion with the family,' Campbell continued, 'but they couldn't think of anyone who'd want to harm him. It's come as a big shock to them and they're obviously very distressed. He seemed a fairly normal lad, no record of him being into anything dodgy at all. We're awaiting the SOCO boys to finish up but so far they haven't found anything significant. Certainly no murder weapon, but, as we said, the obvious place to throw that would be the canal and that'll take a couple of days at least to search. Even then we'd be lucky to find it unless he threw it straight in here,' said Campbell looking down into the dark water. Strong followed his gaze and tried to see to the bottom of the canal but it was too dark and deep and

25

all he could see was his own face frowning back at him and the grey hairs he knew were beginning to show through in his sideburns.

'Okay, it'll be getting dark here soon. Let's do the usual. Interview family, friends, neighbours, see if we can find out any reason why someone would want to kill this poor lad. See if anyone saw anyone around his area. We need a motive. Someone will know something. I'll call a meet back at the station at,' Strong looked at his watch, 'four thirty. We can go through everything then. See what we've got and get a formal case set up.'

And so it starts, he thought. He folded his arms and leant over the canal edge, looking down into the gloomy water and wondered if there were any fish hiding in there. Maybe if they could talk they could tell him what had happened and why. Why had a young man's life been so brutally ended? Having worked in the police for so long he knew there was the rare occasion where there was no logic to these things. People could just happen to be in the wrong place at the wrong time, but that was still the exception and he felt sure they'd find some reason for this violent murder. He had another quick look around the murder scene to refresh the picture in his mind and then strode off back to his car.

Chapter 5

Lucy was excited, but also pretty nervous. She'd applied, and re-applied, her make-up three times already and she was staring at herself closely in the mirror again. It looked okay, she thought but maybe she needed to curl her hair a bit more? She turned her head to the side and back again. Doesn't look too bad, she thought. She turned her head once more, looking again. She liked the lighter highlights her hairdresser had put in. They gave a bit of contrast to her naturally brown hair. She'd always felt her nose was a bit bigger than she might have wanted it to be though. If she'd been more vain, and won the lottery, she might have considered doing something about it, but that wasn't her really. All in all I don't look too bad for a twenty seven year old, she thought.

Not that it particularly mattered how she looked today as she was only going to visit her mum and dad and they wouldn't care one jot, they'd just be pleased to see her. They'd seen her at her best and worst and everything in between. But she so wanted this day to work out well, she wanted everything to be right, so she checked herself in the mirror one final time, again. Although it was winter she'd decided to wear one of her summer dresses, which she knew her mum would approve of. It was a long light blue dress with a white flowery pattern.

The reason Lucy was feeling so nervous today was that her boyfriend, Paul, was going to be meeting her parents for the first time and she wanted them all to get on. Of course she knew they would. Paul seemed to just get on well with everybody. He was so charming - which of course was one of the reasons she was now living with him. He was also funny, good looking and clever, not a bad catch Lucy thought, smiling to herself.

She was still a bit surprised with herself that they were living together though - that had been a big step for Lucy. She'd had boyfriends before, a couple of them serious, but she'd never really thought of moving in with any of them. Paul was her first in that respect. She'd worried about whether she was doing the right thing but it just seemed natural. He'd moved into her flat a few weeks ago and so far everything had been going really well. No underpants on the floor, the toilet seat always down, he seemed to be pretty well house trained – it was all good.

'*Are you sure?*' her mum had asked her, when she'd told her of her plans, '*he sounds nice but you haven't known him that long darling.*' But how long did you have to know someone before you started living together? There were no rules. Her girlfriends had said '*you just know, it's a feeling.*' Although in truth some of *their* track records with men weren't that great. But Lucy knew she had that feeling. Or at least she thought she did!

Once they'd made the decision, the whole process had been really easy. Paul was only renting a place and so it made sense for him to move into Lucy's flat. He didn't own much stuff either so the day of the move itself was really easy, Paul had brought everything over in his car in just a couple of trips. Lucy had hardly had to give up any of her wardrobe or drawer space. Paul was certainly not a big possessions man and the two of them fitted into Lucy's flat perfectly. Since then, living with Paul had certainly had a positive impact on her confidence generally and more specifically in their relationship. Things were looking up and Lucy felt happier than she could remember for a long time

Lucy left the bedroom, with a final, final glance in the mirror on her dressing table, smoothing down her hair as she went. She walked through to the lounge and found Paul sitting there on the settee, as calm as ever, waiting, one leg crossed over the other. He was wearing a pair of black shoes, black jeans and his favourite pink shirt. Dressed but not too dressy, just right to meet her parents. Paul was twenty-eight and good looking, or at least Lucy thought so. She liked that he was clean shaven, so many young men had beards now and they looked good, but for Lucy beards always brought back childhood memories of her grandad's

29

prickly kisses which still sent a shiver down her spine. Like Lucy, Paul also had brown hair, darker than Lucy's but thankfully with no highlights! He was a couple of inches taller than Lucy which was ideal in her eyes as it meant she could wear heels without making him look short.

'You look nice,' he smiled as she walked towards him, 'I love the dress. Are you ready to go?'

'Yep,' Lucy replied smiling, and she picked up the car keys from the wooden coffee table and tossed them across to Paul who caught them one handed as he stood up. They left the flat and walked towards the car holding hands as they went.

Around an hour later they arrived at Lucy's parent's place. It was a white semi-detached house with dark wooden window frames and a small, tidy front garden to the left of the gravel drive where they pulled in and parked the car. Her mum spent a lot of time in the front garden making sure it looked neat and tidy, befitting of the neighbourhood they lived in. The street was quiet today, there was no-one around, but there were quite a few cars parked in the road. More than Lucy remembered from her childhood. The whole area had got a lot busier over the last few years with most households having two, three or even four cars sat outside their houses. It was a cold day and Lucy guessed most people had decided to stay inside their nice warm homes rather than face the low temperature outside.

'Are you sure, you're okay?' Lucy asked Paul for the fifth or sixth time. 'Remember just be yourself and don't let my dad get you sampling his whisky – he doesn't need any excuse, but he doesn't know when to stop.'

'Don't worry,' Paul laughed, 'it'll be fine, I promise you. I'll go easy on the whisky. When have I ever let you down before?'

Never, thought Lucy, smiling, but that also niggled her sometimes. Could this man really be so perfect? He certainly seemed to be up till now. They got out of the car and walked up to the blue front door Lucy knew so well. It had a large, silver number twenty eight half way up it with a matching knocker just underneath. This was the house Lucy had grown up in. She still felt a bit strange pulling back the silver knocker and knocking now, instead of just walking straight in like she used to. But she had been gone almost three years and had her own place now. She had literally moved on.

Her mum had seen them coming and quickly appeared at the door smiling widely. After the usual hugs and kisses with her daughter, she turned to Paul.

'Now then, I guess you must be Paul. Welcome, to our house, I've heard a lot about you, all good,' she said holding out her hand and smiling. She was a good looking woman who obviously took pride in caring for herself as she got older. Every week she attended an aqua aerobics class at the local leisure centre and she was also a member of a small

31

choir which met every Thursday evening in the local church hall.

'It's lovely to meet you Mrs Morris,' Paul replied shaking her hand and offering her a bunch of flowers they'd picked up from a florists near Lucy's flat. They were a mixture of bright reds and yellows, which was about as much as Paul knew about flowers. As he handed them over, he could see the similarity to Lucy in her Mum's face. She was shorter than Lucy and her hair was greyer but they shared the same radiant smile.

'Oooh, lovely,' Mrs Morris replied, 'these are super and, please, you must call me Jean. Come in, let's get out of the cold,' she said standing to one side to let them through, 'I love your dress Lucy.'

Lucy smiled and the three of them entered the house and walked along a light brown, carpeted hallway with a staircase to the right before turning into the first door on the left which was the sitting room. Lucy's dad was already in the room, sitting in a brown leather armchair. He immediately got up and walked towards them, taking his glasses off and giving Lucy a quick hug and kiss on the cheek. He shook hands with Paul and they briefly introduced themselves to each other. Lucy noticed that Paul and her dad were of a similar height and build which somehow gave her a nice feeling. They all sat down, Lucy, her mum and Paul all together on a large brown settee with Lucy in the middle and Lucy's dad sat in his matching armchair opposite. Lucy smoothed down her hair at the side and rested a hand easily on Paul's leg.

'Are you warm enough, you two?' Lucy's mum asked. 'I put the heating on a little while ago but I didn't realise how cold it was outside until you arrived. I can put the fire on too if you want?'

They all looked towards the coal effect gas fire in the middle of the far wall and Lucy spoke.

'No, we're fine mum. It's warm enough, don't worry.'

They spent the next hour discussing the journey, the weather and other non-contentious subjects while drinking tea and eating digestive biscuits. Lucy relaxed, seeing it was all going well. Paul was getting on famously with her dad and her mum seemed equally impressed with her daughter's new boyfriend.

'So I hear you're writing a book Paul,' Lucy's dad said, 'what's it about?'

'Well, it's a sort of crime thriller, I guess,' Paul replied. 'I'm only part way through it though and I still have a fair bit of work to do before it's complete.'

'Sounds interesting,' Lucy's dad replied, 'Is it like that Midsomer Murders thing on the telly? I'd hate to live there, they must have the highest crime rate in the country!'

'Haha, no,' Paul laughed, 'although it would be good if it could make me that sort of money.'

33

'I always wanted to write a book,' Lucy's dad carried on, 'but I've never got around to it. I probably don't have the patience. I think it would take me a long time and I'd probably give up at some point. Have you written anything before Paul?'

'No, not really, it was just an idea I thought of a year or so ago and I decided to give it a go. You know what they say, everyone's got a book in them - so I thought I'd try and get mine out. I've got no great expectations of it selling or anything but it's quite good fun writing it. I find it a bit cathartic in a funny way but it does take time as you say and I find I need to be on my own to be able to focus on it. I spend a bit of time sitting in random cafes and the like,' he said smiling at Lucy.

Paul went on to explain that his Aunt had died and left him some money which had enabled him to give up work and concentrate on writing the book. If it didn't work out in the next year or so then he would probably go back to work but at least he'd know he'd given it a try.

'Well good for you,' Lucy's mum chipped in, 'Do you want some more tea? At least you're giving it a go, a lot of people don't and live to regret it and I'm sure it will be really good. I'll look forward to reading it, perhaps on my summer holiday,' she laughed. 'What's it called, do you have a name for it yet?'

'I'm okay for tea, thanks. Emm, I'm thinking of calling it The Anniversary,' Paul replied.

'Ooh that's funny we were just talking about *our* anniversary, weren't we Dave, it's our Silver one next year.'

'Oh, congratulations, how are you going to celebrate it?' asked Paul.

'Well, we're not sure what to do yet. Dave wants to have a big party at the Social Club but I think I'd rather go away somewhere, just the two of us, maybe a cruise. Dave thinks cruises are just for old people and I say yes, that's us!'

'Oh you're not old, anyway I'm sure whatever you do it will be great fun,' Paul replied, laughing.

'It'd better be, twenty five years is a long time,' Dave chipped in. 'Where do your parents live Paul, are they local?' he asked, changing the subject.

'Oh they em, …I'm afraid they're no longer around. They both died a few years ago.'

'Oh, I'm sorry to hear that Paul, really sorry,' Jean replied.

'That's okay, I don't really like to talk about it much,' said Paul.

'Of course not, bless you,' Jean replied. 'Let me fill you up Dave,' she said reaching across to her husband, teapot in hand.

The room went quiet for a few moments, then Dave suddenly piped up.

'Do you like whisky Paul? Of course you do' he said not waiting for the answer. 'I've got some fine malts we should try' and he got up from

his seat and walked towards the wooden drinks
cabinet in the corner of the room.

'Remember not to drink too much,
especially with your headaches and the tablets
you're taking,' Lucy whispered in Paul's ear.

'Don't worry one or two probably won't
make much difference,' he replied smiling back at
her.

Lucy and her mum took the opportunity to
leave the men to their whisky and picking up the
empty tea things they walked through to the kitchen.
It was a large modern kitchen with a cream coloured
island in the middle of the room. They'd got it done
just before Lucy moved out and Lucy loved it and
wanted to have something similar when she was
able to buy a bigger house. Her flat was only large
enough for a rather small kitchen in comparison.
And certainly no island.

They quickly stacked the dishwasher with
the tea things and sat down on a couple of high, red
bar stools adjacent to the island.

'Paul seems a lovely guy Lucy,' she said to
her daughter. Already he seemed a big improvement
on some of the previous boys, or men, she had dared
bring home. Not that there had been that many, two
or three at most that Jean could remember. She'd
opened a bottle of wine from the fridge and poured
two glasses for herself and Lucy. '*Just a small one
for me, mum, I'm driving.*'Lucy had said. Jean took
a sip of wine before adding,

'Is everything going well now that he's moved in with you?'

Lucy took a sip of her wine before answering with a smile.

'Haha, so that's why you've cornered me in here mum,' Lucy laughed, 'you're going to interrogate me are you?'

'No, no,' Lucy's mum replied, 'not at all. You just seem very happy and he seems to be a very nice young man. Very good looking. Dare I say it much better than your last one.'

'Yes he is mum. I'm really happy with Paul. I know you didn't like Robert and you were probably right but that's all in the past now.'

'I'm glad to hear it,' Lucy's mum replied, 'cheers to that,' and they clinked their glasses together.

Lucy's previous boyfriend, Robert, had never really hit it off with Lucy's mum. The first time they had met was in a restaurant and he'd joined them straight from watching a rugby match in the pub with some of his mates. He was a big man and he'd been a bit drunk, too loud and overly friendly for Lucy's mum's taste. Robert was a very extroverted character and Lucy had some great memories of nights out with him and their friends where he just took over and entertained everyone for the evening but gradually it began to become too much for Lucy. Robert began drinking more and more and sometimes it would get out of hand. There had been a few occasions when they would have to leave places as he was annoying other customers - and other times when she'd had to help him into a taxi and almost carry him up the stairs to his front door which wasn't easy with him being such a big guy. Eventually she started making excuses for not going out with him but he didn't seem particularly bothered by that time and would just go out with his mates and get hammered regardless. After a few weeks, he stopped asking her out and their contact got less and less as they just drifted apart without there being any formal break up. When Lucy told her mum they weren't seeing each other any more she could tell that her mum was secretly pleased but of course she played the sympathetic mum, consoling her only daughter.

'And he's a writer, that's different. Do you think his book is going to be a good one? It must be exciting,' Lucy's mum asked her.

'Well, I don't know,' Lucy replied. 'He's very secretive about it. He hasn't told me much, in fact what he's said today is probably the most I've heard him talk about it. I didn't even know what it was called before he told you. The Anniversary, wasn't that what he said?'

'Yes I think that was it or was it The Wedding Anniversary?' Lucy's mum replied. 'Don't you see him writing it though – where does he do it?'

'No, its funny I don't. I've never seen him writing, although he obviously does. He either writes it in the flat when I'm at work or he often seems to go out and work in cafes. He says it gives him inspiration. He says he can't do it when I'm around. He says I'm too much of a distraction,' Lucy said feeling herself begin to blush.

'Oh, haha, that's a good one. He's a real charmer isn't he!' Lucy's mum exclaimed laughing as she took another sip of her wine.

'Shh..mum, he can probably hear you,' Lucy chastised her mum and they both glanced towards the room where they could hear the low murmur of the two men's voices.

'I hope dad doesn't force him to drink too much whisky,' she said, 'he's had a few headaches lately and its probably not the best thing for him.'

'Oh don't worry, your dad is all bluster, he can only manage a couple himself before his eyes start closing. I just throw a blanket over him, saves him interrupting me when I'm watching Emmerdale,' she laughed.

Lucy smiled at the thought. She'd loved growing up here and couldn't have wished for anything better but she'd also known when it was time to leave and get her own place. It would have been too easy to keep living with her mum and dad, getting everything done for her but equally she needed her independence. Besides she thought it sounded a bit weird when she met people who still lived with their parents. *What, youre thirty next year and still living at home?*

They spent the next half hour just chatting, Jean bringing Lucy up to date with all the latest local gossip. '*Do you remember Tom and Jane Harrow at number fourteen? Well Annabelle, their youngest has just had another baby. Her third I think and Debbie Morton says they've all got different fathers. I think she was a couple of years behind you at school.*'

Their catching up on all things local was interrupted by Paul who came into the room, his cheeks slightly flushed.

'Everything okay love?' Lucy smiled at him as he approached.

'Yes, fine,' he replied, 'but I think I may have bored your dad a bit, he's fast asleep.'

'Oh, no,' the two women exclaimed in unison and they both started laughing with Paul joining in.

A few hours later Lucy was driving home, quietly singing along with the radio. It was one of her favourite Christmas songs, in fact if pressed it was probably *the* favourite. Fairytale of New York. She loved the story in it, more like real life and much better than lots of the other schmaltzy songs that got played over and over at this time of year. Lucy had a good voice and if she'd had a bit more confidence she might have tried to take up singing professionally. When she was young her mum had taken her once a week to an old lady who lived nearby for singing lessons. But Lucy had quickly got bored with all the technical exercises she made her do. Mrs Knight would make her sing musical scales over and over when all Lucy wanted to do was sing her latest favourite pop song. Too many La, La Las. So she eventually stopped going and since then the most she'd done was a few karaoke songs when out with some of her girlfriends - and even then only when she'd had a few drinks to give her the courage to do so. A couple of her friends had suggested she should audition for one of the TV talent shows but that wasn't really her thing and so she'd never done anything about it.

She glanced to her left as she drove and smiled as she saw Paul gently snoozing, his head leaning back and to his left, his face resting on the taut seat belt. He had a nice head, she thought, good shape. Lucy was feeling both relieved and happy. The day had gone well, Paul had got on really well with her mum and dad - it was like they'd known each other for years. Paul and Lucy's dad had made a reasonable dent in the whisky collection which was probably why they'd had to shake her dad awake before they left and why Paul was fast asleep now. Lucy imagined her dad would be back in a similar position not long after they'd gone, asleep in his armchair with a book or the newspaper resting on his lap. Yes it had been a good day and the only slight hiccup Lucy could think of was when Lucy's dad had asked Paul about his parents. But that had been early on and was soon forgotten with everything being fine afterwards.

It did irritate Lucy a bit though that Paul hadn't seemed able to open up to her about how his parents had died. Maybe it just needed the right

41

moment and no doubt that would happen at some point. She needed to keep reminding herself that they'd still only been together for a few months, she always thought it was longer, and Paul probably just needed a bit more time to feel comfortable enough to talk about such a personal event. Lucy couldn't imagine how bad it must be to lose your parents and she felt a shiver go down her spine. She couldn't imagine life without her own mum and dad. Being the only child, Lucy and her parents had always been very close and still were.

A few minutes later they arrived home and Lucy parked the car in her marked bay. She gently woke Paul up and helped him into the flat where he lay down on the bed and promptly fell back into a whisky induced sleep. Lucy relieved him of his shoes and left him there to sleep it off. She worried a bit that it reminded her of times with her ex-Robert. There had been a few times towards the end when she'd had to do much the same for him. But she knew Paul wasn't like that, in fact this was the first time she'd seen him as drunk as he was. And even that didn't seem too bad. It was all her dad's fault, she thought, smiling as she pictured him snoozing in his armchair back home.

Chapter 6
15th December, one year earlier

Chris was feeling a bit fed up, which was unusual for him. He was a glass half full type of guy and always liked to have a laugh and a joke. He always tried to look on the bright side of life. To begin with, he'd had a good night out with his mates but just as it looked like he was going to pull a gorgeous looking bird, great legs and a lovely smile, she'd disappeared. One minute it was all going well, she was laughing at all of his banter, telling him how she liked his blonde hair and he'd gone to the bar to get her another drink and when he came back she, and her girlfriends, had all gone. Nowhere to be seen. What was that all about? Had she just been playing him along? What a bitch!

Now he was back in the car with his mates, on their way home. They'd left the pub, stepped out into the cold air and quickly found the car, turning the heating up to maximum. Jack, who'd chosen the pub, was driving with Dan beside him in the front. Chris was stuck in the back of the car with ginger

43

Jason sitting beside him instead of the beautiful girl he'd been chatting up only half an hour before. Georgia, she said her name was and Chris had liked that. Not too plain but not too exotic. Maybe that wasn't even her real name though?

'Aww poor Chris,' said Jason, 'that bird used you to buy her drinks, she was never that interested in you.'

'You prat,' Jack shouted from the front of the car. 'You never had a chance with her, she was well out of your league.'

Chris ignored them both. It was just lad's banter and he knew he was going to be the brunt of it tonight. Payback time, he was thinking. Definitely from Jack and Jason, but not Dan, he never got involved. They're probably going to make the most of it – it was usually him taking the mickey out of his mates or playing tricks on them. Like last week when he'd unscrewed the top on the salt cellar before handing it to Jason and watching him bury his burger and chips under a mountain of salt. They'd all laughed and even Jason had seen the funny side, albeit not until the following day.

Right now though, Chris was focusing on his phone. The night was still young, well youngish, and there was still time for it finish reasonably well. He'd texted Sam, his on-off girlfriend, currently off, but she'd been responding to his texts and he was working towards getting Jack to drop him off at her house for the chance of a consolation shag. Suddenly Jason grabbed his mobile from him.

44

'Give's it back you ginger dick,' Chris shouted and he tried to grab it from Jason's hand but before he could get it Jason had tossed it over his head and it fell down into the seat well behind the front passenger seat where Dan was sitting.

'Oi you prats settle down, anyone would think you were all pissed!' Jack called out.

'Chris is,' Jason shouted back, 'he's pissed off because he got mugged off. She just played along to get free drinks and now he's texting his ex for an easy shag.'

Chris was searching for the phone down by his feet, he could feel it but couldn't quite see it. He nudged it to the side with his foot and just as he was hooking his fingers around it, he felt the car move and take a hard bump and it threw him off balance. As he fell to one side, he looked to the front and through the windscreen saw a bunch of people, really close, then he saw two faces, really big and bright and he felt himself lurch forward into the back of Dan's seat. He heard someone scream and everything seemed full of colour and then it all went immediately dark.

Chapter 7

DI Strong became aware of a noise and then he was immediately awake. He reached across to the mobile which was buzzing and flashing brightly on his bedside table. He briefly looked at the time before he answered. It showed 6.14am. He hit the green button and a voice spoke.

'Boss, we've found another body,' DS Campbell said without any introduction and before Strong could even say hello. It was one of Campbell's traits, he was always straight to the point. He wasn't one for formalities or politics. It was why he was a Detective Sergeant – he was a good policeman – but not yet a Detective Inspector like Strong. Strong was much better at managing upwards, playing the political game that was needed at that higher level. He'd been through, and passed, all the tests. It was on Strong's mind that he would need to talk with Campbell to help him develop that skill.

'It's a middle-age woman,' Campbell continued, 'we're still trying to identify her but

46

there are some similarities to the one we found yesterday, Peter Wilson.'

Strong was already up, sitting on the edge of his bed, pulling his trousers up his long legs with his mobile levered in between his shoulder and chin. He hadn't slept well, somehow he'd been half expecting this but the victim being a middle-aged woman was unusual. His wife had rolled over onto her side facing away from him, breathing softly, her long brown hair fanned out on the pillow behind her. Like Strong, she'd also grown used to these occasional night time disturbances and she was soon fast asleep again.

'What similarities?' he grunted as quietly as he could, as he stretched down to pull on a sock and thinking he really must do some more exercise. He was still a member of his local gym but couldn't remember the last time he'd actually gone there. Every now and again he would weigh up the pros and cons of cancelling his membership or actually using it. He always concluded that he should get into the routine of going and always vowed that he would do, starting the following week. So far he never had, there was always some reason not to, and the direct debits kept leaving his bank account. He grimaced as his toe caught something sharp on the bedroom carpet and instead of looking, he felt around for it again with his bare foot.

'Ouch,' he said, forgetting he was on the phone.

'What?' Campbell said, caught mid flow. When his boss didn't respond, he carried on.

'Well the body was found lying in Greenside Park, no effort made to hide it, and her throat had been cut, same as Peter Wilson. No sign of any weapon. Doesn't look like she was robbed though, although she may well not have been carrying a purse or any money.'

Strong consumed the information and tossed it around in his head. Despite what it appeared from reading newspapers and the news on television, murders were still very rare and two in two days with similar MOs was even rarer. But why a young lad and then a middle aged woman? He couldn't make the connection.

'Mmm…,' he said back into the phone as he finished tying his shoe lace, 'seems too much of a coincidence not to be related I guess….what do you think?' he asked his colleague.

'I agree, Forensics are on it, but as you know we didn't get much from yesterday so I'm not holding out much hope here either. We're doing some house to house checks locally to see if we can find out who she is, she didn't have any ID on her. It looks like she might have been out for a walk with a dog which is why we think she might not have been carrying anything. She had some of those dog bags on her for collecting, emm.., dog poo, but we haven't found a dog yet either.'

'Okay, I'm on my way,' said Strong as he carefully closed his front door and slid into his car sitting in the driveway, 'keep me posted if you hear any more.' He clipped the phone into the holder on his dashboard and it beeped to tell him it had connected. It was a cold morning and he turned the heating up full, wiping the windscreen with a cloth as he reversed out towards the main road.

Strong drove quickly, but carefully, towards Greenside Park, the car gradually warming up as he made his way along the still quiet streets. He had the radio on and was listening to an early morning news programme. Listening, but not really listening. They were talking about changing the education system and he felt he'd heard it all before. Surely they must know by now the best way to educate children. It always seemed to be that some other country did it better but it wasn't as if that was a new revelation. Strong couldn't understand why they kept changing the process – it just caused confusion for everyone. The same was true of the police force. Every new government brought in new rules, different ways of doing things. In truth, he couldn't think of any change over his years as a policeman that had made a huge difference to most people, be it police, victim or criminal. The basics of good policing would always be the same and all the administration they had to do around that now just made it harder and slower. Sometimes he wished they could go back to the old days when some of the police methods hadn't always been by the book but they got results. It frustrated him but he was experienced enough to know it was just part of how life was and part of his

49

job as a senior police officer was to support it and make it work as best he could without crossing too many lines.

It was still some time before both the rush hour and school run so there weren't many cars on the road and he didn't have to use his siren to get there any quicker. He glanced at the clock on the display and saw he was making good time. His mind was active and he was worried. Murders were still very uncommon and so two in two days was very exceptional. Over the years he'd only worked on a handful of murder cases and he knew they brought their own kind of focus and pressure. When the news broke there would be a lot of people asking questions about what he, and his team, were doing to catch the offenders. The questions would come both internally from his bosses all the way to the top, and also externally from the public and the press. The press especially loved this sort of story and would be sniffing around looking to dramatise it as much as possible. Was there a *serial killer* on the loose? Should the public be worried? What were the police doing to catch him? He'd have to come up with some good answers pretty quickly to keep everyone at bay. This was a part of the job no detective liked, they just wanted to get on with the investigation and catch the criminal without any of these annoying sideshow distractions.

The police questioning and information gathering from yesterday's murder hadn't thrown up any obvious clues or motives as to why someone would want to kill Peter Wilson and from the brief description of today's murder scene it sounded too similar to Strong for his liking. Coincidences rarely applied in Strong's experience and so two murders in such a short time period, with some similarities, most probably meant the same killer. The problem with that was that if he had killed twice already and the police didn't know why, then he could very well kill again and at this point he knew the police had no clue as to who the next victim might be. Murders were very rarely random though and he knew that if his team could find some sort of connection between the two victims then that would be a great step forward in finding the killer. Their key objective would be to find that connection before there were any further fatalities. Strong had faith in his team's ability to do just that.

Strong arrived at Greenside Park and pulled up behind a number of police cars all with their blue lights flashing, reflecting eerily off the trees and bushes in the early morning light. He flashed his ID card and nodded as he walked past the police constable standing by the taped off park gate. Lifting the blue and white striped tape above his head, he walked briskly across the strangely silent park and was soon nearing the murder scene a few hundred metres in. As he approached, he could see that it was surrounded by five or six police officers, standing in a group looking towards him, awaiting his arrival.

51

He easily spotted DS Campbell amongst them. Campbell, was fairly tall, just under six feet, but broad - making him look stocky and slightly shorter than he actually was. DI Strong always thought his DS would have made a good middleweight boxer. Campbell was second generation British / Caribbean – his parents having come to the UK from Jamaica as part of what was called the "Windrush Generation" after the end of the Second World War. Strong knew that he had done well to get to the level of detective sergeant and he had a lot of respect for him in achieving that. He would do all he could to help Campbell progress further in his police career.

The group of policemen were standing just to the edge of a pathway beside a small, bare flower bed, which at this time of year was really just a patch of brown earth. Strong nodded to a couple of them then picked out DS Campbell and pulled him to one side. He was keen to see what they had found out and he ushered his trusted colleague a few steps further down the path, away from the others so they could talk alone.

'Morning. Any more info?' he asked quickly.

'We haven't had official identification yet but we think, from a description of a woman who hasn't returned from a dog walk, that she's called Hilary Potts, lives local.'

Strong shook his head.

'Name doesn't mean anything to me, where's the dog?' Strong enquired.

'Turned up home on his own,' Campbell replied.

'Anything else you can tell me about her?'

'Not yet, she was sixty one but we'll get the body formally identified then start house to house checks. See what we can dig up but nothing unusual at the moment.' Campbell replied, swinging a leg and kicking a stone down the pathway.

'No obvious connection to yesterday's victim, I assume?' Strong asked.

'No. None other than the obvious similarities of her being local and the way she was killed but we don't think the two victims are related in any way. But we'll see what we can come up with when we've done the interviews. Maybe they worked together or knew each other in some other way.'

'Okay, let me know as soon as anything comes up, no matter how trivial. We're going to be under a lot of pressure to demonstrate some quick progress on this one,' Strong replied.

Two hours later Strong walked into what was now the Murder Squad conference room and sat down at the head of the long wooden table. He brushed back his hair with his hands reminding himself that he needed to get it cut soon. The conference room was a sizeable area and it was normally just used for large meetings but when there was an ongoing serious crime investigation, it was quickly converted to focus on that.

Strong opened up his black notebook and placed it on the table in front of him. He quickly looked around the room at his colleagues sat on either side of him. They were a solid crew and he had worked with most of them long enough to know that he could trust them to do a good job. His role was to guide them, to steer them, make sure they were on the right course and to challenge them if he saw any of them deviating. He'd worked with most of them long enough to know their individual strengths and weaknesses – when to rein them in and when to let them take a punt. In some ways his was an easy job as the team did most of the hard work and all he had to do was the tinkering around the edges. But he knew he was good at that and it wasn't something everyone could do well. He had always had the ability to take in a lot of information without getting overwhelmed by it. He could identify the key facts that needed to be focused on and filter them out from the mass of background detail that had to be covered in the course of an investigation. He also knew how and when you could bend the rules and how to make sure you were covered if anything went wrong. This deep understanding of how the police organisation worked was how he had made it to the level of detective inspector.

He looked around and was aware the team were waiting for him to start the meeting. He took a deep breath, checked his notes, looked up and began to talk.

'Okay everyone, so what we have here is two violent murders in two days in the same area. Before we go into detail on each one I want to hear if anyone has come up with anything that connects the two victims. Anything at all. No matter how slight or off the wall. I don't believe in coincidences and at this point any possible connection is key and will help us find the killer.' He looked to his right.

'DS Campbell, you go first please.'

Despite this being a team who worked well together, there was still a very evident hierarchical structure in the police force and when they had meetings like this one, the discussion started with senior ranked officers moving down the chain to the more junior staff unless they were specifically invited to talk first. DS Campbell was used to this, it was the way his boss liked to work. Occasionally Campbell had seen Strong take a more direct hands on approach in a case and dictate the investigation but it seemed this time he was employing his more usual approach of being happy to sit back and oversee his team, guiding them where necessary like a conductor leading his orchestra.

As DS Campbell and the rest of the team put forward their thoughts on the initial question posed by Strong it became clear that they had very little to link the two victims other than that they came from the same area and the families knew each other. Strong looked around the room and could see his team were disappointed. They'd all been hoping there would be some sort of early breakthrough, some sort of connection that they could investigate further. Although this was a first murder case for some of those in the room, all of them had done the training and knew that the first few hours were crucial in identifying a suspect. After that it became more difficult as time moved on and evidence got lost. Although it was likely that Peter Wilson had been carrying a wallet it hadn't turned up anywhere yet. However they were keeping a close eye on his bank and credit cards in case anyone tried to use them. Strong thought that would be unlikely though.

The common view in the room was that it seemed highly likely that it was the same killer and any link between the victims could point them to a reason for the killings and so perhaps some potential suspects. On the other hand, if they were looking for someone who was just randomly murdering people without any motive then that would make things much harder for them to track him down and stop him from carrying on with his killing spree. However Strong, and the other senior officers in the room knew that was the least likely scenario.

As the meeting continued it became obvious that they had also found very little more from the evidence gathered so far on either of the murders. The initial forensic reports had not come up with anything, other than what had been obvious at the crime scenes, although they were still ongoing and

56

so might still yet find something. It was amazing how a small piece of fibre under a fingernail, or a partial fingerprint or a microscopic trace of DNA could prove crucial. No murder weapon had been found for either of the killings and Strong posed the question,

'Was it the same murder weapon used for both murders, do we know? Or at least could it have been?'

A young WPC, put her hand up from the far left hand corner of the room and started reading from her notebook.

'Sir, all forensics will say at this point is that the same weapon is a possibility, but they hope to confirm that later today, one way or the other, I am waiting on their call and they know it's a priority. All they're saying at the moment is that it was a sharp bladed object, most probably a small knife, maybe a kitchen knife.' She put her notebook down and blushed slightly. This was her first murder case and in fact the first time she'd spoken in such a large group. She hadn't really known the etiquette, if there was one, and hoped she'd done things correctly. She was keen to help.

'Thanks, WPC O'Keefe,' Strong replied, 'keep on forensics' case and let me know directly if there is anything to report.'

'Yes sir,' the WPC replied, surprised that the top man knew her name, her face reddening even more and she looked down to her notebook again to try and hide it. Strong continued to address the room.

'Okay, at this point let's assume there is a connection somehow. There's got to be,' he said looking around the room for consensus from his senior officers and a few of them nodded in response.

'As I said, I don't believe much in coincidences. Let's assume *it is* one man and one murder weapon, one knife, which he is holding onto. We need to dig further into the connection between these two victims. You said the families knew each other. How? Did they do anything together, similar clubs, workplaces, schools? Any relationships between any of them? We need to start with the basics and find out as much detail on them that we can. There must be something in there that ties them together. Let's get to it. I want every family member spoken to from both families and any connection at all between them identified and reported back ASAP. Who's keeping an eye on the first victim's bank cards?'

A policeman sitting mid-way down the right hand side of the table raised his hand.

'Good,' Strong continued, 'if there's any action on any of those at all we need to know right away.'

The man nodded and Strong pulled back his shirt cuff and looked at his watch.

'We will meet back here again in four hours time at 4pm. Anything significant comes up before that I want to know immediately. Is that clear?'

There was a general murmur of agreement around the room and then movement as papers were shuffled, seats moved back and one by one the team left the conference room in groups of two or three heading back to their desks.

As soon as Strong had finished speaking he'd immediately left the room and returned to his office. He had a lot on his mind. It was often like this at the start of an investigation with a mass of new, random information and everyone trying to work out what was relevant and what was just background noise. But Strong was confident his team would find something that would lead them to the killer. Although he'd been clever so far, Strong was sure that the murderer would make some sort of mistake. They usually did, and that was always their downfall. Strong knew that time would come, it was just a question of when. He unlocked his top drawer and reaching towards the back, he pulled out a thin brown file. He opened it up on his desk and flicked through the contents before putting it back and locking the drawer again.

'Wilson and Potts,' he said to himself, but wasn't sure what it meant.

Chapter 8

It was another bitter December day. It was cold and bleak. It had been like that for most of the last few weeks. Christmas was coming soon but today was not a day to celebrate. Today was the day of Peter Wilson's funeral.

It was mid-morning but you really couldn't tell. It was one of those grey days where it never seemed to ever get light and so time seemed to stand still. The family of Peter Wilson were all sat together in a church which was full of people generally dressed in dark suits and dark dresses. Most were sat down in the pews but a few remained standing at the back of the church as if they didn't feel worthy enough of getting too close to the family's grief.

Pete's brother Jack was sat in the front row of the church alongside his family, feeling uncomfortable and not just because of having to wear a suit, shirt and tie. The last time he'd had to do that had been at his sister Sarah's funeral and even getting dressed like this had brought back all the terrible memories of that day. The worst by far

60

had been at the start. As a family they'd decided to have Sarah's favourite song playing as people arrived and settled into their seats. It was Songbird sung by Eva Cassidy and Sarah used to sing along to it in her room at home and once or twice she'd sung it when Jack was there too.

"*For you, there'll be no crying...*" it started and Jack remembered that had set him and most of the others off, despite the lyrics.

"*..cause I feel that when I'm with you it's alright..*" it carried on and as tears streamed down Jack's face, he thought back to the times they'd spent together in each other's rooms just chatting and sharing secrets. The best times.

"*... I love you like never before...*" Jack's heart had literally ached then. It was too late now. He'd lost his sister and his best friend and he'd have done anything to bring her back.

Now hardly any time seemed to have passed and he was back here again, his black hair cut short and his beard freshly trimmed, this time mourning the loss of his brother. He turned his head and looked around the room. He knew almost all of the people in the church but he didn't feel that he was really there and he wasn't sure that they were really there either. He was hoping that this was all just a bad dream but the tears rolling down his mum and dad's cheeks were definitely real and he wondered why he wasn't able to cry too. He really wished he could. He needed to, god how he hated funerals.

The priest was standing behind a wooden lectern at the front of the church, talking about Pete. He was a good man, thought Jack. Although Jack didn't think of himself as being religious in any way, he recognised that the priest had done a fine job since all this had happened. Since Pete's murder. It had helped his family, especially his mum, and he felt sorry for the priest having to be part of this again just because that was his job. This was the second time he'd had to do this for the Wilson family. How many times did he have to do this every week with other families like them? All that grief must wear you down surely, Jack thought. Definitely not something he would want to do for a living.

Jack had tried to get a look at everyone who had come along to the funeral. He'd had a strange thought, one of many these days, that maybe the murderer would turn up at the funeral to gloat. However he didn't see anyone that looked out of place, or anyone hanging around at the back of the church acting suspiciously. Maybe that was just something that happened in TV detective programmes, he decided.

While looking around, Jack had noticed a couple of policemen sat at the back of the church. One tall, one slightly shorter and younger. It was funny with policemen; somehow you knew just by looking at them that's what they were. Something to do with the way they held themselves, a bit stiffly maybe, always wearing solid shoes. He recognised one of them as having spent a lot of time with his family keeping them up to speed with the investigation – although it didn't seem to have got very far yet. The other one, he knew, was the detective leading the case although he'd only met him once, not long after Pete was murdered, and then only briefly, and he couldn't remember his name. He made a mental note to himself to see if he could grab him at the end of the service and find out what was happening. Hear it from the top man. Hopefully the police were making some progress. Jack was desperate to find the person who had killed his brother. He needed answers. He needed to know why his brother had been killed.

The priest continued with his sermon. He had stepped out in front of the lectern now allowing everyone to see his colourful outfit, his hands clasped in front of him. He was wearing a long flowing smock, predominantly red and gold with a white background and it reminded Jack of the Pope when he made his New Year's day address on the television. Everyone appeared to be listening attentively to what the priest was saying, although most had their heads bowed and so were perhaps lost in their own private thoughts. Apart from the priest talking, the room was silent.

The priest finished his piece and, as one, without any direction, everyone stood up and sang the final hymn. As it finished and the last note echoed and then faded into the far corners of the cavernous building, row by row, one by one, the congregation all filtered slowly out of the church into the cold grey air outside.

Jack and his family stood in line at the church door and thanked everyone as they left the building. There were people he hadn't spoken to since his sister Sarah's funeral and some for even longer than that. It was a shame it needed something as awful as this to bring them all together. A few of them were in tears and a few of them wanted to say something meaningful, something they'd rehearsed, some story they had of Pete - but Jack couldn't really take in what they were saying and just shook their hands and nodded, thanking them for coming. After the first few it just became a routine.

Out of the corner of his eye he noticed the two policemen walking away down the gravel path towards the church car park, they hadn't come down the line presumably because they were not friends of Pete and not wishing to be intrusive. Jack looked back into the church and saw that there were only a few people left to come out and so he made an excuse and quietly slipped away. He quickly went in pursuit of the two policemen, his shiny black brogues scattering the gravel as he walked. He caught up with them just as they reached the wooden gate from the churchyard going through into the car park. No-one else had made it that far yet, they were all still standing in groups outside the church, so there was only the three of them in earshot.

'Hi there,' Jack called out as he approached the two men and they both turned around at the sound of his voice.

'I just wanted to say thanks for coming, it's appreciated,' Jack said as he caught them up, 'I know you guys are very busy.'

The detective in charge, the taller of the two, nodded and stood forward. Jack could see he had a few grey hairs at the sides and guessed he was somewhere in his mid-forties. The younger policeman stayed a step behind his senior colleague. Both were wearing dark suits and ties.

'Yes, I hope the day has gone as well as can be expected for your family – these things are never easy,' the detective said.

'No that's true,' Jack replied. 'It's hit my mum and dad bad, losing their son, especially so soon after my sister Sarah's death. Losing two of their children... doesn't bear thinking what they must be going through. But hopefully today will help a bit, some sort of closure I guess. At least that's what they say, although I'm not convinced.'

Jack took a deep breath and composed himself.

'I wanted to take the chance to ask you how the investigation was going. Do you think you'll catch the person that did this soon?'

'We're doing all we can,' the detective answered. 'There are a number of ideas we are exploring and as you know we are looking to see if there is any connection between your brother's

65

murder and that of Hilary Potts. As a rule, I'm not a great believer in coincidences and I'm confident we'll get him soon.'

'Have you found any connections? Obviously we knew them but I don't know when Pete and Mrs Potts would last have seen each other. Probably a long time ago, when we were younger. Have you got any, emm…, leads? Any idea who might have done it, or why?' Jack asked.

'As I say we are pursuing a number of leads but I'm sorry there's nothing I can tell you at this point. As soon as we have something positive, I'll make sure you and your family are kept informed,' the detective replied.

'Okay thanks, please do keep us informed, the family I mean, I know my dad appreciates it, gives him something to focus on. I'd hate to think what he would do if he found the guy that did it. Although the same probably goes for me too. Although I probably shouldn't say that,' he added quickly and then, 'Sorry I forgot your name?'

'Strong, DI Strong. We'll be in touch,' he replied and the two policemen turned and headed towards their car.

Thirty minutes later Jack was in the function room of the Horse and Groom pub with the rest of his family and friends who had congregated there after Pete's funeral. He was sat at a table with his best mates, each with a drink and a small plate of snacks and sandwiches in front of them. They'd all loosened their ties and their jackets were hanging awkwardly on the back of their seats.

'I still can't believe it,' said Jason, 'who would do that to Pete? He wouldn't hurt a fly. Why would someone want to kill him? I just don't get it,' he said shaking his head.

'I know,' said Jack, 'I've been going over and over it in my head. Just doesn't make sense. And your mum too Chris, what's the world coming to? If they find the bastard they should give us five minutes in a room with him first. Jail's too good for him.'

'Yeh, I'd like that,' said Chris, 'or bring back the death penalty and make it nice and slow. I'd like to watch him suffer. Doesn't look like that'll happen soon though, the police don't seem to be getting anywhere in finding him. Maybe its Inspector Clouseau that's leading the investigation. I reckon I could do better myself.'

'Yeh, I was speaking to the detective earlier,' said Jack. 'He didn't say much. They seem to think there's a link between Pete and your mum Chris and that it's the same bloke but I don't suppose it takes a genius to work that out. What have they said to you?'

'Yeh, the same sort of thing. They questioned us all a lot about mum and how well she knew Pete and if they ever did anything together, anything in common or that but to be honest we couldn't think of anything. Could you? I think they might be barking up the wrong tree, they don't seem

67

to have a clue,' Chris replied. 'I can't see how mum and Pete were connected in any way. Of course she knew him through you and the family and that but they would hardly have even spoken to each other. Its not like they were having an affair or anything,' he said, and then added 'sorry, stupid thing to say,' as he realised this was not a time for him to be joking.

'Have you heard any more down at the station Dan, any idea if they're getting anywhere?' he said quickly.

Dan looked up from the pint he'd been staring at for the last few minutes with a ring of froth around his bushy, dark beard. He'd been listening to his mates and feeling equally frustrated at what had happened and his inability to make any sense of it all.

'No I haven't,' he replied, pushing up his glasses. 'They're going through their usual processes at the station as far as I can see but it's all done in a special part of the building that only the murder team are allowed in. We're only allowed in there very rarely with special authorisation and only if it's a major IT failure that needs one of us to attend to it in person. Most things we can do remotely from our section.'

'What about the stuff that's recorded on the computer systems, all the case stuff, files and things – can't you see that?' asked Jack, scratching his stubbled beard.

'Nah,' Dan shook his head and rubbed his own beard with the back of his hand, 'it's on a special system, all password protected, encrypted and that. Anyone caught trying to access it would be kicked out right away.'

Nobody could think of anything to add and the table went quiet as, in unison, they all took a sip from their drinks, lost in their own thoughts. Chris finished his drink first and rose from his seat, smoothing back his blonde hair.

'I'm going to make a move Jack, I'll say goodbye to your mum and dad and then head off. We've still got to arrange a few things for mums next week. I'm not looking forward to it, but I guess I'll see you all there.'

His mates all nodded and stood up and they shook hands, one by one. Jack gave him an awkward hug and thanked him for coming.

'Do you need a lift next week Jack? I can get one of my cousins to pick you up on the way if you like?' asked Chris.

'No, it's fine,' Jack replied, 'Dan is driving, aren't you?' he said looking across the table and Dan nodded in reply.

'Ok, see you later then. Hopefully they'll have caught the bastard before then,' said Chris as he walked away.

There was a general murmuring of agreement from the other three sat back down at the table but inwardly none of them had much faith that would be the case.

Chapter 9

'Morning Guv,' said DS Campbell as he strode into Strong's office, pushing the half glass door shut noisily behind him, his arms swinging by his side as he approached Strong's desk. He was a big man and he sat down awkwardly, squeezing into the brown plastic chair facing Strong's desk. Campbell had come straight from his early morning session at the gym, he was a great believer in a healthy body creating a healthy mind and he liked to stay fit. Most weeks he'd be at the gym twice a day, every day going through his set routine. He always tried to get a visit in first thing in the morning as it helped him get his brain in shape for the days challenges ahead. He'd usually try and fit a second session in at some point in the evening to help him wind down. While he was doing his exercise he found he was able to think more clearly and put things in perspective. Sometimes he could clear the clutter from his mind and come up with a new idea on whatever was troubling him, usually an unsolved case at work. Although he'd never openly admit it, lately he'd also found himself spending longer at the gym as an excuse not to go home.

DI Strong looked up from the paper he was reading laid out on the wooden desk in front of him. He peered above his reading glasses at his colleague and thought, yes, DS Campbell definitely could have been a boxer. He took his glasses off and put them on the desk.

'Good morning, what is it you wanted to see me about, any new developments?' he asked, eager to know if his DS or any of the team had come up with anything useful.

'Well, I'm not sure,' his colleague replied, shifting awkwardly in his chair. 'But I think I may have found something. It's a bit tenuous, but I think I might have come up with some sort of connection between the two victims and I just wanted to run it by you, see what you think.'

'Go on then,' said Strong, sitting forward, keen to hear what his colleague had to say.

'Well, we know they both came from the same area and that they sort of knew each other through family and friends and that, but nothing more than that. Nothing concrete. So I started thinking if there was anything else, less obvious, that tied them together in any way. And, well there may be something that does connect them a bit more directly although I can't quite see how yet, or what it means.'

'Go on, what is it?' asked Strong, looking attentively at his colleague, wondering if he'd found something that would help them break this case. With two people dead, no apparent motive and no clues as to who had done it or why, he was under a lot of pressure - personally and from his superiors, the public and the press to find the murderer. Or, if not to find him, at the very least to show some sign of progress, of which he knew there had been very little so far. He knew Campbell was a good cop, a good fact finder, and so if anyone could make the breakthrough it could well be him. He pushed up his glasses and leaned further forward ready to hear what his colleague had to say.

Campbell was looking at him, thinking, hesitating, making sure he had the right words to make sense of what he was about to tell his boss. He had come up with this idea during his morning gym session and it was still quite raw and undeveloped. He thought he had something but didn't know whether he, himself, believed in it enough and he needed Strong to understand his logic so he could get his opinion, which he knew through experience was always valuable.

'Okay, bear with me on this one, I just thought about it earlier this morning, let me try and explain it and then see what you think,' Campbell said.

He took a deep breath and started to try and describe his theory. Strong sat and listened, letting his colleague have the time to talk it through. He knew that Campbell was a clever detective and anything he had to say was usually worth listening to. They'd worked together for over four years now and Strong had learnt to trust Campbell's judgement and listen to his hunches. Sometimes they came to nothing but more often than not there was some substance to them. They often led to something worth investigating further. It would be interesting to see what he was thinking here and Strong was glad Campbell had come to him first so he could stay in control.

Campbell explained what he'd been thinking. It was apparent that the two victims hadn't known each other directly, or not that anyone knew of, but some of their respective family members did know, and associate with, each other. Campbell had thought more deeply about this family connection and realised that both of the families had a son of much the same age who were close friends with each other. Jack Wilson, brother of the first victim, Pete Wilson and Chris Potts, son of the second victim, Hilary Potts were good friends who regularly hung around together. In fact they'd gone to school and had grown up together and were still close friends now regularly spending time together.

'Okay I get there's a connection, between those two, albeit I agree it's a tenuous one,' said Strong, 'but why do you think it's related to the murders? Do you have anything more?' he asked watching his colleague closely.

'No, not yet, I've just been running this around in my head the last couple of hours and wanted to pass it by you and get your opinion.

73

Might be nothing. Do you think there might be anything in it? Do you think I should dig a bit deeper, maybe have a talk with the two lads and see if they can tell us anything? I don't know what, maybe they're involved in something they shouldn't be and its escalated into some sort of feud?'

Strong sat back in his chair, thinking. He pushed his long legs out under his desk. In truth there wasn't much here and he didn't want to waste time and resources on something that was very weak and would probably not lead them anywhere. However, at this point they didn't have much else to go on and he didn't want to be seen to be discouraging Campbell. He liked Campbell and knew he had good instincts and he also knew that he looked up to Strong. He was a good guy to have in your team, he'd never cross you and he respected Strong's ultimate authority. DI Strong sat forward again and looked at his colleague across the desk.

'Okay, there's not much here to be honest but it may be worth a shot if we don't find anything else soon. But let's keep this contained between just a few of us for now. Take DC Jones with you and go and talk to the two lads separately. See what you can find out. Look for a link between them, something that could lead to violence, to murder. Brief Jones and let him ask the questions, you listen, see what you can hear. Watch how they say it. Watch their body language. Anything suspicious, or anything that doesn't look quite right to you. After

that if you think there's something, come and tell
me, otherwise we drop it. Okay?'

'Sure, I'm on it,' said Campbell and he
quickly got up, turned and left the room, the door
banging shut behind him. DI Strong sat back in his
chair, slowly turning a pen between his fingers and
staring into space.

A few hours later, DS Campbell and DC
Jones were outside the home of the Wilsons.
Campbell stepped forward and rang the bell on the
green front door with the number fifteen on it. After
a few seconds it was opened inwards and a young
man stood in the doorway looking out at them. He
had short dark hair and was unshaven and looking
tired. From inside the house Campbell could hear
sounds of people talking, a woman's voice agitated,
possibly crying. For a second it reminded Campbell
of his own home. It had been a difficult time for him
and his wife lately as they were trying to start a
family and the stress was beginning to tell
emotionally on his wife.

The man at the door looked at Campbell and
Jones, waiting, as if it was too much effort for him
to speak. He guessed they were policemen, he'd
seen quite a few lately and they had a distinctive
look. DS Campbell broke the silence.

'Hello, I'm DS Campbell and this is my
colleague Detective Constable Jones. Is Jack Wilson
in, we'd like to talk to him if possible,' he asked.
The man on the doorstep looked like Jack Wilson

from a photo Campbell had seen, but not having met him before he didn't want to be presumptive.

'I'm Jack,' the man answered gruffly, then cleared his throat. 'What do you want, have you found out who, em, who done Pete? DI Strong said he'd let us know.'

'No, not yet but we're working on it. I work for DI Strong and I just wanted to ask you a couple of questions to see if you can help us. Can we come in? Would that be okay?' Campbell replied.

'Of course, come in,' said Jack, 'but I don't know if I can help you. I've already said everything I know to your colleagues and believe me if I had any idea who had killed Pete I'd be right on it.' Jack stepped to one side to let the two policemen through.

'Who is it?' a man's voice shouted from somewhere inside the house.

'It's okay,' Jack replied, 'just the police. They want to ask me a few more things about Pete. I'll take them in the front room.'

'Have they found the bastard yet?' the voice responded and a woman's voice told him to be quiet.

'No, not yet,' Jack called back, silently mouthing *"sorry"* to the two policemen.

Campbell stopped in the hallway with Jones behind him and they turned around to await Jack as he closed the front door. Jack eased past and showed them through a white door into the first room on the left off the hallway. It was some sort of sitting room with a couple of light brown fabric sofas and a wooden glass topped coffee table in the centre of the room. The room had a faint, stale smell and the table was covered with used cups and mugs, some still half full of brown liquid, indistinguishable as tea or coffee. Jack moved the cups into a group in the centre of the table and then sat down on one of the sofas. He motioned for the two policemen to sit on the other sofa opposite him. Jack sat leaning forward, his arms crossed, resting on his knees. He looked and felt tired.

'I'm not sure if there's anything more I can tell you,' he said, 'like I told the other fellas, cops, Pete is, was, a good lad. I don't know why anyone would want to do this. It's not right. Just not right.' Jack's head dropped forward and he stared at the floor, his hands tightly clasped in front of him.

'I know,' said Campbell, 'I'm very sorry. We just wanted to ask you a couple more questions. Just in case there's anything we've missed. Sometimes there's something that might not seem important at the time,' and he turned to look at DC Jones and nodded for him to speak.

'Jack, I wanted to ask, do you know a lady called Hilary Potts?' Jones asked. This was the first time DC Jones had spoken and his voice took Jack slightly by surprise, it was somehow higher pitched than he'd expected and there was the trace of some sort of accent in there, maybe Irish or Welsh? Jack couldn't quite fathom it out.

Campbell had sat back in his seat, keeping his eyes fixed on Jack. Jack had sat still for a few seconds as if digesting the question. He scratched at his beard, then sighed and repeated the name, as if questioning himself.

'Hilary Potts...Hilary Potts. Yes, of course that's Chris's mum isn't it? Sorry I didn't really recognise her first name, always called her Mrs Potts or Chris's mum.'

'Yes, that's right Chris Pott's mum. He's a good friend of yours isn't he?' Jones asked.

'Chris, yeh, we grew up together, went to the same school and that. He's a good lad, a real mate. A real joker. He's always trying to play pranks and stuff. He should have been a comedian. We play football together, go out for drinks and stuff. Shocking what happened to his mum as well, I can't believe it still. She was in her sixties, who would want to do that to an old woman?'

'So you and Chris still see each other, go around as mates?' Jones prompted.

'Yeh sure there's a group of us, half a dozen or so all good mates. We all play football and go out quite regularly for a few beers and a laugh. Nothing more than that. Why do you ask?' Jack replied, thinking there was definitely a hint of a Welsh in the policeman's voice.

'Can you think, have the two of you ever been in trouble? Maybe upset anyone, had a few too many drinks, got into a fight, anything like that you can think of?' DC Jones asked.

78

Campbell was watching Jack closely. He thought he saw a flicker in Jack's eyes, a slight tensing of the body, something there, something he was thinking of. Something that had happened.

'No, nothing,' Jack replied. 'Why, do you think it's got something to do with us, me and Chris? Is that why they got killed?'

'We're just exploring a number of possibilities and as you and Chris are both good friends and have the closest connection between your two families we just want to see if there's anything that's happened that might be important. Can you think of anything at all that the two of you have done that might have upset anyone, even if it seemed trivial at the time? Don't worry you won't be in any trouble if there was anything. We're all trying to catch the murderer and anything you can think of might help,' Jones responded.

'No I really can't,' Jack replied looking down at his feet, 'I honestly can't think of anything like that. We're just mates. We play football, hang around together, me, Chris and a couple of others, that's about it.' He looked up briefly and then immediately lowered his head again.

Jones looked across to Campbell and the DS gave him a slight nod.

'Okay,' said Jones standing up, 'well thanks for your time and if you do think of anything else please give us a call.'

79

'Yes of course I will, I really hope you catch him soon,' Jack replied getting up too, realising the meeting was over.

Jones and Campbell left the house and walked in silence along the path back to the car. As they drove off Campbell shared his thoughts with his colleague.

'There was something there. Something. I don't know what, but he was holding back.'

'You think so? Jones replied, 'I couldn't see anything.'

'It was when you asked him if they'd upset anyone, I saw it then, he was thinking of something, something that had happened. I could see it in his eyes, in a slight hesitation, a slight movement. Maybe he doesn't want to bring it up in front of us, we being the police. But there's definitely something. Lets go back to the station and you have a look at the records - see if either of them have been in any sort of trouble before.'

It was getting late but DS Campbell didn't particularly want to go home yet. He did genuinely want to look further into the background of the two young men but he also knew, guiltily, that he was using it as an excuse to stay out a bit longer. He and his wife were having problems trying to start a family and they had just undergone another cycle of IVF which had been unsuccessful. This had been the third failure and his wife was taking it harder every time. He'd heard her sobbing in the bathroom as he'd left early that morning for the gym and he didn't really know what to do to make things better for her. Campbell lived his life in a practical way and helping someone, even his wife, emotionally didn't come easy to him.

Back at the station, he logged on to his system and cleared a few outstanding emails before looking at his watch and deciding he could fit in another quick visit to the gym before heading for home. It was getting late and DC Jones had gone straight home deciding that it would be okay to have a look at the Police Records database in the morning.

<u>Chapter 10</u>

Lucy was busying herself in the flat, tidying up – although compared to many of her friends' houses, her flat was never really that untidy. She sometimes worried slightly that she might be a bit OCD, but she didn't think she was that bad. It wasn't like she went around straightening up the towels or putting the tins in line in her kitchen cupboards. It was probably just in her genes that she was a tidy person. Her mum and dad's house was always pretty clean and with her flat being quite small it didn't take much time to do the same here. Even after Paul had moved in not much had changed in that respect, he didn't seem to leave anything lying around and so the flat was still generally very organised with nothing out of place.

She'd switched the television on and it was playing away in the background. It was an early evening quiz show which she could half watch and listen to while doing other things. It was one of those programmes where you could tune in an out and not really miss anything. Like most TV really!

Paul wasn't home yet. That was becoming a more regular occurrence over the last few weeks. Before that she'd often get home from work to find that he'd already prepared dinner and there was a nice glass of cold white wine awaiting her arrival. She really loved that but it wasn't happening so much lately. Paul's explanation for this recent change of behaviour was that he was out doing more research for his book, that he was really getting into it now, and Lucy couldn't seem to get any more from him than that. When she tried to find out what that meant, what he'd actually been doing as this '*research*', he became vague, not defensive so much, but saying he'd just been walking around or sat in coffee shops. His explanation was that just watching people and observing their movements and habits helped give him more context to the actual story he was writing. He said it was amazing what new ideas you could pick up from just doing that. It sounded a bit weird to Lucy but Paul said it enabled him to develop the story better than just sitting at his laptop at home all day. He needed to be out seeing people to get ideas and inspiration. After a few attempts at getting more information from him, he usually managed to deflect the conversation, or Lucy just gave up.

Lucy went into the bedroom and looked in the laundry bin to see if there was anything needing washing but there were only a few items in there, not enough for a load yet. She remembered that Paul had run a wash the day before – another bit of housework he was good at doing, she smiled as she thought of him. Lately he seemed to have got into a regular routine of doing the washing, so much so that Lucy couldn't remember the last time she'd had to do it herself. When she'd commented on it, Paul just smiled saying that he just wanted to do his bit around the house, especially when she was working and so, in these metrosexual days, she couldn't really fault him for that. She couldn't imagine her dad doing that though. He was from a different generation, one that had a clear distinction between man-jobs and women's work. Even though he was now retired, he would say that his jobs were to take the bins out, mow the lawn, do the driving and any simple DIY tasks. Anything more complicated meant a call to their local handyman, Geoff, who they'd been using for years. Lucy's dad still regarded "housework" as very much a woman's task so her mum would do everything else, which she seemed happy to do. Lucy had never seen her dad making anything in the kitchen and doubted if he could even boil an egg.

As Lucy returned to the lounge, she heard the key turning in the lock and went to meet Paul as he came through the front door. He put his bag down on the hallway floor and they both smiled, hugged and kissed each other on the lips.

'That was a nice welcome,' said Paul grinning and he pulled Lucy towards him again and they kissed once more, this time longer, Lucy pushing up on her tip-toes.

'You're looking good, what have I done to deserve that?' he said as he pulled back, noticing that Lucy was wearing a light blue, short sleeve top and grey jeans, as if ready to go out.

'Oh nothing special,' said Lucy smiling back at him. 'I just thought it would be a nice welcome, a break in our normal routine. And…. I thought we might do something different tonight.'

'Oh yeah? Sounds good,' Paul said. 'What do you have in mind?' he said raising his eyebrows suggestively.

'No, not that!' she laughed. 'At least not right away anyhow. I thought we could go out. I've booked us a table at a nice restaurant, somewhere different for a change. You've got half an hour to get ready, that's twenty minutes longer than you normally take.'

'Great, sounds good' said Paul. 'I just need to take a quick shower and get changed and I'll be ready. I am feeling quite hungry.' He let Lucy go, picked up his bag and disappeared into the bedroom.

A few minutes later Paul was drying himself in front of the tall bedroom mirror which was set in a silver frame, at an angle in one of the corners of the room. He liked the way Lucy had designed the bedroom. It wasn't a large room but with the position of the mirror and the fact she'd decorated it brightly, it made the room look bigger than it really was. In fact she'd done the same all the way through the flat, making it as light as possible. Paul had often thought that she would have made a

85

great interior designer, she seemed to have an eye for things and how they would look in a room. Maybe in another life that's what she would be.

He finished drying off and threw his towel down onto the bed. Opening the wardrobe he looked at his row of shirts trying to decide which one to wear.

'Where are we going tonight then? Are you going to tell me? I need to know what to wear,' he called out to Lucy, 'or is it a surprise?'

'No, not a surprise. It's an Italian place over in Harden, it's supposed to be lovely. It's got a good reputation,' she called back to him.

'Oh…, it's not the Bella Vista is it, the one on North Street?' Paul asked.

'Yes, that's the one. Of course I forgot you used to live over that way didn't you. Have you been there before then?' Lucy asked.

'No, I haven't, but I'm not sure if it's very good. I seem to remember some bad stories about it. Maybe we should try somewhere else? We could stay local?' Paul called back.

'No it's fine, it'll be good to go somewhere different for a change' Lucy said as she came into the bedroom. 'Apparently it's got new owners and the reviews on-line are all very good. Natasha at work also recommended it to me, she's been a couple of times and says its very nice. She said they do really tasty fresh pasta.'

'Okay, if you're sure,' Paul replied frowning.

'Come on don't be a grumpy,' Lucy said, leaning forward and kissing him lightly on the lips. 'This girl's taking control and taking you out. What more could a man want?!' she said giggling.

A few minutes later they were driving to the restaurant and Lucy was in a good mood, singing along to the radio. For a change it wasn't a Christmas song this time, it was Queen singing *Don't stop me now* and the lyrics seemed to reflect how she was feeling. She was glad she'd organised this "date night", she hadn't seen so much of Paul lately and she was looking forward to having a couple of hours with him where they could just chat, like they used to do when they first started going out.

She looked over at Paul sat in the passenger seat smiling as she sang along, and she thought what a good looking man he was. She'd done well. Paul was wearing a dark blue shirt, black jeans and black deck shoes. He had his sunglasses on, which was unusual for him, although there was still some late evening sunshine, and it made Lucy think about them going away on holiday. The two of them, somewhere hot, sitting in a beach bar watching the sun go down. That would be fun. Maybe they could do that soon. Maybe this summer. They hadn't made any plans yet, but maybe Lucy could start the conversation tonight as they dined.

The traffic was light and they soon arrived at the restaurant. Lucy took a left turn and pulled into the restaurant car park, finding a free space in the far corner. It was a good sign that the car park was busy, she thought, it must mean the place was popular. She switched off the engine and turned to look at Paul who was sitting quietly.

'Do you want to have a quick drink first? There's a pub next door,' she asked.

'Nah, let's just go in, we can have a drink in here can't we? It'll be more comfortable at the table,' Paul replied.

They went into the brightly lit restaurant and Paul took the lead speaking to the waiter who led them to an alcove table in the far corner of the restaurant. They sat down and ordered a pre-dinner drink.

'Maybe you should take your sunglasses off now,' Lucy teased him. 'You don't normally wear them.'

'Oh yes, sorry I forgot I had them on. I had a little bit of a headache coming on so I thought I'd shade my eyes a bit, it's okay now though,' Paul replied, taking his sunglasses off and putting them in his jacket pocket.

'Oh sorry love, I didn't realise. Are you okay now?' Lucy asked and Paul smiled and nodded in response, reaching across and squeezing her hand.

Soon they'd ordered their food and they ate it as they chatted about their respective days. Paul had been working on his book again and seemed to have spent most of the day sitting in a café somewhere with his laptop. He seemed quite positive about it though, making a comment that things seemed to be happening and the story was beginning to take on a life of its own.

'That's good then,' Lucy replied, pleased that he seemed to be making progress and secretly hoping that she might actually see some evidence of it soon.

Paul was sitting with his back to most of the other tables with Lucy sat opposite, facing out towards the centre of the room. The restaurant was pretty busy with most tables occupied with families, groups of friends or couples like themselves. At one of the tables to Lucy's right there were three couples and as they caught Lucy's eye line she noticed that one of the men seemed to be looking across at them. Over the course of their meal it seemed to her that each time she looked up he would often be glancing over at them and, although she couldn't be sure, it looked like he might be talking about them to his friends at the table. She mentioned it to Paul but he didn't seem that interested and didn't look round so she didn't make any more of it. He seemed quiet though, not his usual self.

'Are you okay sweetheart?' she asked him.

'Yes fine,' he replied, 'I just can't quite shake this headache though,' he replied.

'Do you think you should go back to the doctor? You seem to be getting them more frequently now,' Lucy said. 'Maybe you need another check up?'

'No, I'm fine,' Paul replied, 'the doc gave me some pills to take last time and they seem to help. It's not that bad really, just lingers for a bit sometimes' he said reaching across and squeezing Lucy's hand.

Lucy smiled and decided not to say anymore. She had seen the pills he was taking one day when he'd left them out in the bathroom and she'd looked them up on the internet. They seemed to be fairly strong painkillers and it had worried her that he was taking them, but she reasoned that if the doctor had prescribed them then they must be the right thing. If it was anything worse then surely he would have been referred to a specialist? When she'd asked Paul about it he'd reassured her by saying the doctor had said it was just one of those things that would pass in a year or two. They thought it was some sort of virus that eventually just passes.

'I was thinking earlier about holidays,' she said tentatively. 'I was thinking we might look at going somewhere in the summer, somewhere hot and sunny. Just the two of us. What do you think?'

'Yeh, sounds good,' Paul replied smiling back at her.

'Anywhere you fancy?' Lucy asked.

'No. not really,' Paul replied. 'Maybe we can have a look after Christmas.'

'Okay,' Lucy replied, not sure if Paul had seemed that enthusiastic, but maybe she was just reading too much into it, as usual. She knew he wasn't feeling a hundred percent tonight.

Just then, Lucy noticed the table with the three couples seemed to be getting ready to leave and she asked Paul if they should just get the bill too as they were almost finished and Paul was still very quiet.

'Do you mind?' Paul replied, 'I'm just a bit tired and we're pretty much done anyway, aren't we? You don't want anything else do you? We can always have a coffee at home, if you fancy?'

Lucy said she was fine and so they called the waiter across and paid the bill, adding on a reasonable tip as they did so. It had been a good meal and both Paul and Lucy agreed that it was well deserved. They were just finishing off the last of their drinks when Lucy noticed the man from the other table approaching them. He looked about the same age as them but a bit shorter and chunkier looking than Paul. He walked towards their table purposefully with a wide grin on his face. As he reached them, he tapped Paul on the shoulder and Paul turned around and looked up at him.

'Andy, I knew it was you,' the man said, 'where have you been? No-one seemed to know what had happened to you. Somebody said you'd gone abroad? How are you mate? Its been ages.'

Paul smiled up at the man and said,

'I'm sorry mate, I think you've got the wrong person, but no problem,' he smiled at the man then looked across to Lucy, frowning.

91

'Shall we go?' he said and started to get up.

The man was still standing there staring at Paul, seemingly not quite sure what to do or say but not yet ready to leave.

'You're not Andy? Oh I'm really sorry. I could have sworn you were. You're the spitting image of one of my friends. Different colour hair and he has a beard but you really....your face, I could have put money on it. I haven't seen him for a while and thought he was you. Andy Austin. Do you know him? He's not a relative is he?'

'Sorry, no, never heard of him,' Paul said smiling as he edged past the man and moved towards the restaurant door. Lucy gathered up her things and hurried after him leaving the man still standing there at their table. She caught up with Paul outside and they walked together in silence until they were back in the car.

'Thanks for a lovely evening Lucy,' said Paul, 'I really enjoyed it. Sorry if I was a bit off, it's just this headache is getting a bit worse,' and he leaned across and kissed her.

'Oh don't worry, it was fine,' Lucy replied. 'Wasn't that weird at the end, that man coming over and thinking you were someone else? Andy something I think he said.'

'Yes, strange,' Paul replied, 'how could there be someone else as good looking as me?' he said laughing.

92

'Ha ha, exactly, one of you is enough!' Lucy replied laughing along with the joke and she started the car and set off for home.

Chapter 11

It was Dan's turn to get the coffees in. He'd been there long enough to know the drinks order by heart, as did most of his fellow IT technicians, or "The Techies" as they were commonly called. They had all done the coffee run so many times before it had become like an automatic pilot routine for them. No-one had left the department for as long as Dan could remember, and no-one ever changed their drinks order. The coffee from the machine tasted awful, no matter which one you chose, but that didn't seem to matter to any of them. Dan had a suspicion that the machine just spewed out the same drink regardless of which button you pressed.

However, doing the coffee run was a good excuse to get a break from the desk, stretch the legs and do something else, even if just for a few minutes. It was a chance to clear the head a bit from the daily IT drudge and get a view outside of the grey IT office. Some non-techy air. It was either that or going for a cigarette and as Dan didn't smoke, the coffee run was his only option.

The coffee machine was in a different part of the building from where the IT technicians were based. It was located in a communal area mid-way between where the technicians worked, along with the other admin staff, and where the police themselves were actually based. They occupied most of the right side of the building with different departments based on different floors. Dan knew that most of the police on his floor were part of the Serious Crime team, responsible for things like murders and rapes. The clue was in their departmental title.

Dan knew the numbers he had to punch in the coffee machine, two thirty fives which were cappuccinos, two twenty sevens, for Americanos and one regular coffee – a number twenty. In truth when they came out the machine they all looked much the same dirty brown colour and all tasted equally bitter and disgusting. But at least the walk there and back broke up the day to some extent and so he didn't mind taking his turn. Dan had worked here for over four years now. He'd started straight from University on the graduate trainee scheme (aka the slave labour scheme) and worked himself into a full time job. He wasn't sure if it was what he really wanted to do – at university he'd envisaged himself working for a gaming company or an entertainment company, or even starting his own business. He'd had some good ideas on new bits of software that he saw a gap in the market for and had even started writing some in his spare time but he never quite completed any. Besides he knew people like him didn't run their own companies, he wasn't the type. Not extrovert enough. Besides it was alright working here. There were some advantages. It was steady work and it had a good pension scheme.

As Dan walked along the corridor towards the coffee machine he saw two men already there apparently getting coffees for themselves and some of their colleagues. They were dressed similarly, both in grey suit trousers and white shirts with the sleeves rolled up to the elbows. Dan assumed they were from the Serious Crime Squad and he slowed down his pace, approaching quietly. He stopped a few paces away, and leant his shoulder against the corridor wall crossing his feet, prepared to wait his turn. Although Dan had seen the two policemen before, as a general rule the admin staff and police didn't really mix, there were too many rules and regulations around data protection and confidentiality on the cases the police were working on. When Dan started working for the police he'd had to sign all sorts of confidentiality documents and he knew that any leaks, anything traced back to him could mean severe penalties, including him losing his job.

Dan stood there silently, waiting his turn. So far it had been a pretty boring day in the IT department, when was it not lately he was thinking, and so an extra couple of minutes hanging around waiting for coffees was actually a good break for him.

One of the policemen was reading numbers off a scrap of paper and the other was punching them into the machine and, as each white cup appeared and filled up with liquid, placing it on a Formica table on the far side of the coffee machine. While the machine did its business the two policemen were carrying on a conversation and Dan couldn't help catching some of it as it travelled along the empty corridor towards him.

'So DS Campbell asked me to look into any connection between the two lads, Jack and Chris. The only thing I could find on the system was that they were both involved in some sort of car accident a year ago,' he heard one of the men say.

'Can't see why that would be important,' his colleague replied, 'road rage doesn't usually go on for a year and the victims now weren't even in the car accident were they?'

'No, I don't know, it was a pretty serious accident though, some people were killed. The lad called Jack was driving and the one called Chris was a passenger in the car. As I say that's the only thing we have on them in our database so I don't really know. If I get a chance I'll bring it up at one of the team meetings or drop a note into Campbell to tick the box that I've done it. But like you say I can't see how it's relevant.'

The two men gathered up their coffees and walked down the corridor in the opposite direction to Dan. They stopped to punch in a code on the metal door at the far end of the corridor before it

opened and they disappeared through into their part
of the building.

Chapter 12

Later that evening Dan, Jack and Jason all met up for their usual weekly game of five a side football. Chris was a good player and he usually played too but had understandably pulled out this time due to his mum's death. Dan wasn't really a footballer so he usually ended up playing in goal which meant he could keep his glasses on. He'd tried playing without them once but everything was just a blur and he kept running into the other players.

Jack had also had doubts about whether he should play, or even if he wanted to play. But in the end he felt he needed to get out of the house and do something normal. He felt guilty but he needed to escape from his family, even if it was only for an hour or two. He loved them dearly but he needed some space to breathe. And he also felt he wanted to do it for his brother Pete to show the bastard that killed him that life carried on. However hard that was, he knew it had to.

After the game they followed their normal routine of a quick shower, a spray of deodorant, some hair gel, a change of clothes and a short drive to a nearby pub for a post-match drink and general ribbing of each other's performance on the pitch. Jack felt better, more refreshed, and he was glad he'd decided to come out. The pub was still old fashioned, not one that had been converted into a gastro pub selling posh food. They had been coming here for years and it had stayed true to its roots with a long bar, a darts board at the far end and several large TVs dotted around on the walls showing various sports from around the world. The pub usually had the same half dozen or so customers who were mostly all middle aged or elderly men with the only women generally being those working behind the bar.

After some discussion about the game, who had scored the best goal, who had made the worst mistake and a general analysis of each other's performance, the young men's conversation inevitably moved on to the recent murders. Neither Jack or his family had heard anything further from the police and from that they assumed they hadn't made any progress in finding Pete's killer.

'I don't think they're any further forward to catching the guy,' Jack said, 'or they would have told us something. They didn't seem to have anything when they came to see me. I read somewhere that if they don't get the guy in the first forty eight hours then the trail begins to go cold and the chances of solving the case reduce to less than fifty-fifty.'

As usual Dan had been sitting quietly at the table, letting the others do the talking, but he suddenly looked up from his pint,

'Actually I did overhear something about the investigation today, but it wasn't much I don't think,' he said. 'I'm not sure I should really say anything either,' he said nervously looking over his shoulder.

'Come on,' said Jack, 'you can't leave us hanging like that, you know we won't say anything to anyone that would get you in trouble.'

His two mates looked at him expectantly, both slightly surprised that Dan had actually spoken, and Dan took a gulp from his pint and looked around once more before leaning into the centre of the table. As usual he'd left a ring of froth around his beard. He spoke quietly over the top of his pint, explaining what he'd overheard in the corridor by the coffee machine but he again concluded that it didn't seem to mean much.

'I think it's just standard stuff,' he said, 'just what's on the database.'

The three of them discussed it for a few minutes more but reluctantly agreed they couldn't think of any connection. They all went quiet for a few minutes and sat there just sipping their drinks, each seemingly lost in their own thoughts.

The conversation moved on to what they were all doing at Christmas although both Dan and Jason felt uncomfortable and didn't want to talk too much about their plans as they knew that Jack's family would still be in mourning for his bother Pete and wouldn't be looking forward to Christmas this year.

Sensing the mood change, Jack got up from the table and went to the bar to get another round in before they all headed home. It hadn't been their usual after football banter in the pub and he wondered if it ever would be again. As he waited at the bar for the drinks he began running everything through his head once more. Like the rest of his family, they had all become quasi detectives now, all analysing every little detail, every nuance, every possibility all ricocheting around in their heads, trying to make some sense of it all. But he always came to the same frustrating conclusion that it didn't make *any* sense. He began trying to think about any new information, maybe looking at it differently somehow. Maybe come at it from a different angle, because straightforward was getting him nowhere. It always seemed so easy in police dramas on the television where there was usually something obvious uncovered at the end of the programme that had actually been there all the way through if only you had picked it up. Was that the same in real life, or just TV?

He remembered the detective at Pete's funeral saying that he didn't believe in coincidences and that they were looking at any connection between Chris's mum and Pete. Then another detective had come back and questioned him about it again and they'd done the same with Chris. Then he thought about what Dan had said earlier about the policemen discussing the accident. That was definitely a connection between them that was memorable, for all the wrong reasons. It couldn't be though, could it? Had he started something that was somehow now coming back to haunt him?

He picked up the three drinks and headed back towards the table, a bottle of cold lager each for himself and Jason and a diet coke this time for Dan who was driving tonight. He handed round the drinks, sat down and began to voice his thoughts,

'I was just thinking, when I was at the bar, about what Dan was saying. What if there was some connection with the, em, accident we had and what's happening now?'

'Like what?' Jason replied, 'what sort of connection, what do you mean, I don't get it?' Jason's face was still red from playing football, it often stayed like that for a good hour after he had done any form of exercise.

'I don't know,' said Jack, 'what if it was some sort of karma thing. Maybe somebody thinks we got off lightly and wants to make us pay somehow.'

'But why would they take it out on Pete and Chris's mum? Why kill them? Jason responded. 'Surely if it was to do with the accident, they'd go for you as the driver. Sorry. Why Chris's mum, and where do me and Dan fit in? All four of us were in the car. It doesn't make sense to me. The more I think about it I just think it's some sort of random killer on the loose. He'll probably kill someone else that's nothing to do with any of us.'

'Yeh, I suppose so,' said Jack, rubbing his beard. 'I guess it's not a big place we live in so the chances are that someone would know someone else, it's just so frustrating, there must be something we can do though. We can't let him get away with it whoever he is.'

Dan had been sitting quietly listening, as he often did.

'You know when you…, sorry we, had the accident,' he piped up. 'There were four of them, em, …died but there was also another one there wasn't there? He didn't get hit much, he managed to get out the way and was alright I seem to remember.'

'Yeh, that's right, now you mention it I remember seeing him at the trial. He just sat there looking at you Jack, and at us, in the public gallery. It was a bit weird,' Jason added, 'what was his name again?'

'Andy Austin,' said Jack quickly, 'yeh I remember, a bit older than us, with a beard. You're right, he was just sitting there looking at us. I didn't want to look at him.'

'I think they were all his family that got hit,' Jason added, scratching his nose. 'They were all related in some way. Wasn't it his mum and dad I think and a couple of others, maybe brothers, I don't know.'

'That's right,' said Dan, 'Andy, that's it. So what if he decided to get some revenge or something?'

'Yeh but why Pete and Chris's mum, they'd nothing to do with it,' said Jason, 'and if he did want to do something surely he'd have tried right away, not years later? It doesn't make sense. I still think its some random sicko. As you said Jack, this isn't a big place.'

Jack was sitting quietly, thinking. It couldn't be Andy Austin, could it, surely not. He wouldn't go to that extreme would he? Jack was just beginning to get over the accident, surely it wasn't coming back to haunt him again?

'Mmm,' said Jack, 'I can't see it being him but maybe it would be interesting to find out where this Andy Austin is now, maybe check him out. At least it would give us something to do rather than sitting around here in limbo, doing nothing.'

'If you really think so, maybe you'd better tell the police, one of the detectives, see what they say?' Dan suggested.

'Nah, I don't really want to bring it up with them and go through all the accident stuff again. It sounds like they're already on it anyway. What's the harm in me just looking him up, see where he works and lives and that. As I say it'd give me something to do and god knows I need to do something just to get me out of the house. You never know, and if he is connected in some way we could have a quiet word with him before the police get there.'

'You'd better be careful, if you do try and find him though,' said Jason. 'Even if he's not involved in any of this he's still not going to want to see you after all that happened.'

'No, I'll be discrete, 'Jack replied. 'I wont tell anyone what I'm doing and I'll let you know what I find, and don't worry Dan, I won't mention your name to anyone.'

Chapter 13

The police team were all assembled back in the incident room, sitting around the long table. Strong was at the head of the table, sat up straight in his chair, with Campbell perched on an uncomfortably small chair immediately to his right, looking shorter than he actually was. They were going through all the latest developments one by one and discussing them, questioning them, challenging them to see if there was anything important or anything they'd missed that needed further investigation. This was a part of the job that Strong really enjoyed. Getting his team together and having an open discussion, regardless of rank. It was a great way of getting the whole squad working as a whole and he really believed there was an exponential benefit in running the operation this way. It brought them all up to speed on what they had learned so far and also the format allowed a variety of views and ideas to be aired without the worry of ridicule. Strong quickly shut down any negative comments in this type of meeting and his team had grown to understand that and the benefits that brought.

107

Several times he'd seen the synergistic benefits of the team working together and potentially coming up with new leads or lines of inquiry. He really believed in the idea of people building on, and adding to, others original thoughts and ideas. He knew cases were rarely solved by one person; it was usually a combination of several ideas followed up by a lot of good old fashioned, hard police work

Today's meeting had come up with some interesting ideas, a few of which might be worth investigating further but in reality, Strong and the other senior policemen knew that they hadn't made much progress since the last briefing. Strong could sense everyone was getting frustrated and he, himself was becoming under increasing pressure to find a suspect. He now had to brief the Chief Constable on a daily basis and he knew their meeting later today was likely to be an uncomfortable one for him as they hadn't made any notable progress in the last twenty four hours. Such was the nature of working on a murder case.

DS Campbell had reported back on their further questioning of Jack and Chris, looking for some link, some common connection that would provide a reason for the killings. Although he felt Jack had been holding something back, he hadn't been able to find anything further and so he concluded that it was looking like a dead end. They'd discussed the fact that both Jack and Chris were on the police database as having been in a car accident with fatalities and that Jack had lost his driving licence as a result of that. One of the junior officers had been given the task of tracking down the sole survivor of the accident, Andy Austin, just so they could cover him off. However the officer was apparently still looking for him and so there was no further update on that and the discussion ground to a halt. Although that was frustrating for Strong, he couldn't see that there was much else they could do until the officer assigned reported back with his findings.

As a standard routine, they'd also looked back at previous murder cases over the last ten years with any sort of similarity and found that one of those convicted had recently been released from prison on parole. It was decided that they should look into his movements over the last couple of weeks and see if he could be a possible suspect. Other than that there were no new developments and so Strong finished the meeting and went back to his office to plan what he was going to say to his Chief Constable in a couple of hours time.

Although he didn't believe it, he'd already decided his best bet was to focus on the recently released killer as a major new line of enquiry. He knew the Chief Constable would want to see some progress and, at this moment, that was all that he could give him. He started making some notes. The previous murderer had also used a knife to kill his victim in an apparently random attack with an excuse that he was high on drugs. If he talked it up a bit it would keep the Chief Constable off his back for at least for another twenty four hours but that would be the most he could hope for. The Chief wasn't stupid and he'd soon see through Strong's story if there was nothing in it. Hopefully by that time his team would have come up with something, or the killer would have made a mistake. In Strong's experience, they usually did. Strong knew that they only had a short time left to make some breakthrough before he'd have to come up with some sort of Plan B. He shuddered at the thought.

Just as he was about to wind up the meeting, the door opened and a man came into the room holding a piece of paper. He looked at Strong and Strong nodded.

'Sir, this has just come in. About an hour ago, someone tried to use one of Peter Wilson's bank cards to withdraw cash. It was at an ATM on the High Street and we are hopeful there'll be CCTV. A couple of the lads have gone down there now and I've told them to call me as soon as they get there.'

A buzz went around the room.

'Good, good,' Strong said, 'come and see me as soon as you hear. This could be the breakthrough we need.'

Chapter 14

Paul was seated, sipping a cup of hot coffee in front of the warm log fire. It was cold outside and he found it cosy and peaceful to just sit there and think. And he had a lot of thinking to do. It was peaceful here, ironic really when he considered why he was using it. This place had been a good find but he knew that it would soon be time to move on to the next chapter of his story - and he knew that wasn't going to be easy.

But he had planned it well. He'd been working on this for a while now and so he was confident that he'd succeed. Nevertheless he still felt stressed and that was starting to bring on one of his headaches. He reached into his bag and took out his bottle of pills. He popped two into his mouth and washed them down with a gulp of coffee, relaxing back into his chair.

As he sat there in front of the fire, looking at the orange flickering flames, his mind began to drift and he started to think about Lucy again. She'd gone out with some friends on a girl's night out and told him not to wait up for her. She said they'd planned to go to a club and so she wouldn't be back home until the early hours of the morning. Lucy was a problem he'd been thinking about more often as things had progressed over the last few weeks. It had been great fun when he'd first met her and she fitted exactly what he needed at that time. She'd given him a steady relationship and she didn't ask too many questions with the added benefit of a place for him to live pretty much incognito. However he hadn't foreseen how quickly and how deeply their relationship would grow. From just being a useful companion, he now realised that she'd become much more than that. At this point he didn't know how he was going to handle that. A serious girlfriend had never been part of his carefully thought out plan and maybe that had been his only mistake so far.

There had been a few occasions lately where things had got a bit difficult between them. She had started asking more about where he'd been during the day and he'd had to come up with some good explanations about writing his book. She'd also been quizzing him about the book itself and he could sense that she was suspicious about his answers and his reluctance to show her anything that he'd written so far. Some sort of evidence. How could he though, when there was nothing to show? He could see the time coming soon when she would demand to see his writing as some sort of proof point that they were in an honest, trusting relationship. And he couldn't blame her for that. If their positions were switched he'd probably do exactly the same.

Then there had been the incident in the restaurant. That had been a close call. That idiot coming over and claiming that he knew him. That he was someone else, not Paul Smith. Somehow he'd managed to smooth that over with Lucy but he knew that something similar could easily happen again soon and she wouldn't be so easily fobbed off a second time. If she remembered the name she could have looked it up on the internet, although Paul had taken precautions and wiped all his previous history as much as he could. He was lucky that there was an American country and western singer with the same name and he took up the first few pages of any search results.

Paul was beginning to wonder if he was he doing the right thing though. Maybe Lucy was the one for him and he should change his plans. Maybe he and Lucy could have the sort of relationship his mum and dad had when they were younger. He wished they could have met her, they'd really have liked Lucy. She was the first woman he'd met where he could imagine a long term future. Him and Lucy getting married, having children and living a long and happy life together – just like his parents had, or at least did, until last year. Maybe that was still possible if he stopped now.

But then he remembered what had happened to his parents. What was the point of it, all those years together, if it was just going to end like that?

113

He owed it to his mum and dad to carry on. He loved Lucy but he couldn't live with her under such a huge lie. This was just too important. It was more important than anything else. He felt he had to do it. He didn't have a choice.

As he sat in front of the warm fire he felt more relaxed and his headache was beginning to ease. The pills were already kicking in and he took another sip of the warm coffee. He began to feel less anxious, besides he only needed another week and his plan would all be done. All except for the Lucy part. He still didn't know what he was going to do there, or he did but wasn't yet ready to admit it to himself.

For now though he needed to concentrate on getting the next part of his plan right. He'd rehearsed it over many weeks and knew the routine but he also knew that something unexpected could come up and he'd need to be ready for that. He'd thought through a number of possibilities of things that could go wrong and was confident he had a good plan B in place to be able to cope with any of these should they happen. He'd been doing his exercise routine daily and felt fit and strong. As strong as he had for a long time and he was confident he'd be able to cope with any physical activity needed. He picked up his sports bag and checked that everything he needed was inside. He looked at his watch and decided it was time to go. He didn't want to be too early and risk being seen waiting but it would be worse if he was late and

114

missed his chance completely. It had to be done today. Taking one final glance around the room to make sure there was nothing out of place, he switched the lights off and left the farmhouse. He walked along the driveway and around to the side of the house where a dark grey van was parked, obscured from the front approach.

Paul opened the van door and threw the sports bag across onto the passenger seat, climbing up into the van. He checked himself in the rear view mirror, flattened down his hair and then started the van up and drove off around the front of the house and back down the long driveway leading to the main road.

Chapter 15

There was a knock on Strong's office door.

'Come in,' he called and the door opened. It was the policeman who had been tasked with monitoring Peter Wilson's bank cards. Strong was impatient to see what he had found out.

'Well, did we get anything from the CCTV?' Strong asked, pulling his chair in closer to his desk.

'Yes sir, we did,' the policeman replied. 'We got a clear shot of the man from the Bank's camera at the ATM.'

'That's great.' Strong replied, 'lets get that circulated so we can see if we can find out who he is.'

'Well sir, in fact we already know. He's already known to us, he's….'

'Really?' Strong interrupted in a surprised tone.

'Yes sir, he's a bit of low life scum, a well known drug addict. His name's John Davies but everyone calls him Junkie John. We've picked him up and a couple of the lads are bringing him in now,' he glanced at his watch, 'should be here in ten minutes or so. Shall we put him in one of the rooms for interview?'

'Yes, please do, is Campbell still around, does he know?' Strong asked.

'Yes, I believe so sir.' And just at that point, as if by magic, DS Campbell came marching into Strong's office.

'You've heard the news?' Strong asked him.

'Yes sir,' Campbell replied.

'What do you think?' Strong asked.

'I'm not sure, lets see what he has to say but initial thoughts are that he doesn't fit the bill of being a double murderer. From what I hear he struggles to tie his shoe laces most days. Do you want to interview him?'

'Mmm, okay, no you can do it – I'll watch in from the side room, let me know when we're ready to go.' Strong replied.

Thirty minutes later Strong was sitting in the side room looking at the three screens in front of him. He was stretched comfortably across one of the chairs watching closely. All three screens showed the same scene but each from a different angle. They were showing the interview room where DS Campbell and DC Jones sat on one side of a table across from the man they had brought in, known as John Davies. Davies had already declined the offer of a legal representative to be with him and he was lounging in a grey plastic chair, his legs stretched

117

out in front of him, crossed at the ankles. He was wearing a grey hooded top, some baggy tracksuit trousers and a pair of scuffed and torn trainers. In contrast to Davies, DS Campbell and DC Jones were dressed almost identically, both wearing black shoes, grey trousers and white shirts. Campbell's sleeves were rolled up and he was leaning forward, directly opposite John Davies. DC Jones was sat next to Campbell and he was leaning back in his chair, partly obscured by Campbell on one of the screens.

'So, John, tell me how did you come by this bank card?' he asked, pushing a polythene bag across the table towards Davies. Davies's head moved slightly as he glanced down at the item in front of him on the table.

'No comment,' he replied.

DS Campbell sighed and looked towards DC Jones. He then turned back to face Davies and pulled his chair in so that he was as close to the table as his large frame would allow. He leaned forward and looked directly in Davies's face.

'Okay John, let me cut to the chase. This bank card belongs to a man who was found murdered. We have video of you using the card at an ATM the following day. Right now I'm sure you can see how that looks John. In short it puts you are in a serious position. I'll ask you again John, how did you get this card?'

Davies shifted slightly in his chair and mumbled something.

'What was that John?' Campbell asked.

'I said I found it, that's all.' Davies replied.

'Where did you find it John?' Campbell asked.

'I dunno, in the street somewhere. It was just lying there. I picked it up and was gonna hand it in to you guys.'

'Which street John, its important for you that you remember,' the detective persisted.

'I dunno, down by the canal I think. It was just lying there like someone had dropped it.'

Campbell turned sideways to look at Jones again and Jones pushed another plastic bag towards him. Campbell pushed it across the table to rest next to the bank card.

'When we picked you up John, you also had this wallet on your person. Where did you get that?'

'It was a present,' Davies replied.

'I see,' Campbell responded. 'If that was the case John, why does it contain several other cards and documents belonging to Peter Wilson, the man who was murdered? Do you want to spend the rest of your life in prison John, because from where I'm sat that's what's going to happen unless you start talking John and tell me the truth because I'm quickly running out of patience.'

Davies pushed himself up in his chair and exhaled loudly.

'Look, I didn't kill no-one,' he said. 'I didn't even know he was dead. He just looked like he was asleep to me and his wallet was just lying

119

there. It must have fallen out of his pocket or something. I just picked it up. I was gonna hand it in. Just haven't got round to it yet.'

Looking on from the side room, Strong pushed his chair back, stretched his legs out under the table and interlocked his hands behind his head, remembering that he still needed that haircut. As he continued to listen in on the interview, he became more and more sure that this man was not the killer they were looking for. It appeared he was simply an opportunist thief who had robbed a dead man of his wallet undoubtedly so that he could buy himself some more drugs. Davies had not seen anyone else on the towpath and it appeared from what he was saying that it was likely he had stumbled on the body a few hours after the murder had actually taken place. They would still have to spend some time and resource confirming some of what Davies had told them, but as Campbell had thought from the start, this was highly unlikely to be the double murderer they were seeking.

Chapter 16
15th December, one year earlier

Jason knew he was drunk. But he felt good drunk. Not ill drunk. Not the kind of drunk that he couldn't speak or was about to throw up. He was just happy drunk so that everything seemed much brighter and a lot more funny. He'd had a good night out with his mates. Mates he'd grown up with. The best. Now he was on his way home in Jack's car, slumped in the back seat with Chris. Chris the comedian. Jack, who was the same age as him, was driving and Dan a year older and the biggest of all of them in both height and weight, was squeezed into the passenger seat up front. As usual he wasn't saying much.

As always it had been a funny night, a lot of piss taking between them, but they all knew it was just friendly banter. If any of them ever got upset with things going too far they'd all give that person a hug and things would be back to normal. They all looked out for each other and always had done since they were little.

Jason was wedged up sideways against the door and he could see the bright lights flashing past him as Jack drove them home. Street lights, car lights and lots of colourful Christmas lights. They were all really vibrant. The Council had gone to town this year, decorating all the trees and lampposts in the town centre with colourful lights - reds, blues, greens and whites. They all sped past Jason's eye-line glowing radiantly reminding him it would soon be Christmas and making him feel warm and cosy inside. Jason loved Christmas. He always had done since he was a little boy. Every year his family had made sure it was special – especially his dad who would dress up as Santa and hand out all the presents to him and his brothers and sisters on Christmas morning making it seem magical to them. He still did it, even now, although they'd all long since discovered the truth about Santa, it was still a family tradition and no-one wanted to break it.

The car went over a bump, probably a pothole that the council had been too busy to repair whilst putting up the Christmas lights, and jarred Jason out of his Christmas thoughts. He looked across at his mate Chris. He was the one that the women seemed to like. It was his blonde hair. Jason looked at his reflection in the window and wished he hadn't been born ginger headed with freckles, but knew he couldn't do anything about that. Chris was looking glum, he'd thought he was going to pull a girl he'd met in the pub but Jason thought she'd just been playing him all along.

'Aww poor Chris,' Jason said looking at his mate, 'that bird used you to buy her drinks, she was never that interested in you.'

'You prat,' Jack shouted from the front of the car. 'You never had a chance with her, she was well out of your league.'

They all laughed but Chris ignored them. He was doing something on his phone and so Jason reached over and snatched it from him.

'Give's it back you ginger dick,' Chris shouted and he tried to get it back from Jason, but Jason was too quick for him and before he could get it he'd tossed it back over Chris's head where it bounced off the seat and onto the floor of the car. Jason was in hysterics.

'Oi you two settle down, anyone would think you were all pissed!' Jack called out from the front of the car, glancing in his mirror as he did so and Jason caught the reflection of his dark hair, open mouth and newly grown beard. He'd taken a bit of ribbing for that but Jason had to concede it actually suited him.

'Chris is,' Jason shouted back, ''he's pissed off because he got mugged off. That bird just played along to get free drinks and now he's texting his ex, begging for an easy shag,' he said laughing.

Chris bent forward to try and pick up his phone and as he did so, Jason went to push his head down but suddenly felt the car lurch and he was

123

thrown up off his seat slightly with his head bumping into the side window. He was about to shout something to Jack when he was distracted and confused by a dark shape passing by outside his window. Suddenly he was thrown forward and his head hit the back of the passenger seat in front of him and everything went quiet and black.

Chapter 17

Bill Reynolds was in his local pub, the Horse and Groom. It was Saturday night, where else would he be? He'd been coming here for years, only missing the odd Saturday night when he was on holiday or ill, and even that had been very rare. Once, a few years ago, new neighbours had moved in next door and invited Bill and his wife to a barbeque at their house on the Saturday evening. Of course Bill had gone but he'd been a bit grumpy all night, missing his usual pint in his usual local. It wasn't even a proper barbeque, it was a gas appliance, they might as well have cooked it in the grill indoors, he had said to his wife afterwards. In Bill's eyes a real barbeque had charcoal and smoke and black bits of chicken. Also when he'd asked for a beer, he'd been handed a bottle of some fizzy lager and had been made to feel odd when he asked if he could have a glass to drink it out off. At least they hadn't asked if he wanted a straw. Luckily it had been a one off and they'd never been invited back again. Bill was 58 and he'd had a number of different jobs since he'd left the army twenty five years ago. Mostly manual work on building sites, anything that brought in a few pounds for him and his family. He'd always worked hard and made sure they never went short.

But now even the pub wasn't the same anymore. Not like the old days. It used to be packed in here, back in the days when he was younger. And back then Bill had known every one of the people in the pub. Not now though. Now, it had changed. And not for the better, in Bill's opinion. When he looked around, he could count the people he knew on the fingers of one hand. A lot had changed in the last few years and, in Bill's view, most of it was not for the good. There didn't seem to be any friendliness now, no sense of community or togetherness. Everyone was just looking out for themselves nowadays. In his younger days the pub had been the heart of the neighbourhood, especially for the young men. They'd all meet there, exchange stories, have a laugh and do things, it was their lives. They had been like one big family. If someone was going through hard times they'd all chip in and help out where they could.

That didn't seem to happen now though. Everyone seemed to be looking at those bloody mobile phones nowadays or walking around with headphones on. What was that all about? Couldn't they listen to music in their homes, in their bedrooms like he used to do when he was younger? Or in the pubs or discos when they were out at the weekend? Why did they have to have it on when they were outside, cutting themselves off from

126

everyone else, living in their own little cocooned world. No-one seemed to care about anyone else anymore – who they were, what they were up to in their everyday lives – it no longer seemed to matter.

And the pub had changed too. His pub. The one he'd spent a lot of time in over many years. It wasn't really a pub anymore. It was more of a restaurant. They almost made you feel guilty if you only came in for a drink. Like there was something wrong with you. '*What? You don't want a table, you don't want to see a menu?' 'Are you some kind of weirdo, someone that comes to a pub just to drink?*' That's how it felt sometimes now. But he still came. Every Saturday night. It was his place and he still knew a few others that did the same, although they were getting fewer and fewer as the years rolled by. He could see the seats they all used to sit in by the bar gradually disappearing, one by one.

He looked at his watch, it was just gone ten o'clock, and then looked at his pint which was almost empty. He could have another one, or head for home now and be back in time for Match of the Day on the television. That might be more interesting. There weren't many people he knew in tonight so he had spent the last couple of hours standing at the bar, mostly on his own. He drained his pint and put the glass down on the bar top.

'Another one mate, same again?'

Bill looked up and saw a young barman, dressed in a white shirt and needing a shave, standing in front of him with a glass in one hand and

127

his other hand poised over the beer pump ready to pull it towards him. He was smiling at Bill and eager to start pulling the pint. Bill looked at him. He'd been coming here for almost forty years now, before this guy was even born; when he knew all of the bar staff by name and they all knew him too. They had all been his friends, his extended family even. But Bill didn't know this guy's name and he doubted the barman knew his either. Not like the old days when Fred had run it. Fred knew everyone that came into his pub and most of their business too. There wasn't much going on in the area that Fred didn't know about. The barman was still poised, waiting.

'What's my name?' Bill asked the barman.

'What, your name? Sorry I'm new here, it's emm…, John isn't it, I'm not sure? Do you want another pint?' he replied smiling.

Bill smiled back wryly and shook his head. He pushed his glass back across the bar and turned away. Picking up his coat from the back of the chair he slipped it on and walked towards the pub door. The barman watched him as he went. Strange old guy, he thought to himself as he quickly turned to serve the next customer.

'Another one mate, same again?' he said with a big smile.

As Bill stepped outside, the pub door swung heavily shut behind him and the cold night air hit him sharply. He stopped and fumbled for the buttons on his coat, doing them up as quickly as he could. His fingers weren't as nimble as they used to be. But then neither was most of his body now, although he was still quite fit for a fifty eight year old. All that time working on building sites had certainly built up his muscles. He reached into his pocket and took out his woolly hat pulling it tightly over his head and ears, a few, what were once ginger but now white, hairs sticking out at the sides.

It would soon be Christmas and they were forecasting snow this year. Lovely, thought Bill, a white Christmas, just like the old days. It had been a few years since it last snowed properly. Back then, all the families would be out in the street building snowmen and having snowball fights. That never seemed to happen now though – kids weren't allowed to play in the streets anymore. Too dangerous apparently. Safer to keep them inside and let them play games on their computers and not talk to anyone. He walked on, his hands pushed down deeply into his coat pockets, burrowing for warmth with his head bowed forward against the cold December wind. He walked slowly, his hip playing up a bit in the cold weather.

He knew the way well, the road back home. He'd walked it many times over the years and definitely on most Saturday nights through sun, wind, rain and the occasional snow. Whatever the weather threw at him, he always made it out for a pint or two, or occasionally a few more. It was tradition. What else would he do on a Saturday night?

129

As he turned the corner into Ridley Road, he glanced up and noticed a dark van parked mid-way down the street with a man standing next to it talking on one of those damned mobile phones. He could see the glow from the screen shining up from the man's hand but it was casting a shadow across the man's face. The van was parked mid-way between two street lights so Bill still couldn't make out if it was anyone he knew as he walked towards him. The man's head was bent down into the phone with his face turned slightly away from Bill in the shadow. He was wearing a dark hooded jacket or maybe a sweatshirt.

'Good evening,' Bill said, nodding to the man as he walked past him. He still couldn't see his face but didn't think he knew him. He didn't look familiar. Truth be told, he seemed to know less and less people in this area now. There had been lots of incomers, not like the old days when everyone knew everyone.

However Bill always made a point of saying hello to people as he passed them, whether he knew them or not. He just believed it was polite and the right thing to do. He especially liked to do it when they were on their phones or had headphones in, just to make a point. The man didn't answer, which Bill always thought was rude but he had come to accept that's what people were like nowadays and anyway he was more focused on getting home and out of the cold wind.

130

As Bill walked on a few paces he suddenly felt a sharp pain on the back of his head, his knees buckled and he momentarily saw himself falling forwards towards the pavement and into nothingness. He was unconscious before he hit the pavement.

Paul looked around, reassuring himself that there was still no one in sight. He slipped his phone into his jacket pocket and quickly opened the rear doors of the van. He bent down and rolled Bill over onto his back, taking his hat off and unleashing a shock of white hair. His nose was bleeding and his freckled forehead was scraped as he hadn't been able to stop his face hitting the pavement when he fell. Paul checked he was still breathing and was relieved to find he was. He knew that there was a risk he might have killed him when he hit him on the back of the head with the metal bar but thankfully he was still alive. Everything was still going to plan.

He hooked his hands under his arms and half dragged, half carried him towards the van. He struggled a bit as Bill was a big man but it didn't matter as there was no-one else around to see what he was doing. He'd done his homework, driven the route a few times before and knew that this was a very quiet street. The quietest road between the pub and Bill's house. As he hoisted Bill into the back of the van, one of his boots banged hard against a rear light, smashing the plastic covering and several pieces dropped onto the road. Paul slid him along

131

the metal floor towards the front of the van and scooped up several larger pieces of the broken light, throwing them in behind him. He then climbed inside and pulled the doors closed behind him. He sat for a moment getting his breath back, glad that he'd kept up his exercise routine. He hadn't realised Bill would be so heavy, he was a big man, solid. He switched on the rear light and opened his sports bag which was lying on the floor against the headboard. Taking out some cloth and tape, he worked quickly to gag and tie Bill up before he came round. Finally he secured him to two hooks on the inside panel of the van with a piece of rope. He sensed Bill was beginning to regain consciousness and so he reached back into his sports bag and took out a small brown bottle and a white cloth. He carefully poured some liquid from the bottle onto the cloth and then held the damp cloth against Bill's nose. After a few seconds he felt his body begin to relax and he took the cloth away and gently laid him back down on the floor of the van. Paul checked Bill's breathing again and was satisfied it was normal. He pulled on the rope, checking it was tight then zipped up his bag and took it with him as he left the rear of the van. The street was still empty as he got into the front of the van and drove away.

The roads were quiet and he was making good time, heading back to the farm. Everything had gone to plan and he was feeling pretty satisfied with himself. In some ways this was always going to be a harder part of his plan, there was more that could have gone wrong. It wasn't like the first two when he was able to just do the business and leave. He knew there was still more to be done with his load in the back of the van but so far everything had gone well. He turned right at the traffic lights and glanced at his watch. He was now out in the country and should be home in about twenty minutes, he thought, which meant he had plenty of time to unload the van and get him safely secured in his new abode, as it would be for the next few days. The dose he'd given Bill should mean that he'd still be asleep for at least another hour. He turned the radio down and listened towards the rear and sure enough all was quiet. He turned the radio back up again and glanced in his mirror where, for the first time, he noticed a police car immediately behind him. He felt his heartbeat increase slightly and he looked again. It was probably just a coincidence, there was no reason for them to be interested in him and he eased off his speed slightly to make sure he was well within the speed limit. As he glanced up again at his mirror he thought he might have seen a flash of light. Did the police just flash me, he thought? He wasn't sure so he kept driving but he kept one eye on his rear view mirror. This time he saw it clearly, the police car definitely flashed its headlights. There was no other traffic around so Paul knew it must be him they were flashing at. "*Shit*" he thought, "*what am I going to do?*"

He decided he had better stop and find out what they wanted, he didn't think he'd been speeding but he didn't think there was any way it could be anything to do with Bill in the back of the van. He was positive no-one had seen him abduct him, but maybe he was wrong, maybe someone had and they'd phoned the police. But if that had been the case surely they wouldn't just be flashing him to stop. Abduction was a serious crime and warranted a more robust police response than just a flash of the headlights. Paul set his indicator and pulled into the side of the dark country road, turning off his engine. There was no other traffic around and the police car pulled in behind Paul's van.

Paul stayed in the van, watching the police car attentively via his rear view mirror. There were two policemen in the car and neither had yet moved. As he continued to watch the driver side door opened and one of the policemen emerged from the car holding a torch. He held it out in front of him and started walking towards Paul's van. As he approached, Paul switched his view to his side mirror and after a few seconds he saw the policeman walking up the side of the van towards him. As he got closer, Paul pressed a button and his window slid open. The policeman was now level with Paul and he bent down to look at him.

"Good evening sir, how are we?' he said in a neutral tone.

'I'm fine, officer,' Paul replied, thinking was that right, was that what you call them. He'd never actually been stopped by the police before. He felt his face getting hot. 'How can I help you?' Paul asked, keen to find out what the issue was.

'Is this your van?' the policeman asked.

'Yes, well, its actually hired. I just needed it for a couple of days, for, em, a job I'm doing,' Paul replied and immediately thinking shut up, too much information.

'Oh right, what is that then, what job?' the policeman enquired.

'Oh I was just helping a friend move some stuff to his new flat,' Paul replied quickly.

'I see,' said the policeman. 'Is it in the back of the van?'

'What?' Paul responded, taken aback, he still didn't know why he'd been stopped.

'The, em, stuff you're moving for your friend,' the policeman replied.

'Oh, that, oh no,' Paul said, 'that was earlier, its empty now, I'm just heading home.'

'I see,' the policeman replied and he shone his torch around the front of the van. 'Do you know one of your tail lights is broken?' he asked.

'Oh, yes sorry, that happened earlier tonight, when we were, err, moving the stuff. We caught it with something, a lamp I think and it broke. I'm going to see if I can get it fixed first thing tomorrow. I'll need to ring the rental company. I've got the broken bits in the back,' Paul said, immediately regretting it. Why couldn't he stop talking?

135

'I see,' the policeman responded, 'can I just take your name please?'

But before Paul could answer there was a sudden crack of static and the policeman's radio burst into life. Paul watched as the policeman stepped a couple of paces away from the van, turned his back and spoke into it. At the same time he noticed a movement reflected in his wing mirror and he saw that the other policeman had got out of the car and appeared to be beckoning his colleague. The first policeman gave a nod and turned back to face Paul.

'Okay, make sure you do get that fixed sir, you know it's an offence to drive with a broken tail light but take this as a warning and get it sorted before you drive again,'

'I will do officer, thanks,' Paul replied.

The policeman walked back to his car and Paul sat there until they'd driven off and were out of sight. He exhaled deeply and ran his hands through his hair before taking another deep breath. He looked at his watch and concluded that he still had plenty of time to do what he had to do and get back to the flat before Lucy got home from her girl's night out. He started the engine and, watching in his mirror, he drove carefully back out onto the road.

Chapter 18

Strong was sitting in his office reading emails. Although it was the weekend police work never really stopped and many of his team were in, working on potential leads for the double murder. Strong had promised his wife that he would try and get home as soon as he could, but they both knew from experience that there was no guarantee. Strong skipped through most of his correspondence and tried to give as brief answers as possible to those that really needed a response from him. Whilst he appreciated the benefits technology brought to the process of police work, he was also aware that the amount of information floating around could also swamp an individual - making them miss some key elements of an investigation. He'd seen it happen to colleagues of his who had let the technology dictate them rather than the other way around. Up till now he had been pretty good at keeping it all under control and separating the wood from the trees. He was about to read an email from the Chief Constable when his phone rang.

'Hello, it's Maria from the Chief's office, he'd like to see you. Could you pop along now please?'

'Sure, Maria,' replied Strong. 'Any idea what it's about?'

'Sorry, no he just popped his head out and said to give you a call.'

Ok, I'll be there in two minutes,' Strong replied and replaced the receiver.

He clicked on the Chief Constable's email but it wasn't anything important, certainly not anything that would require an immediate face to face with him.

In Strong's experience a meeting at such short notice was rarely good news. If he was a betting man, which he wasn't – other than a yearly flutter on the Grand National, he would put his money on this being some sort of bollocking for him. He guessed it would probably be to do with their lack of progress on solving the recent two murders. His last meeting with the Chief hadn't gone particularly well and he knew that he only had a limited time left before the Chief suggested bringing in another DI to review the investigation and that was something he definitely didn't want. Strong knew the Chief Constable had faith in him and his abilities as a detective but he also knew the Chief Constable was no fool. It was obvious that the Chief hadn't been convinced of the idea that the recently released murderer could be the prime suspect and Strong had found it hard to put forward any evidence to persuade him. In truth that was mainly because Strong didn't believe it himself but he was just trying to buy some time until the team uncovered something more concrete that would lead them to the real killer. They'd also wasted time interviewing and following up on the petty thief, John Davies. The Chief had got wind of that also before they realised that Davies wasn't the killer and Strong knew another false lead wouldn't have impressed him.

He left his office and walked along the corridor to the elevator. The Chief Constable's office was on the top floor of the building, which was commonly known as the "Golden Mile" because of its more stylish layout and décor. It would seem that more money had been spent on this floor than the rest of the building put together. Where Strong had a small office with a metal filing cabinet, the Chief Constable had a suite of rooms with leather sofas and oak cabinets and tables. It reminded Strong of a top end furniture showroom.

Strong exited the elevator and walked through the outer office past a line of three desks all occupied by staff working on their laptops. He made his way through an open door, tapping lightly on it as he passed, and arrived in the Chief Constable's inner room. The Chief was sitting behind his desk with a pile of papers randomly spread out in front of him. Strong had worked for him for the last five years and knew him well in a professional sense, but he had never engaged with him personally. He stood

139

up as Strong approached, he was shorter than Strong, in his late fifties and approaching retirement with a bald head and a larger stomach perhaps reflecting the many social events Strong knew he had to attend as part of his role. He met Strong on the other side of his desk.

'Shut the door please,' he said picking up one of the sheets of paper from his desk. 'Have you seen this?' he asked loudly, not waiting for a reply. 'The bloody papers have got it – its going to be all over the headlines tomorrow morning. Killer on the loose. Double murderer. God knows what else they'll come up with. Makes us look like we don't know what we're doing! I have two questions. What are we doing and how did the papers get a hold of this?'

Strong stepped forward and took a deep breath. He'd seen the Chief like this before, his face flushed, and he knew he needed to be careful what he said and that he needed to get through the next few minutes until the Chief calmed down and became more rational again. He decided to answer the second question first and hope that would take up most of the time he needed.

'I haven't seen what the papers have got. I'm guessing its just what's known publicly and a bit of speculation on their part? Is there anything in there that could only have come from us?' The Chief sighed and handed the sheet of paper across to Strong to look at. He scanned it quickly and satisfied himself that there was nothing sensitive in there.

'Just normal paper stuff as far as I can see, putting two and two together and making five. I'll get a statement out reassuring them that we're working on a number of leads and that the public do not have any reason to be alarmed. The usual stuff.'

'What's happening with the guy who was recently released from prison, any more on that?' the Chief Constable asked Strong

'We're still checking out his movements sir,' Strong replied.

'And this Davies guy, the junkie, what about him?'

'We're pretty sure he just stumbled across Peter Wilson's body and stole the wallet from him. He's been charged with theft and is in custody awaiting trial, but he's of no further interest to us in regard to the murders.'

Just at that moment, there was a knock on the office door and Maria popped her head around it.

'Your car's waiting out front sir, shall I tell them you're on your way?'

'Yes please Maria,' the Chief constable answered and Maria disappeared closing the door behind her. He turned to look at Strong.

'I don't need to tell you that the pressure is ramping on this one, especially now the papers are on it. They'll be looking for something new every day and if we don't have any progress for them,

141

they'll make it look bad for us. We need to get this one sorted Mo,' he said quietly, his eyes locked on Strong's, 'And we need to do it quickly. You know what I'm saying.'

Strong nodded and turned to leave. He knew he'd got off pretty lightly this time but it was telling that the Chief had called him by his first name. He rarely did that and Strong knew he had been making a point on how serious this one had become. He was making it seem personal, which it felt like for Strong anyhow and he knew he needed to decide on what to do next. He hoped his team would come up with some sort of breakthrough soon or he might have to get more deeply involved himself instead of letting DS Campbell and the team manage it. He made his way back down to his office and sat at his desk thinking through a number of different scenarios.

Chapter 19

Jack was making his way to Andy Austin's workplace. He was dressed sensibly, but casually, in a blue jacket, white shirt, black trousers and shoes. Since he and his friends had been talking in the pub he hadn't been able to stop thinking about him. At first it had just been something to focus his mind on, away from the dark thoughts, but it had now become a bit of an obsession. The truth is he was annoyed with himself for not thinking about this possibility before. Although he knew that if he took five minutes and thought about it rationally, he'd conclude that it was highly unlikely that Andy Austin was the murderer. In reality Austin was just a normal guy with a normal job and an ordinary life. People like that didn't murder other people did they? But at this point Jack didn't want to think rationally; he just wanted to do something. Besides, stranger things did happen, or at least they did on TV and especially on the internet.

After the pub discussion he'd gone away and done a bit of digging for information. He'd got onto the internet and looked up newspaper reports from last year about the accident and his subsequent court case. It had been difficult reading for him but he persisted as it made him feel like he was actually doing something to track down his brother's killer, assuming it could be Austin. The articles brought back memories of what had been a very difficult time for Jack and one that he had only just begun to move on from. But reading the newspaper reports had brought it all back and with some of the pieces including graphic detail about the accident, it made him feel sick. He knew he'd made a mistake and this was just reminding him of that.

It also brought back memories of some of the journalists who had tried to dig up dirt on him and his friends – often offering people they knew hundreds of pounds for a story. Any story. Anything that could add to the distress of what had already happened. They didn't seem to care. But in truth there wasn't much to uncover, they were just four normal guys and no-one had been tempted by the money to make anything up. So in the end the journalists finally all just gave up, concluding there wasn't anything else they could write about regarding the Austin family and Jack and his mates and it had just been as it seemed – a tragic accident. Eventually the accident and court case had become yesterday's news. In fact, he remembered the national papers had moved on from the story quite quickly as later that week a well-known television newsreader had been caught having an affair with a senior politician and it had taken over the headlines for a few days. "*Cabinet Minister caught on the News,*" was one particular headline Jack remembered seeing. Even the local papers had relegated the story about his accident fairly quickly and so, as Jack was finding out, there was only limited reporting of the trial, distressing as it was.

To avoid having to read the worst details of the accident over and over, Jack got into the habit of scanning through the information as quickly as he could. He focused on just looking for the name "Andy Austin" but surprisingly he had only found it a couple of times. It seems Andy Austin had also avoided the press although he could probably have made quite a bit of money if he had sold his story as the only survivor.

'*The man whose family was wiped out.*' Jack could imagine the type of headline the tabloids would have come up with telling Andy's story. Alongside would be a picture of him looking sad or maybe angry, depending on the theme of the piece. Although this made Jack's current task more difficult, he was relieved that Andy hadn't been tempted to sell his story. It had been bad enough for Jack going through the court case, hearing the details of the accident, making him sound like a mass murderer, without it then being splashed all over the tabloid newspapers. During the court case, he had to keep reminding everyone that it had been an accident and that he wasn't some sort of evil criminal. People didn't seem to realise that the accident had been as bad for him as anyone else. He

145

was the one that had been driving and now he had to live with that for the rest of his life. He didn't mean to kill the four people walking along the pavement. It had been an accident. He couldn't explain how it happened, maybe there was a fault with the car or he hit a pothole or he just took his eyes off the road for a few seconds. They'd asked him over and over again – the police, journalists and even his friends and family but he couldn't give them an answer. It had all happened in a split second, like a reflex, and there was no rational explanation for it.

He remembered feeling relieved when the court case was over and the journalists, realising there was nothing else to be had on this one, moved onto their next story of human tragedy. Or at least that of the newsreader and politician's affair.

Back in Jack's bedroom, although he wasn't enjoying reading the newspaper reports, now that he'd started down this road, he was determined to see it through. The fact that he was actually doing something was giving him some sense of purpose. At the very least it had stopped him sitting around just thinking and coming up with all sorts of nightmarish visions of Pete's murder. Last night he'd woken up from a dream, seemingly just at a point where he was about to see the face of Pete's killer. The man had just stabbed Pete by the side of the canal and somehow Jack was there too, standing behind him, but not moving. Why wasn't he moving? Why didn't he try and stop him? He was just standing watching like some sort of silent spectator watching a horror movie. The man started to turn around and as he did so he began to pull down his hood. That was when Jack woke up. He thought he knew him somehow but he couldn't place him.

His duvet had been kicked off on to the floor and he'd lain uncovered on his bed for ages trying to think what the dream had meant. Why hadn't he stopped the man? Why didn't he see the man's face? Did he know him? Was that what the dream was trying to tell him? He tried over and over to recreate the dream in his head and then run it on past the part when he'd woken up, but he couldn't. It always stopped at the same bit when the killer was just about to reveal himself to Jack. It was hopeless and he was happy that at least now he was doing something to occupy his mind on something more constructive.

Although he was in some way grateful that Andy Austin hadn't sold his story to the newspapers, it also meant that there was very little information on him in the actual newspaper reports. There were no photos or any quotes from him and it didn't appear he'd spoken to any journalist. All in all, it appeared he had been pretty anonymous. In fact the only useful piece of detail Jack found was a brief reference to a financial investment company he worked for in one of the broadsheet newspapers. Jack had then tried to confirm that by looking at Linked In but he couldn't find Austin on there, nor could he find him on Facebook or any other common social media platforms. It seemed he wasn't a social media fan. A couple of Jack's friends were like that too, they said they didn't see the point of it. Jack, himself was a bit fifty-fifty about it, he had accounts on a few of the sites but didn't post anything and only occasionally looked at them. He did use WhatsApp a lot though with different groups for the different areas of his life. He pretty much ran his life through WhatsApp with various groups covering his family, his friends and several others including a football group and a work related group.

Jack had looked up the financial investment company on the internet and got their office address through their website. They seemed to have one main office and so he assumed that would be where Andy Austin would work. He felt quite proud of himself at that point – this detective lark was quite easy, maybe he could become a private investigator? That could be fun!

He felt good that he was doing something in the hunt for his brother's killer even though when he really thought about it, he couldn't believe that it actually was this guy. He worked for a financial investment company. He was just an ordinary bloke, like Jack. Surely he wouldn't have gone to that extreme just because of the accident?

Having gathered the information on Andy Austin's workplace, Jack hadn't been sure what best to do with it - or even what best to do next. He didn't have any grand plan but after thinking for a few minutes it seemed the obvious thing to do was to go to the company's offices and see if he could find out any more about Austin. At the moment, where Austin worked was the only thing Jack knew about him and so following that trail seemed to be the logical next step.

He thought it best not to give advance warning of his visit in case someone told Andy he was coming. He knew that was a risk and there could be all sorts of repercussions from that if they came face to face. Who knew how Andy might react? If he was the killer, he might even be armed. From what Jack knew both murders had been committed using some sort of knife. However, even if Austin didn't have a weapon on him, it would still be a strange encounter, him meeting Jack a year after the accident.

"*Ah, Mr Austin, the man who accidentally killed four of your family is waiting for you in reception.*" Who knew what Austin would do? That might be a story for the tabloids.

So not being able to come up with a better plan, but determined to at least do something, he'd decided just to go along to Austin's offices, maybe ask a few innocuous questions and see what he could find out about him. It was a start. Perhaps someone had noticed him acting strangely these last few days? Maybe Jack would discover what time he finished work and follow him home. That could help him get a better picture of this man. Was he married, did he have any family? Jack couldn't

149

remember seeing anyone with him in court but he didn't suppose it was the sort of occasion you brought the family to. If he found out where he lived though, he could maybe ask the neighbours about him and see if they'd noticed anything suspicious. It was worth a try and he'd nothing else to go on.

He was getting nervous as he approached the offices where Andy Austin worked. He'd zipped and unzipped his jacket a few times, finally, after looking in a shop window, deciding the unzipped look was better. He still wasn't sure how this was going to pan out and he began to have second thoughts about not telling the police. Maybe he should have. They would have known how to do this best, it was their job, what they'd been trained to do. But Jack wanted to be in control and he was frustrated at the police's lack of progress in finding Pete's killer. He also thought it might be best to keep this little project to himself until he found out some more. There might be nothing to find and the last thing he wanted was the police questioning him unnecessarily about the accident all over again. In truth he didn't expect much to come of his investigative work but it made him feel better that he was at least doing something rather than just sitting waiting.

He had told Jason and Dan some of what he was planning to do, not much though as he didn't know much himself, and although they'd raised some doubts, they understood he had to do something. However he'd decided not to tell any of

150

his family until after he'd found out if there was actually anything to tell. He knew they'd try and talk him out of it and insist he told the police.

He found the offices easily, the big company sign on the front of it had helped, and he walked past the door looking into the reception area as he did so. He stopped about twenty paces past and looked back. It was a four storey building, lots of glass, with dark grey aluminium surrounds to the windows. He guessed there must be a couple of hundred people working in there and he found himself trying to guess which floor Austin would be on. The second or the third he concluded, with no rationale he could think of. They were just the numbers that he had in his head. He walked back towards the building entrance, slowly this time, watching it as he did so and taking care not to bump into the other pedestrians all walking purposefully in different directions. All headed for their own very important liaisons. He reached the door and inside the building, he could see a big open space with lots of fluorescent lighting set in a grey, tiled ceiling. No-one else had gone in while he walked up and down the street and the reception area looked quiet inside. He could see a seating area with two black leather settees and two black single chairs surrounding a round glass table with, what looked like, a number of magazines lying on it. Across from that was the reception desk where two young looking women sat turned towards each other, talking animatedly.

This looks like a good time while it's quiet, thought Jack, it's now or never, and he strode into the building decisively, making his way quickly and directly to the reception desk, his shoes clacking on the tiled floor as he walked. The young woman sitting on the left swivelled her chair around to face him and smiled. She was wearing a dark blue jacket with a lighter blue blouse underneath and her teeth were brilliantly white.

'Hello, how can I help you?' she said.

'Good morning,' Jack replied, putting on his most charming voice. 'I was wondering, do you have an Andy Austin who works here? I'm an old friend of his and was just passing when I remembered him saying, I think, that he worked for you?' Jack surprised himself by saying that. It had only just come to him as he stood there.

While Jack had been speaking, the receptionist had started typing something on her keyboard. Jack put his hand in his jacket pocket and felt an old sweet wrapper tucked away in the corner. The receptionist appeared to be frowning at the screen and then she looked back up towards Jack, still with a frown on her face.

'Well it looks like we did but he doesn't work here any more, I don't think. I think he must have left. I mean his name's on the system but it's greyed out which usually means the person's gone,' she said giving Jack her best sympathetic smile.

'Oh,' said Jack, 'that's a shame, I really wanted to see him. Did you know him at all?'

'No I'm afraid I didn't. I've only been here a few weeks. I'm with an agency and most of the staff here just walk past. You don't really get to know them much. Everyone's pretty busy I guess. Some of them don't even speak.' She turned to face her colleague.

'Sara, do you know...' she glanced at her screen again, 'Andy Austin? He used to work here. Probably left earlier this year as his name's still on the system but in grey.'

Sara looked up from her screen and shook her head.

'Sorry, no, doesn't ring a bell. What did he do?' she asked, looking at Jack.

'Oh, em some clever financial stuff I think. He was always clever at school. He was good at maths.' Jack replied, thinking "*did I just say that? Good at maths?*" He carried on trying to recover his composure, subconsciously rubbing his beard.

'I think he might have been an analyst or something,' he said, remembering that's how he'd been described in one of the newspaper reports.

'You wouldn't know where he's gone or perhaps where he lives do you? It'd be a shame to miss him, I'm only in town for a day or two, just passing through' Jack lied, but impressing himself again with his continued creativity.

'I'm afraid I don't, I didn't know him' the receptionist repeated.

'You could try asking David Brown, the HR guy, he's usually pretty good with things like that

153

and always quite helpful,' her colleague Sara suggested and Jack noticed she blushed slightly as she spoke.

The first receptionist nodded, turned back and punched a few numbers into a phone on the right side of her desk. She was wearing a headset and after a few seconds she started talking into the microphone piece. Jack could hear her half of the conversation which after her initial query was mainly "yes", "thankyou" and accompanied by a few nods of her head.

'Hold on,' she said and looked up at Jack, 'what's your name?' she asked.

'Name, em, it's em, Chris, em Chris Potts,' he said, feeling himself reddening. Shit, why had he given Chris's name, that was stupid but he didn't want to tell her his name and Chris was the first name that came to mind.

The receptionist repeated the name into the phone and said a final thankyou before reaching over and pressing the end call button on her console. She smiled at Jack.

'Mr Brown is going to pop down...ooh that rhymes' and the two women broke into a fit of giggles.

'Sorry,' she said composing herself, 'it can be a bit boring here sometimes. If you'd just like to wait over there, he should be here shortly.'

Jack sat down on one of the sofas and took his jacket off, laying it across his knees. A few minutes later he saw a middle aged man in a dark grey suit appear from the elevators and walk across to the reception desk. He was wearing a white shirt with a bright red tie and he was carrying a brown file under his arm. Jack watched as he said something to the two ladies and they both laughed again. The one who had dealt with Jack then nodded in Jack's direction and the man turned round and looked across towards him. Jack noticed he was going bald on top but had his hair cut short to make it less noticeable. He appeared to make a final comment to the two women, which set them off laughing again, before turning and walking across to where Jack sat. He held out his hand as Jack stood up and said,

'Hi, please sit down, I'm David Brown, HR director here. I believe you are a friend of Andy Austin?' he said as he sat down opposite Jack, his tie coming to rest between his legs.

'Yes, that's right,' said Jack, 'Chris Potts, I'm an old school friend actually but I haven't seen him for a few years and I was just passing your offices and remembered him saying he worked here. I thought I'd pop my head in and see if he was around, but I hear he's left.'

'Yes, that's right he did work here, but he left about six months ago. I'm not sure when you last spoke with him. Did you know he was involved in a car accident? He was okay but unfortunately I believe some of his family died in the accident.'

'Yes, I did hear about that,' Jack replied keeping himself focused on the man opposite him, hoping his face wasn't giving anything away but he felt it was burning bright red and he gripped the sofa cushion tightly with both hands.

'Well he left a few months after that,' Mr Brown carried on. 'He had time off to recover but I'm not sure he ever got completely over it, the accident. Maybe you never do. He just came in one day and resigned. No-one I know has seen him since. I guess he just needed a change, maybe try and start again somewhere else.'

'Oh no, I didn't realise...do you know where he lives?' Jack said looking pointedly at the file resting on the HR director's lap. 'It's just I'm only here for the next couple of days and I'd really like to see him, especially after the accident and that. Maybe that'll help, seeing an old friend again.'

Mr Brown looked at him and smiled ruefully.

'Well I'm not really supposed to, confidentiality rules and all that. You wouldn't believe what we have to do to meet the data protection laws nowadays,' he laughed. 'But seeing as you're an old friend of his, it would seem churlish not to. Maybe you can hold this file while I talk to the receptionist about something for a minute,' he said winking at Jack, which Jack found slightly unnerving but he understood the intent.

Mr Brown handed Jack the brown cardboard file and walked back across to the reception desk. Jack quickly opened it up and scanned through the contents. It was pretty light, nothing of any interest other than a sheet of paper with his address, phone number and next of kin. Jack recognised the next of kin name as one of those who had died in the accident. He took out his phone and took a photo of the one sheet and as he put his phone away Mr Brown reappeared.

'All done?' he asked, exaggerating another wink at Jack to ensure he knew they were co-conspirators.

'Yes thanks,' Jack replied, handing back the file and resisting a return wink. 'I really appreciate your help.'

The two men shook hands briefly and then Jack left the building, partly frustrated that Andy wasn't there but also partly relieved. He was somewhat satisfied that at least he'd got something else to follow up, a home address to go and check out. Something to keep him going. He looked up the address on his phone and calculated he could be there in about twenty five minutes. Might as well go and have a look, he thought, see if he could find out anything else. At this point he'd nothing better to do with his time.

A short while later he was walking down the street where Andy Austin lived. It appeared to be a normal street with odd numbers on one side and even on the other and he was walking on the opposite side of the road from where he'd reckoned Andy's house to be. He was walking slowly, not looking directly across the street, but with his face turned slightly away, his jacket zipped up to his neck. Maybe he should have brought his sunglasses, he thought. Every now and again he looked across the road to check the house numbers and soon he realised he was only a little way away from where Andy lived. He stopped by the next lamppost and, using it as partial cover, had a good look across the street. He soon worked out which house was Andy's. He could see it quite clearly and he stood for a minute taking it in and then wondering what to do next. Like all the houses in the street it was set back from the road slightly with a small frontage and a path leading to the front door. The house itself was pretty ordinary looking. Apart from the green front door there was one double window to the right hand side as Jack looked, probably a living room he guessed. Up above there were another two similar sized widows all with painted white frames. Like most of the other houses in the street it was semi-detached and the one adjoining it was a mirror image.

Jack just stood by the lamppost for a few minutes, the street was empty but he wasn't sure what to do now. He'd come this far but he was beginning to feel nervous and didn't know what would be the best course of action from here. Maybe he should just back off and hand it over to the police now? It would be a shame after coming all this way but he knew he could get into all sorts of trouble if things didn't go well. He decided to walk on further down the street to gather his thoughts, but as he arrived directly opposite Andy's house the front door suddenly opened. Jack stopped and turned his face away quickly looking in the opposite direction. He heard some voices and slowly turned his head to look back across the street. A man, a woman and two children had left the house and were walking down their pathway towards a red car parked by the side of the road. The man was not the man that had stared at him in court. He wasn't Andy Austin. Realising that he was holding his breath, Jack breathed out in some relief. That had been close. Panic over, he decided to take a chance and see if he could find anything out from these people. Maybe they could tell him something about Andy Austin? Presumably they knew him as they had just come out of his house. He crossed the street and approached the family just as they were getting into the car.

'Excuse me,' he said walking towards the man, unzipping his jacket as he approached. The man stopped and looked at him with a puzzled expression.

'Sorry, I wonder if you can help me' said Jack, 'I'm looking for an old friend who I think might live round here. I was wondering if you might know him? His name's Andy Austin.'

The man looked at him for a second, not used to strangers asking him questions in the street unless they were asking for money or trying to sell him a magazine. This young man didn't appear to be doing either so after a few seconds, he replied.

'No, sorry, don't think so, not a name I recognise' he replied, opening his car door.

'Wait…, did you say Austin?' the woman called from the other side of the car. 'Andrew Austin? Wasn't that the name of the man we bought the house from? Wasn't it Raj?' she said looking at the man.

'Oh yes, it could have been, now you say it, I think I saw it once on the documents,' he replied and turned back towards Jack.

'We bought the house, but we never actually met him,' he explained, 'it was a bit strange but it was all done through his solicitors. I think they said he'd moved abroad or something.'

'Yes that's right,' his wife added. 'Didn't he go to Australia, or maybe it was America….I'm not sure.'

'Oh, ok,' said Jack, 'Did he leave a forwarding address by any chance?'

'No, nothing I'm afraid. We didn't have any contact with him. It was all done through the agency. Look I'm sorry but we have to go, kids swimming lessons,' he explained motioning his head towards the two children sitting waiting in the back of the car. At that, the two adults quickly got in the car and drove off leaving Jack standing there all on his own.

Jack stood for a minute, alone in the street, his hands stuffed into his pockets. That's it then, he thought, I've got nothing. This guy, Andy Austin, has just disappeared. How can that be? And Jack suddenly felt very sad and completely alone.

Chapter 20

The police team were all assembled back in the incident meeting room, awaiting Strong and Campbell's arrival. The two senior policemen had been delayed by the Chief Constable's daily briefing which he'd brought forward that day due to 'another engagement.' Probably a boozy lunch or a round of golf thought Strong but of course he didn't voice that thought. It had been a tough meeting, the Chief Constable was getting angry and frustrated by the lack of progress and Strong had had to exaggerate a bit on some of the lines of enquiry they were pursuing. Especially on the suspect who'd recently been released from prison. The Chief Constable had forced them to the point where they'd had to say he was their prime suspect although both Strong and Campbell knew at this point that they had no real evidence to suggest that he was involved in any way. Strong knew that if the team didn't come up with something significant soon there was the danger that the Chief Constable would helicopter in another DI to "review" the case. He may even have planned that already, Strong thought. If someone

162

else was brought in Strong knew that he would be seen as a failure and he was desperate not to have that blemish on his record, not at this late stage in his career. He knew it was getting risky now, if there was any sign of someone else being brought in then he would have to rethink his current approach, and quickly.

The two detectives entered the meeting room and took their normal places at the table. Strong sat at the head and Campbell was again positioned awkwardly in his usual seat immediately to Strong's right. Strong kicked the meeting off with a summary of where they were and then most of the meeting was spent reviewing what they knew and had found out about their 'prime suspect.' But despite detailed investigation and interviews there was nothing that indicated that he'd had any involvement in either of the two murders. Even worse was that for the murder of Pete Wilson, the suspect appeared to have a watertight alibi. He claimed to have been at a party in a local working mens club held to celebrate his release from prison. This had been backed up by several other people at the party and although they might not be regarded as the most reliable witnesses, there were also several photographs on social media which would seem to confirm his presence there. On the basis that the police believed it was the same person who had committed both murders, this appeared to rule him out completely.

Strong could sense that his team were getting more and more frustrated by the lack of progress and they needed some sort of breakthrough to revitalise the investigation.

'Ok, what else do we have?' he said looking around the room, hoping for some inspiration.

'Sir?' a young police officer spoke up from the back of the room.

'Yes?' Strong replied, 'what is it, go ahead.'

'Sir, I've been looking into the whereabouts of Andy Austin, who you may remember was the survivor from the road accident last year that killed four members of his family. Actually I think you may have been involved in it Sir. Emm, I mean, not the accident but, emm, your name was on a couple of the interview sheets. You may remember him?' There were a few murmurs around the room and the young policeman could sense everyone looking at him. He was beginning to feel uncomfortably warm.

Strong didn't answer and the young policeman took that as a hint to quickly carry on.

'Well, Sir, the driver of the car that hit them was a Jack Wilson, the brother of Peter Wilson, who we know was the first victim. Well I'm afraid I've been unable to track down Andy Austin so far. He left his job and sold his house and, well, he just seems to have disappeared. At this point no-one seems to know where he is and there are no records of him doing anything recently. No bank transactions, nothing. One other thing I found out was that someone else has also been trying to find

Andy Austin recently. He went to where Austin used to work and on further investigation it would appear that it was Jack Wilson. He'd met the HR Director, a David Brown, but he couldn't remember his name but he did recognise him as Wilson from a photo I showed him.'

Strong sat silently for a minute taking this in. Of course he remembered the accident and the subsequent case but thankfully he'd only played a minor part in it. The records would show that he had just helped a colleague by sitting in on a couple of witness interviews. However maybe this could be the breakthrough he was hoping his team would make and the timing couldn't be better. They needed to catch this man, two deaths was too many and Strong had no idea what he might do next.

His thoughts were interrupted by DS Campbell who had left his seat and was now pacing around the room, thinking out loud. He was slightly hunched over and resembled a caged animal looking for a way to escape.

'So Austin has disappeared. Why would he do that? Maybe he just needed to get away from it all? But why not tell anyone where he was going? And then why was Jack Wilson also looking for him? I knew he was keeping something from me. I knew it. But what?'

'Who else was in the accident?' Campbell barked at the young policeman.

165

'Emm,' he said looking down at the notes he held in his hand, 'there was Austins' family, his mum and....'

'No, not them,' Campbell interrupted, 'who else was in the car with Jack Wilson when it happened?'

The policeman looked back down at his notes his face burning red as he realised the whole room was looking in his direction. He'd only been in the force a few months and this was the first time he'd had to speak in front of the whole team and now it appeared that he may have found something interesting. He shuffled the papers he had and some of them fell to the floor.

'Oh, em, here it is,' he said quickly, hoping he still had a job. 'There was Jack Wilson, Dan Sears, Jason Reynolds and Chris Potts.'

'Chris Potts, Hilary Potts son,' said Campbell excitedly, 'we knew that, so that's two relatives of the lads in the car that have been murdered. What about the other two, what do we know about them?'

'Sorry I don't have any more information, I can go and find out,' the young policeman replied.

'I suggest you do,' DS Campbell replied. 'Find out where they live and let me know as soon as possible. We need to have a chat with them.'

Neither DI Strong nor DS Campbell believed in coincidences and Campbell was beginning to believe there was something there. He knew that Jack Wilson had been keeping something from him and although he still couldn't quite piece it together he felt they were getting somewhere. This accident had something to do with it. He continued to pace around the room thinking. There was a few seconds of silence around the rest of the room as the whole team churned this information around in their minds, trying to get to something that made sense. Then the murmurs began as thoughts were exchanged. Strong sensed they were looking towards him for some sort of answer. He was thinking of what to say and he held his hand up to silence the room.

As he was about to speak, he became aware of someone else leaving his seat at the table and heading towards him. He looked up and recognised it was one of the duty sergeants walking purposefully straight to where he sat.

'Sir, you should see this,' he said handing DI Strong a piece of paper. The detective looked down at the document in front of him and saw it was an incident report of a missing person, a man called Bill Reynolds. He scanned the report and looked back up at his Sergeant questioningly.

'What is this?' he asked with a frown.

'Bill Reynolds, the missing man, he didn't come home from the pub on Saturday night. When I heard the name Reynolds just now it rang a bell so I looked it up. His son is Jason Reynolds. One of the passengers in Jack Wilson's car.'

This news started off more murmurs around the room and DS Campbell was the first to speak. He was excited.

'Shit, that's it. It's got to be. That's three of them now all connected to the accident. It's gotta be something to do with it. We need to find this Andy Austin and we need to get him quickly.'

More whispers and nods of agreement rolled around the room and Strong moved his head forwards in agreement too. He held up his hand again to regain control.

'Okay let's find Andy Austin then. He's now our number one priority. Maybe he's on some sort of revenge kick or something?' He nodded to the young police officer.

'Good job lad, solid police work. The stage is yours. Tell us everything you did and what you found out. Don't leave out anything no matter how trivial it might seem. We need to find this guy quickly.' Strong leant back in his chair, hands crossed behind his head and smiled. He knew this day would come; it was inevitable and it was always just going to be a matter of time. They were on the right path now and he was convinced they'd get him soon. In Strong's eyes, this had gone far enough.

Chapter 21

However, the next twenty four hours turned out to be a period of continual frustration for the police. After the initial buzz of identifying Andy Austin as being connected to, if not himself, the actual killer, every potential road leading to finding him seemed to be a dead end. Nobody at his work had heard from him or had any idea of where he'd gone. DI Strong and DS Campbell had been to his offices and met the HR director, David Brown.

'Hi, come in, please sit down, how can I help you?' Brown smiled and motioned to two seats set back and open in front of a meeting table. He sat in a similar chair on the opposite side.

'We'd like to ask you about one of your former employees, a man called Andy Austin,' said DI Strong.

'Ah, yes Andy. There's been a few people interested in him lately. He was a good man, worked here for five or six years in Sales. Good, solid employee, no problems at all with him. He left about a year ago, not long after the tragic accident, I assume you know about that?'

'Yes, we do,' Strong replied, 'what can you tell me about him at that time, his state of mind. It must have been very hard for him. What were his reasons for leaving?'

'Yes, I remember some of it, he was off for a bit after the accident, understandably. I don't think he himself was badly injured, physically at least. Then he came back to work one day and just handed in his resignation. I never saw him again after that and I think we all just assumed that losing his…, losing his family like that in such a tragic accident had all been too much for him.'

'Did he talk to anyone about it? Any colleagues he was particularly close to?' Campbell enquired.

'No, I'm sorry, not that I know off. I don't think anyone really knew what to say to him to be honest. We do have a counselling service available for employees but he didn't make use of that,' Brown replied.

'Do you know if he went to work anywhere else?' Strong asked, 'Did you hear anything?'

'No nothing. Strange that, usually these sales guys pop up at a competitor, it's a small world. But maybe under the circumstances he just needed to get out. A life changing thing like that, maybe he needed to escape and start again,' Brown replied.

'Yes, could be,' Strong replied. 'Do you have an address for him?' he asked.

'Let me get his file,' the man answered and he got up and walked out of the room. Strong and

Campbell waited in silence. Campbell got up and paced around the room as was his usual way. Strong stayed seated, noting that the office of the HR Director was bigger, brighter and much less messy than his own back at the station. In the corner there was a large green plant in a cream coloured pot set against a similarly cream coloured wall. The plant looked very healthy and Strong remembered he'd had a plant in his office a couple of years ago but it had died, and with the cut backs on expenditure he hadn't felt it right to spend money on replacing it. Not that it bothered him as he had always forgotten to water it, or maybe over-watered it, which is probably why it died in the first place. Plants and Strong just didn't seem to go together well.

The door opened, breaking Strong's train of thought, and the HR Director came back into the room holding a brown paper file.

'I'm sorry, I didn't ask if you gents would like a tea or coffee? Can I get you one?' he asked.

'No thanks, we're fine. Do you mind if we have a look at the file?' Strong asked impatiently, keen to see what it held.

'Sure,' he replied and handed the document across to Strong who immediately passed it to Campbell. DS Campbell opened it up on the table in front of him and began quickly scanning through the documents.

'Same address...same telephone...next of kin one of the deceased...nothing else I can see,' he said as he turned over the final page.

171

'Have you had anyone else asking about Austin recently?' DS Campbell asked.

'Yes, actually we did,' Brown replied. 'I mentioned it to your constable when he came in. He was a young guy, said he was an old friend trying to look him up. What was his name again....? I'm afraid I couldn't tell the guy anything about Andy Austin though, data protection and all that. I'm sorry I can't remember his name, maybe it'll come to me, I think your constable had a photo of him,' Brown smiled ruefully.

DS Campbell reached into his jacket pocket and took out his phone. He scrolled through a few screens before holding it up in front of Mr Brown, showing a photo of Jack Wilson.

'Was it this man?' he asked.

Brown looked carefully at the screen for a few seconds and then nodded,

'Yes, yes I believe it was. Looked a bit scruffier, needed a shave but I'm pretty sure that's him.'

Driving back to the station in Strong's car they made a few phone calls to get an update from the rest of the team. They learned that Andy Austin's only surviving relatives were distant ones and none of them had had any contact with him since the funerals of his family last year. He'd sold his house and none of his old neighbours knew where he had gone, in fact some of them hadn't even known him in the first place. Nobody from his local area, or in any of the cafes or bars near his work, had seen him for a long time. He'd stopped going to the gym where he'd been a member around nine months ago and no-one there had seen or heard of him since. He'd cancelled his credit cards and closed his bank accounts and seemingly left no public record of himself for the last nine months. He didn't appear to have any social media accounts, or if he did have they had been erased. It seemed that Andy Austin had managed to completely disappear.

'I think we have to assume that he's somehow changed his identity,' DS Campbell said.

'You could be right,' Strong replied.

'But that's not such an easy thing to do for a bloke like Austin,' Campbell carried on, voicing his thoughts. 'He worked for a Financial Services company for Christ's sake. You need contacts, criminal contacts, how would he have known them? He was just an ordinary bloke working in an ordinary job. He hasn't got a record. How would he have done that so completely so that he's just disappeared?'

'Mmm, it's either that or he's got someone helping him, someone supplying him with cash. You can't live without a credit card or bank account. What do you think about Jack Wilson looking for him?' DI Strong said, changing the subject.

'I think he's probably come to the same conclusion that we have and wanted to check Austin out,' DS Campbell replied, 'With everything that's happened he probably thinks he can play detective. I'll get one of the team to warn him to stay well

173

away. At least we've got something to tell the Chief now,' he added, glancing towards his boss.

'Yes, thank god for that. Hopefully he'll let us carry on with our jobs now and track down Austin. He used to do this job himself so he knows it's never easy. He was definitely getting some pressure from above though so this should certainly help. I'll update him as soon as we get back.'

Back in the office, Strong had managed to get the Chief Constable on the phone and briefly tell him of the progress they had made. He could sense the Chief's relief on the other end of the phone and he knew he'd bought himself another day or two, but probably no more than that or the pressure would be back on again if they didn't find Austin in that timescale.

Strong was now sitting alone in his office waiting for Doctor Collins to arrive. Doctor Collins was a police psychologist who had been assigned to the case to try and help build up a profile of the killer. Strong didn't like psychologists but he knew it was standard procedure in a serious, high-profile case like this and so they would have to go through the process. If he could do it quickly he could probably get it over with in an hour and then get back to proper police investigative work. He thought of police psychologists as being towards the far end of the spectrum of usefulness. Not as bad as psychics who often contacted the police saying they had information from 'the other side', but not too far removed from that. When Strong had lost his parents in the hit and run, he'd been assigned to a psychologist as normal police routine as part of his recovery process - and he had attended a few sessions as directed. But he didn't have any confidence in the process and just played along until he was able to stop going. He didn't believe it could help in any way. Of course he was sad, he'd lost both parents to some idiot driver but how would talking about his childhood to some complete stranger help him? He did the required minimum number of sessions then never went back.

Just then his thoughts were interrupted by a knock on the door.

'Come in,' he called and the door opened and a woman entered the room. Through police habit, Strong instantly assessed her. She was good looking, probably late twenties. She had long, straight brown hair and was dressed smartly with a light blue blouse and dark blue skirt and black shoes. Maybe trying to fit in with the police, Strong thought. She had a silver necklace and bracelet and two rings, but no obvious engagement or wedding ring. Still young, Strong surmised, building a career, probably not long out of university.

'Good morning, DI Strong' she said walking towards Strong's desk, her hand outstretched in front of her, 'I'm Doctor Sam Collins, police psychologist assigned to your murder case. I trust you were expecting me?'

Young, but confident, thought Strong as he replied and shook her hand firmly. He picked up his phone and called DS Campbell. He trusted Campbell and he liked to have another perspective on any meeting to make sure he himself was doing everything right and wasn't missing anything. It wasn't that Strong didn't have confidence in himself, but he'd learnt it was best to cover his back in case it was suggested that he had made any error in procedure. These days everyone seemed to be looking for someone to blame, looking for a mistake they could pick you up on.

Campbell arrived a few minutes later and Strong noticed that he was looking tired. There were dark bags under his eyes – that's what a case like this does to you Strong thought. He'd seen many a good officer burn out in the past and he made a mental note to have a chat with Campbell later about making sure all was well and he was getting enough rest.

The three of them sat around Strong's desk. Doctor Collins took a blue folder out of her briefcase, opened it up and laid it on the desk in front of her. She explained she had reviewed everything that they knew about Andy Austin including police records, medical records and various statements from people who knew him. She did it in a methodical fashion starting with general points and, where required, she drilled down into specific details. Strong and Campbell both appreciated that as it fitted with their normal logical way of thinking and their everyday police work of processing masses of data.

176

After Doctor Collins had gone through all the details and confirmed with the two detectives that they understood and had no further questions, she then moved on to what she called her initial findings. She explained that they used certain techniques, based on scientific modelling methods which had been developed and refined over many years using historical data and enhanced with new data from more recent cases as it became available.

'The scientific bods have these clever algorithms now, modelling techniques that take data and learn from it, refining the output as it develops. They call it machine learning. Soon the machines will be doing all our jobs,' she laughed but Strong and Campbell stayed silent. She looked down at her papers again and carried on.

'So using these methods, here is a summary of my main findings at this point. Just to emphasise that none of this is hard fact. It is merely an educated indication based on scientific analysis of the most likely outcomes.' Doctor Collins looked up towards Strong and he nodded, impatient to hear what she had to say. Although he'd initially been sceptical of the usefulness of this meeting, now that he was in the midst of it he was interested to hear what Dr Collins had concluded to see if it could help them in any way. Campbell was thinking the same, now that they were here, he realised that there was nothing to lose by at least giving her a hearing.

'Okay so the first key point is that Austin sustained a head injury during the accident.'

177

Both Strong and Campbell sat forward. This wasn't something either of them had picked up or maybe they had but just not thought it was significant. Dr Collins carried on.

'Unfortunately this was never fully assessed by the medical staff as he discharged himself from the hospital only a few hours after arriving there. This was against the attending doctor's advice but it was noted that Austin insisted on leaving to be with his family who were elsewhere in the hospital. After he left, there is no record of him seeking any further medical help or advice.' Doctor Collins paused to allow Strong and Campbell to take this in.

'However, various statements from colleagues and friends suggest that Austin then went through some sort of personality change over the following weeks. It was noted by a number of people that he became quieter, more reserved, withdrawn even, which of course is perfectly understandable after such a traumatic incident. However it is also possible that this change in personality could have been medically linked to the head injury he sustained. An injury to the head and indeed the brain can act as a catalyst for many personality changes or disorders. You will have heard of post-traumatic stress disorder or PTSD?' she looked up and both Strong and Campbell nodded. They'd both heard of it in relation to the armed forces but they'd also attended police briefings on the subject and knew that some of the terrible things that ordinary policemen and

178

policewomen had to deal with could equally cause a similar reaction.

'Well there is a similar type of affliction which is known as post traumatic embitterment disorder or PTED. In simple terms this is a pathological reaction to a major event in a person's life. As the name would suggest it's almost always a negative event and a negative reaction and causes the sufferer to seek some sort of culpability or perhaps even revenge for the original incident. In short they want, or even need, someone to blame and perhaps they do not believe that justice has been fully done. They often believe that *they* have suffered most from what happened and that is clearly not fair to them. In some cases this can develop to become the most important thing in their life and their point of focus can then become some sort of equalisation. That is, they will want someone to suffer in the same way that they have - so that person or persons might fully understand what they have gone through. In extreme cases, and I must emphasise extreme, this can result in the sufferer undertaking violent acts in an attempt to gain some feeling of recompense for his pain. However even when that happens, it is not certain that this clears the underlying condition, the PTED. Because of the brain injury it may be that the person will still continue to suffer with PTED. At this point there are not enough defined or recorded cases of this particular disorder to be able to make definite conclusions on the longer term effects.'

179

Strong realised that Doctor Collins had stopped talking and that he'd been listening attentively to her summary. Surprisingly he'd understood it and actually found it quite interesting. Doctor Collins had sat back in her chair, crossing her legs.

'Okay,' he said, leaning forward, his hands interlocked and his forearms leaning on the desk in front of him.

'So what you're saying then is Austin got a bump on his head, this changed him, gave him PTED. He didn't feel justice was done for the deaths of his family. The driver only got a twelve month driving ban so you could argue he does have a point I guess. And now, a year later, he's started running around killing various people connected to the incident. Relatives of the young men that were in the car. Some sort of revenge. He wants them to suffer like he has suffered. He lost some relatives so they have to as well so that they understand how he feels?'

'Yes that's pretty much it,' Doctor Collins replied, pleased that Strong seemed to be taking her seriously. She'd been warned that he wasn't a great supporter of psychologists helping with his investigations and so she'd prepared well for this meeting to make sure she did her job as best she could.

'So why is he doing it now? Why wait for a year before enacting his revenge though?' Campbell asked forcefully, looking directly at Doctor Collins.

180

'Well that's an interesting question,' Doctor Collins replied, confidently, pleased that he'd asked that question.

'I had to dig a bit deep into some of the data for this one but I did find something that may explain it,' she said.

'Go on,' Strong prompted and both he and DS Campbell straightened up in their chairs, awaiting the doctor's response.

'Well, in a few similar cases we have seen of PTED, the sufferer can latch onto one specific thing and somehow that becomes of exaggerated importance to the patient. In a few of these cases, mostly in the States, it was the date of the original critical event that seemed to be important. In this case, Andy Austin's accident happened on the fifteenth of December. As you know, Peter Wilson, his first victim was killed on the same date exactly one year later.'

'Shit,' Campbell exclaimed, standing up, 'so you think he's taking his revenge on the same date, the anniversary of when he lost his family?'

'Yes, but it may be more complex than that,' Doctor Collins replied, enjoying the focus she was getting from these two senior policemen. She was beginning to feel really confident now.

'Looking back at the medical records from a year ago, Andy Austin's brother died at the scene, so on the same day, the fifteenth of December. The other victims however survived the original accident and were all taken to hospital. His mum hung on

181

and died in hospital two days later. His dad died a week and a half after that and then his cousin passed away a couple of days after Christmas, twelve days after the accident.'

Doctor Collins was into her stride now, she brushed her hair away from her face and looked directly at DI Strong. She knew the next part by heart and didn't need to refer to her notes any longer. But before she could speak, Campbell, who had now got up and was pacing the room, jumped in.

'So looking at the four boys in the car, we have a brother killed the same day, same date, exactly one year later. Then we have a mum killed two days later. The same as happened to Andy Austin's mum. So next would be a dad, ten days afterwards, on the twenty fifth, Christmas day, and shit, we've just heard that one of the other lad's dads has gone missing. He's going to kill him in a few days on the twenty fifth of December? Then the fourth guy, he's going to lose a cousin next week on the twenty seventh? Is that what you're saying?' Campbell asked excitedly from somewhere over Doctor Collins' shoulder.

'It's a possibility, yes,' replied Doctor Collins, looking around at Campbell, and making an effort not to smile. 'As I said at the start of our meeting, none of this is hard fact but the theory would seem to have some foundation to it. And certainly the first two victims would appear to comply with this possibility.'

'We need to get the team together again boss,' DS Campbell said, as he came forward towards Strong's desk. The detective inspector was leaning back in his chair with a wry smile. The psychologist had surprised him, her theory seemed to hold some water and DS Campbell seemed convinced. He was also right that they now needed to share this theory with the rest of the team. Maybe he was wrong about psychologists – maybe they did know their stuff after all. He thought he'd test her a bit further while she was here. There were some things that had been bugging him because even he didn't know the answers himself.

'Okay, it's certainly an interesting theory we should consider,' he started, non-committaly.'I have a couple of questions,' he carried on, looking directly at Doctor Collins. 'He lost four relatives so will each of the lads need to lose four relatives as well? To satisfy his revenge, to equalise his suffering as you put it?'

'It's a good point but my guess is no,' Doctor Collins replied, 'I think he sees it as one incident so he thinks of all the inhabitants of the car as one single body needing to suffer like he did. Otherwise the logic says that he would have killed a brother of each of them on that first day.'

'Yes, makes sense,' Strong agreed, 'and what happens after the twenty seventh? If we haven't caught him, is that it? Does he stop there?'

'I think so….but taking both your questions together there is the possibility that the date is so

183

significant to him that he will do the same next year and subsequent years on that same date. I hope not but I just don't know, there's not much precedent. There is also another possible outcome in that if he is unable to finish his task, as he sees it, this year he may believe he still has unfinished business, which by his logic he can only try again same time next year. Assuming the date is so critical to him.'

'Bloody hell,' DS Campbell responded, 'if what you're saying is right, we could have an anniversary killer on our hands then.' He turned and looked across at his boss, suddenly remembering something.

'Hey, you've met this Andy Austin before, haven't you?' he said looking excitedly at DI Strong. 'What was he like, did he say anything that might be relevant to this?'

Strong sat back in his chair, thinking.

'Mmm, I didn't see him much. I think I sat in on a couple of the interviews after the accident, maybe even just one. He seemed a normal sort of guy, mid-twenties, good-looking, a bit of a beard I think. I was helping out DI Williamson at the time, it was his case. It might be worth having a word with him see if he has any thoughts.'

'Oh. So you've actually met him?' Dr Collins asked, 'I didn't know that. It might be worth going over it with me to see if it can help prove or disprove any of the theory we are working on.'

'I doubt it,' Strong replied, 'I think we should just focus our time on finding him. As I said

I only spent minimal time with him. There's nothing I can add. Overall, it was a sad situation and I felt sorry for him, losing his family like that and it just being an accident with nothing he could do about it.'

'It looks like he's doing something now though,' DS Campbell replied.

The Anniversary

Chapter 22

Bill woke up slowly, forcing his eyes open. He felt like he'd been in a ten round boxing match and lost. It'd been a long time since he'd done that. Not since he'd been in the army. And even then they'd not usually lasted many rounds and he usually won. He'd been a good boxer in his day.

His mouth was dry and he licked his lips, trying to get some feeling back. He tried to focus but all he could see was a roughly painted white wall directly ahead of him and the brightness was burning his eyes. He moved his hands so he could feel what he was lying on. It seemed like a hard bench and he looked slowly downwards and saw that it *was* a bench, a wooden slatted one like the ones he'd seen in the park. He looked around and saw he was in a small, rectangular room with four plain, roughly painted, white walls. There was a grey metal door in one wall, but no windows. Up above there was a similarly roughly painted ceiling with a single, solitary light bulb hanging from it. He looked away as the light brought more pain to his eyes. The most overpowering thing about the room

186

though was the smell. There was a distinctive smell of animals or hay, something 'farm-like' but he couldn't quite nail it down.

He was confused. He didn't know where he was or why he felt like he did. The last thing he could remember was being in the Pub on Saturday night. Had he drunk more than he thought and been arrested? He didn't think so. He'd never had a hangover as bad as this before, his head was throbbing. He reached up with his hands and tentatively felt the hair at the back of his head. It felt sticky and he there was also a lump. So at least that explained his sore head, he'd bumped it somehow. Either someone had hit him or maybe he'd fallen. He stood up gingerly, checking his balance which seemed okay. He looked around the room trying to work out where he was. It seemed like some sort of cell, but it wasn't a police cell – he had spent a couple of nights in police cells in his youth and they never smelled like this one. He walked to the door, turned the knob and pulled. Nothing happened. He tried again, this time pushing but again there was no movement. The door was firmly locked. He made a fist and banged twice on the door shouting 'hello' as he did so.

'Hello, is there anyone there, HELLO,' he shouted more loudly and banged on the door again, this time harder. He banged the door again but the metal was solid.

He listened for any sound from the other side of the door, but heard nothing. He repeated the

187

process and pressed his ear against the door, feeling it vibrate slightly from his banging, but again he couldn't hear anything from outside. Where-ever he was it appeared, for the moment at least, he was locked in and on his own. He turned around and sat back down on the wooden bench. He needed to think. How did he get here, what had happened?

He focused his thoughts and remembered being in the pub and leaving to go home and watch the football on television. He retraced the steps in his head. He recalled turning into Ridley Road and walking along the pavement. There was the parked van, the man standing by it on his phone. And then nothing. That must be it, thought Bill. The man with the phone must have hit me and knocked me out and then locked me in this room. But why? He racked his brains to think of any reason why someone would do that to him. He hadn't upset or offended anyone recently had he? Not that he could think of. He was a man in his sixties, just a normal bloke. His days of getting into any sort of mischief or trouble were long gone. He wasn't a criminal and he didn't have any money to speak of. Kidnapped? Things like that didn't happen to someone like Bill. There must be a mistake. Maybe it was just a case of mistaken identity. He banged on the door and shouted as loud as he could.

'HELP!' He banged again, and again, until his hands turned red and then he kicked it over and over till the sound reverberating around the room was too much for his aching head.

The Anniversary

He stopped and took a closer look at the door. He bent down and looked at the gap between the door and the frame. He could just make out the lock. It looked pretty big and solid. He shook the door a few times and watched to see if the lock moved. If it did it was only very slightly. He felt in his pockets for anything that could help him but found they were empty. He looked around the room again but there was no sign of his coat. He turned his attention to the other end of the door and examined the hinges. There were two metal hinges, one towards the top and the other near the bottom. He knelt down and examined the lower hinge, picking at it with his fingers. It was quite big and solid and covered in the same white paint as the walls. As he picked away at the paint he could see steel underneath. He tried to move the hinge up and down and then side to side but with no success. It was firmly stuck. He stared up at the top hinge and it looked exactly the same.

He gave up and sat back down on the wooden bench. It looked like he was going to have to wait until someone came and opened the door to find out what was going on. He assumed that if he was being kidnapped that they'd at least give him water and food for some time until a deal was done, or whatever it was they were holding him for. At least that was what he'd seen happening on the television.

As it turned out he didn't have to wait long as only a few minutes later, without any warning,

189

the door suddenly opened outwards. A man stood there looking at Bill. He looked like he was in his twenties; pretty fit looking with short brown hair. He had a steel pole in one hand and looking beyond him Bill thought he could see a kitchen sink.

'Don't move,' he said, 'just sit where you are.'

Bill stood up defiantly.

'Sit down please,' the man said 'or else I'll lock the door again and leave you.'

Bill weighed up his options and decided to sit down, for now. He wanted to hear what this man had to say. He was younger than Bill, probably about half his age, Bill guessed. He looked quite fit but Bill knew he would take his chances with him if needed.

'Who are you and why have you locked me up here?' Bill demanded as he sat back down on the bench.

'My name's Andy,' the man replied, 'your son Jason was one of the four men who murdered my family. Specifically he killed my brother, my mum and dad and my cousin. He's shown no regret or remorse for that since and he needs to understand what he did, and the impact it had.'

Bill was taken aback and didn't quite know what to say. He still didn't understand who this guy was and why he was here. He must have got it wrong.

'My son never killed anyone, what are you talking about? What is it that you want?' he asked

190

frowning. 'I don't have any money, apart from my pension and you can have that. You think you're clever locking up an old man do you? What is it that you want?' he asked again, still feeling as confused as before but ready to jump up if the chance came.

'It's quite simple really. Your son and his mates need to know what it feels like to lose someone they love. You might call it revenge. I prefer to call it justice. At the end everyone is equal.'

At that he stepped to one side and picked up a tray and placed it on the floor inside the door. He edged it forward with his foot before pushing the door closed and locking it again. Bill was on his feet and over at the door in seconds but he was too late. He thumped it hard with both fists and shouted.

'Come back. Open the door. OPEN THIS DOOR.'

After a few more bangs on the door he conceded that the man was not coming back. At least not for now. Bill turned around, picked up the tray and sat back down on the bench. There were a couple of sandwiches, a bag of crisps and a can of coke. He realised he was ravenous and began to eat, finishing it all in a few short minutes. He immediately felt better with some food inside him and he began to assess his situation. It seemed this man, Andy, had some beef with his son Jason. He seemed to think Jason had murdered his mum and dad – but that couldn't be right. Bill knew his son and he definitely wasn't a killer. In fact he didn't

191

have a bad bone in his body. Bill had made sure he'd brought him up properly to respect other people. He thought back to what the man had said again. What was it exactly? He'd said something about Jason and his mates and justice. Had they done something that he didn't know about?

Wait a minute, he thought, could it be anything to do with Jack's car accident? That was the only thing Bill could think of where Jason had been involved and of course some people had unfortunately died in the accident. Maybe it was something to do with that but he couldn't think why. That had happened last year and was history now. Wasn't it?

After a few minutes he decided that it was a waste of time trying to work out why this guy had locked him up, he was obviously crazy. He refocused his mind back on how he could get out of this situation. First things first, he needed to escape. He needed to get out of this room, this cell, he was trapped in. He looked at the tray he'd been given and quickly decided there was nothing useful on it, no cutlery or anything sharp, but the tray itself might be a useful weapon. It was only plastic but it was a reasonable size and if he managed to jab it in the guy's face it might give him a few seconds to follow up with a kick or a punch. He put it to the side and re-examined the whole room, walking around it touching the walls with his hands, but he couldn't see or feel any weak spots. It just appeared to be some sort of plain store room, maybe on a

192

farm he thought which would explain the smell. Although he wasn't an expert in kidnapping, he guessed a farm might be a good location to hold someone. Assuming it wasn't a working farm it would be quiet and probably remote from any other buildings or people.

He presumed the man would come back to see him at some point and so he decided to wait for that and see if he could overpower him when he did. He had noticed that the man had some sort of steel looking rod in his hand when he'd opened the door but with a bit of luck he might be able to take him by surprise before he was able to use it against him. If he managed to knock him down and get out then he might be able to raise the alarm and get help.

Without his watch, Bill couldn't be sure of the time and it seemed like a couple of hours before the man came back. But Bill was ready. His eyes had been laser focused on the door for some time and as soon as he heard a slight sound from the other side and sensed the door opening he was ready. The door opened outwards and the man stood in the entrance just like before, holding the steel rod. Bill was on his feet at an angle to where the man stood about ten feet away. He threw the tray, spinning it like a Frisbee as hard as he could and it flew across the room, hitting the man somewhere in his face. As soon as the tray had left Bill's hand he charged forward, crouching down like a rugby player and three seconds later he hit the man shoulder first, somewhere in his midriff, carrying

193

him backwards till they both crashed across the floor outside the room. The steel rod clattered noisily and slid away to one side. Bill was up quickly, back on his feet throwing punches at the man's head as he lay half dazed on the floor in front of him. The man had his arms up protecting himself and most of Bill's blows were glancing off his arms. Bill wasn't as fit as he used to be and he was breathing heavily with his punches gradually becoming weaker and less frequent.

The man was beginning to push himself up off the floor and trying to fight back, kicking upwards as he rose. Bill decided to make a run for it and after a parting kick at the man's midriff which sent him back to the floor, he turned and ran across the room as fast as he could. He ran through an open door and found himself in a corridor, he kept running until he reached a wooden door at the far end. It was unlocked and he pushed it open and found himself outside in what seemed to be a farmyard. He kept running across the open space, shouting for help as loud as he could as he ran.

'HELP, HELP' His words echoed around in the air, but there didn't seem to be anyone else there, the place looked deserted, just a collection of old farm buildings.

He passed a couple of grey, wooden barns and rounding a corner he saw a house about fifty metres ahead. He was breathing heavily and sweating but he kept going, determined to make his escape. He reached the house and banged on the front door with both fists, shouting for help. He tried opening the door but it was locked and he couldn't hear any movement inside. He stepped back a few paces and tried shoulder charging the door but it was solid and wouldn't budge. He moved back from the door and looked around. To his right, beyond a brown field he thought he could see a road. He stared for a few seconds and saw a red object moving from left to right. It was a lorry or a van. He started jogging towards the field until he reached a wire fence with a ditch in front of it. He stepped over the ditch and stood on the lower wire of the fence pushing himself upwards but the wire wouldn't take his weight and he fell forwards onto the fence before tumbling over it into the field, landing head first in the ploughed earth on the other side of the fence. He shook his head, spat some earth out of his mouth and tried to get up, but he couldn't. His left foot was still caught in the fence wire and he couldn't free it. He shuffled backwards on his bottom towards the fence to get a better view. He could see where his foot had caught and reaching up awkwardly with his right hand he tried to untangle it. His foot was caught between two pieces of the fence wire and he managed to grab the bottom part and pull it downwards. He pulled on his leg and could feel some movement. Suddenly his foot broke loose as his shoe fell off landing on the other side of the fence and rolling down into the ditch. Bill stood up and looked back over the fence. He could see his shoe but it was out of reach. His

195

gaze took him beyond that, back towards the house and he could see the man now running in his direction, carrying what looked like a piece of wood. Bill turned away, scrambled to his feet and started running across the muddy field. It was hard work and his shoeless foot kept sinking into the ground slowing him down. He was breathing hard and could feel his pace dropping with every step. He looked around and saw that the man had got over the fence and was gaining on him. He was in the field now, running freely and making up ground quickly. Bill was still fifty or so metres from the far side of the field and the road beyond. He could see cars travelling along the road and he started calling, hoping that some of them might have their windows open and be able to hear him. He tried to up his pace but he was struggling. He'd now lost his sock and his foot was just a ball of mud. He glanced back and could see the man was closing in fast, only a few metres behind him now. Bill realised he wasn't going to make it to the road in time and so he jinked sharply to his left, stopped and turned to face his pursuer. Bill was breathing heavily but he wasn't going to give in easily. He knew his life might depend on it. He stood in the muddy field, one shoe missing and defiantly shouted,

'Come on then son. Let's see what you've got. You piece of shit.' Bill still didn't know what was going on but he was angry. He was angrier than he'd been for a long time and he was not going to give up. Bill raised his fists in a classic boxer pose

196

at the same time noticing that what the man was carrying was a golf club. The man took a step forward and swung the club at Bill, but he was ready and he ducked under it. He tried to counter the man and catch him off balance with a punch but he couldn't move his feet quickly enough out of the mud and he missed. The golf club came swinging towards him again and this time it caught his right forearm and knocked him backwards and to the right. Bill staggered and struggled to keep his footing. The club swung again this time catching him in the ribs and he doubled up winded, his legs beginning to buckle. Before he could do anything the next strike caught him on the back of his head and he fell forwards, face first, into the muddy field losing consciousness.

On the road, about fifty metres away, a young man in the front passenger seat of a red Vauxhall Astra was looking out his window across the field towards them.

'Jesus, did you see that?' he asked the driver.

'See what?' said the driver.

'Just back there in the field. Looked like a couple of guys having a fight. One of them hitting an old bloke with a stick or something. Maybe we should stop and go back see if he's alright?'

'Nah, we'll be late for the game if we stop now. Besides it's probably just those farm folks, they're crazy round here. It's all the inter-breeding, I guess,' the driver replied.

'Ha-ha, yes you're probably right,' his passenger said as they passed a copse of trees and lost sight of the field, 'I reckon we'll beat them three nil today.'

Chapter 23

It was Saturday morning and Lucy was sitting in the kitchen on her own, wearing an old sweat shirt and jeans, bare footed, eating a bowl of cornflakes. That was her usual breakfast choice. She'd had cornflakes for breakfast when she was little and it still had some sort of comforting element for her, even now she was an adult. When she'd lived on her own she'd occasionally, somewhat guiltily, also had cornflakes late at night when she'd been curled up on the couch in her pyjamas watching TV.

Today, Paul had gone out early, before she had even woken up. He'd left her a note on the kitchen table saying he had more research to do on his book and that he'd be back sometime after lunch.

Lucy had been disappointed when she'd got up and discovered the note. She'd been hoping to spend some time with Paul today. It seemed over the last couple of weeks she'd hardly seen him at all. He always seemed to be out somewhere working on his book. His bloody book! He'd better finish it soon so they could get back to being a proper couple again.

199

The more annoying thing though was that she still hadn't seen anything that he'd produced so far that looked anything like a book. She hadn't seen any notebooks or pieces of paper lying around anywhere. Wasn't that how authors worked – constantly writing down each new creative idea as it came to them on scraps of paper so they wouldn't forget it? Paul had told Lucy that the way he worked was that he gathered ideas in his head and tapped them into his mobile or laptop, but thinking back she'd rarely seen him doing that when she'd been with him. He told her it would be some time before he could link all his ideas together to form a proper story. Then he'd have to spend some time editing it over and over. Only after that would he have a draft that he promised Lucy she could see. He said he wanted her to be the first person to read it but that he wanted it to be a complete draft before she saw it, otherwise it wouldn't make sense. She sort of understood that. Kind of, but not really. When he gave her one of his smiles, she couldn't help but let him off.

His timescale for getting to a draft stage however were vague at best, a few months, maybe next year….She'd felt a bit guilty keeping asking him, maybe she was indirectly putting pressure on him and she didn't want to do that. So in the end she'd mainly given up asking.

She was still disappointed though. And bored. Surely he didn't have to work on his bloody book on a Saturday. He had all week to work on it.

Weekends should be their time to spend together. If you're your own boss you choose which days you work and Lucy definitely wouldn't choose a weekend day. Oh well, she thought, when he's turned it into a best selling novel I guess all will be well and the likes of today will be a distant memory.

She put her empty breakfast bowl in the dishwasher and resolved to put her free to time to good use and spring clean the flat. It wasn't a big flat and as both she and Paul were quite house-proud, it was actually already pretty clean to begin with. So after only just an hour she was finished and back in the kitchen making herself a cup of coffee. She glanced up at the big, round, black kitchen clock. It was still only 11am, Paul could be another couple of hours yet. Maybe more. She needed to do something else. She couldn't sit around for another couple of hours waiting for him to turn up. She looked out the window and saw it was raining and there were leaves blowing around in the street making it look wintry and cold. She didn't fancy going out in that.

She decided to clear out her wardrobe. It was getting full with the rail bending in the middle and she resolved to throw out anything she hadn't worn for the last year. Twenty minutes later the wardrobe was now distinctly emptier. The wardrobe rail was a bit less stressed and there was a large pile of her clothes lying on the bed.

She looked at the pile and picked out a long purple dress with a low cut front.

'How the hell did I ever buy this?' she said out loud laughing to herself as she threw it back down on the bed. She did the same with a yellow, flowery jump suit she remembered she'd only worn once to a friend's party when it may have been trendy. She had been single at the time and looking for a man – it hadn't helped though. She then picked out a couple of dresses that, although she couldn't remember the last time she wore them, she couldn't bear to throw out. They just needed the right occasion, she thought, as she hung them back in the wardrobe.

She picked up the remainder of the pile and made to leave the bedroom to look at them better in the lounge but a silk dress on top of the pile slid off and landed on the floor at her feet. As she bent down to retrieve it a glint of light caught her eye. She looked closer and saw it was coming from the key to Paul's small wooden filing cabinet in the corner of the room. It was the only piece of furniture Paul had brought with him and it was so small that it easily fitted into Lucy's bedroom. Lucy looked at the key, it was still in the lock. She'd never noticed that before. Lucy was sure he usually kept it with him. The key was in the drawer which he told her he used to keep the notes for his book and he was always very protective of it. Lucy stopped and stood there, thinking for a second, but the temptation was too great. She put the pile of clothes back down on the bed and reaching down she turned the key and slowly opened the drawer.

202

She had expected to see some sheets of paper with notes written on them, or maybe a few notebooks, like how she imagined authors worked - but instead all that seemed to be in the drawer was a slightly dented white, cardboard shoe box. She carefully took the box out and sat down on the bed resting it on her lap. The flat was completely silent. Holding her breath, Lucy slowly took the lid off the box and looked inside. It appeared to contain some papers and what looked like several newspaper cuttings. She put her hands in the box and, at the bottom, she could feel what she guessed was a small notepad. She lifted everything out carefully, placed it on her lap, and started looking through the individual items. Her attention was immediately drawn to the newspaper cuttings. There seemed to be about half a dozen of them and she began to scan through them quickly, one by one, placing each on the bed to the side of her as she finished. There were several articles about a road accident whilst others seemed to be reports of a court case.

Before she had time to read them properly, she heard the front door opening and Paul's voice calling her name. She quickly put everything back in the box, satisfying herself that it looked just as she'd found it, put it away and locked the drawer. With a final glance she reassured herself that all looked just as she had found it then picked up her pile of clothes and called back,

'Hi, just coming, been doing some spring cleaning,' she said, as she left the bedroom. She put

203

the clothes down on the sofa in the lounge and hugged Paul as he came in, catching the familiar aroma of his aftershave.

'Blimey, that is a clear out,' he said looking at the clothes. 'Are they all for the charity shop?'

'Yes, pretty much I think. I just need to have one final sort through in the light and make sure I'm happy to get rid of them. How did it go today?' she asked. 'Did you get anything useful for the book?'

'Yes, it wasn't bad,' he replied. 'You've done well there,' he said motioning his head towards the pile of clothes. 'I need to do the same with mine sometime.'

'I guess so, but you don't really have that many clothes to sort out. Not like me, I've become a bit of a hoarder,' Lucy laughed. 'So where have you been, around town?' she said, not wanting to let it drop.

'Yeh, around and about,' he replied picking up an envelope from the coffee table in front of him and opening it to look inside.

'See anyone in town?' Lucy enquired.

'What? No,' Paul replied distractedly, 'I was out of town a bit.'

'Oh whereabouts?' Lucy persisted.

Paul appeared not to hear her, he was reading the contents of the envelope, and didn't answer.

'Where were you,' Lucy persevered, 'anywhere nice?'

'What? Oh no,' Paul replied, putting the envelope back down on the coffee table, 'just out driving around bits of the countryside, looking at a farm, a bit of research for the book, nothing much.'

'A farm?' Lucy replied intrigued, 'Is your book set on a farm then? You've never really told me much about it.'

Paul put the letter back in the envelope, 'Blooming estate agents,' he said, 'where do they get your details from? I'm going to have a shower, do you want to go out for lunch, I found a nice country pub when I was driving around,' and before Lucy could reply he left the room.

A little while later they were sat at a table in the country pub that Paul had found. It was one of those pubs that wasn't really a pub anymore. In the past it had been a proper pub where people went just to drink beer but now it was really a restaurant. Paul and Lucy were sat at a square wooden table on high stools, enjoying an early afternoon lunch. They were both casually dressed in t-shirts and jeans.

'This is lovely,' said Lucy for the fourth time since they'd arrived 'How did you find it, is it near that farm you were talking about earlier?'

'Yes, I just passed it when I was driving around. Do you want another glass of wine?' he asked nodding towards Lucy's almost empty glass.

'No, I'm fine. It makes me tired drinking in the afternoon,' she smiled. 'Besides I want to see if I can get rid of all those clothes when we get back.'

They finished their meals and ordered two coffees. Lucy was still thinking about what she'd found in Paul's drawer, trying to make some sense of it and she decided to try and steer the conversation back towards his book.

'I spoke to my mum and dad earlier, they want to invite us round again' she began. 'They were asking for you. I think dad wants an excuse to drink more of his whisky with you. I told them you were out doing some research on your book. They couldn't believe you were doing that on a Saturday morning,' she laughed. 'They said you must be keen.'

'Haha, no, I just woke up and didn't want to disturb you so I decided I'd go out and do a bit. How are they, both well?' Paul replied, drinking his coffee.

'Yes they're both fine,' Lucy fibbed, not actually having spoken to them, 'Dad remembered you telling him the book was a crime thriller, called… The Accident wasn't it? He was asking me if I could tell him any more about it. The plot and stuff I guess. But I said you'd not really told me anything yet. Is there anything I can tell him, what it's about or that? I think he's just interested and been talking about it with some of his friends.'

''Ha, Ha, it's called The Anniversary. Tell him he'll have to wait a few weeks,' Paul replied smiling. 'Let's keep him in suspense. You know I don't want to say too much about it until I've got it all clear myself. I'm not quite there with it yet.'

206

Lucy pouted and replied,

'Okay, I know let's play a little game then. You don't have to tell me anything but I'll ask questions and you can say yes or no, just to give me a few clues.'

'All right,' Paul replied laughing, 'go on then, if we must.'

'Okay…..question one….am I in it?' she asked, gripping her coffee cup tightly.

'No!' Paul replied laughing. 'It's a crime thriller….I didn't have you down as an evil murderer. Or a middle aged detective.'

'Ah, so there's a murderer,' Lucy replied. 'Right, question two then….Does the murderer get caught and taken to court?' She raised her cup, taking a drink, but all the while watching Paul, waiting for his response.

'Well, he might,' Paul replied, 'but he's a clever bloke and so he might also get away with it. I haven't finished it yet, so even I don't know the outcome.'

'So there might or might not be a court case….hmmm,' Lucy replied quickly, pleased that Paul was taking part in her little "game." 'How many people get killed?'

'That's not a yes or no question,' Paul said smiling across the table at Lucy. He glanced at his watch, 'Oh, look at the time, come on we better get moving, it's getting late. You need to get back before the charity shop closes.'

'Okay, okay, hold on, let me have one final question….Let me think. I know…is there a road accident, like a car crash or something in the story?'

'A road accident? Why do you ask that?' Paul responded quizzically, 'sounds a bit random? It's a crime thriller not an episode of Casualty.'

'I know, I don't know….I'm running out of ideas on what to ask and that just came to me,' Lucy replied. 'So come on, is there? It's a yes or no question.'

Paul smiled ruefully and hesitated before answering.

'Yes strangely there is a sort of a road accident, but it's not really an accident. That's all I'm saying, You'll have to wait till I've finished,' he said smiling and he stood up to leave.

'Come on, let's go,' he said. 'We need to clear that pile of clothes before you change your mind and keep them all!'

Lucy finished the last of her coffee and followed him out the door into the car park, not sure what, if anything, she'd managed to find out.

Chapter 24

DS Campbell strode confidently into Strong's office with a large brown envelope in his hand. He made his way to the desk and waited till his boss looked up. He was feeling excited and impatient at the same time.

'There's been a letter, came in today.' he said simply.

'A letter?' Strong replied, raising his eyebrows. Campbell still looked tired but perhaps not as bad as the day before. Strong hadn't found the time to check if he was okay yet.

'Yes, well it's a sort of fake medical report actually,' DS Campbell replied. 'It's a bit weird. It was delivered to Jason Reynolds, the son of our missing man, Bill Reynolds. You'll remember Jason was one of the gang of four in the car that wiped out Andy Austin's family. Well it was delivered last night or early this morning. We think probably sometime early in the morning. We think by hand. No-one in the Reynolds household heard or saw anything but they were late to bed and understandably not sleeping well. It seems to have

209

been just pushed through the letterbox and they found it lying on the doormat this morning. When they read it they called us straight away. We're talking with the neighbours to see if they saw anyone around the house but nothing has come up so far. Of course there's no CCTV nearby as its pretty much a residential area.'

'What does it say,' Strong asked with a touch of surprise in his voice. He hadn't expected this development.

'Here, it's probably easier if you just have a look,' Campbell replied as he passed the brown envelope across the desk to Strong. 'Forensics have seen it,' he added, 'but it was completely clean, no prints, apart from the Reynolds family who all read it.'

Strong took the envelope and looked at it closely, turning it around in his hands but it appeared to be just an ordinary brown envelope with nothing on it. He turned it upside down with one hand, letting a single white sheet of paper slip out which he caught with his other hand. He put the envelope down on his already busy desk and started reading the note. He read it through quickly and then a second time, more slowly, reading some of the content out aloud as he read.

'Critical   condition...stable...in   good hands...too   early   to   say...being   closely monitored...will report any change.'

As Campbell had said it was written in the form of some sort of crude medical report. He read

210

it a third time, again quickly, and then put it down on top of the envelope.

'What do you think?' he said, looking across the desk at his colleague.

Campbell was ready for the question. He knew this was often how his boss liked to work and in this particular case he seemed to be letting Campbell take more responsibility. He'd seen Strong do this many times before where he'd ask for other people's opinions first before he made any comment himself. It seemed he often liked to get as full a picture as he could before he made any judgements and it appeared that was how he was running this particular operation. Although Campbell appreciated the opportunity to take on more of the lead and the potential that would give him for promotion to a Detective Inspector role, part of him was also wishing that it wasn't at a time when things weren't going so well at home. His wife was still suffering badly with their IVF failures and although Campbell wouldn't readily admit it, it was also having an impact on him. He had always been a good sleeper but now he was waking up in the early hours of the morning with all sorts of negative thoughts going on inside his head. It was difficult to separate his family problems and his work problems but he knew at this moment he needed to try and give his full focus to solving the two murders. Once that was over he could then work out the best way forward for him and his wife.

He was aware that Strong was waiting for him to respond.

'Well, it would appear to be referring to our missing man, Bill Reynolds,' Campbell started. 'As you know, he disappeared last night. He didn't come home from his usual Saturday night out at his local pub. The letter was delivered to his son, Jason, one of the four guys, and so I think we have to assume it's come from our man Andy Austin. Looks like he's playing some sort of game, taunting the Reynolds family, or maybe us? I'm not sure what the purpose is in giving supposed details of his injuries though.'

Strong moved backwards in his chair with the paper in his hand in front of him. He was staring into space, thinking.

'Mmm…I didn't expect this,' he said. 'Let's get Dr Collins back in and see what she makes of it. She did a lot of digging into what happened before, maybe she'll have some insight to what this means and what our man Austin is playing at. Did either of you speak with DI Williamson to see if he could help at all?'

'Yes, we both did,' Campbell replied, 'but as you said he didn't really remember much about it. It was just another road traffic case to him I think, although with a tragic outcome obviously. There wasn't anything more he could offer. Did you have any further thoughts from when you met him?' he asked Strong.

'No,' Strong replied, 'All I can remember is feeling sorry for what he was going through but that's about it.'

Strong picked up his desk phone and punched in a number. DS Campbell squeezed into the chair on the other side of his desk and waited while Strong finished the call to Dr Collins, filling her in on the letter and its contents.

'She's making her way over now, should be here in about thirty minutes,' Strong said glancing at his watch, 'you okay to wait, I'd like you to hear what she says?' he asked Campbell.

Campbell looked at his phone then replied,

'Sure, just got to make a quick call first,' and he got up and left the room.

DS Campbell walked along the corridor, looking for a quiet place to make his phone call. He was supposed to be going with his wife to see the fertility consultant at the hospital to discuss what their options were after their last failed attempt at IVF. He knew his wife would be upset if he didn't make the appointment but he tried to convince himself that they'd discussed it between themselves enough already and they knew what they wanted to ask so his wife should be able to do that without him if he couldn't make it in time. She knew he was a policeman and she'd understand how important it was for him to be fully working on this high profile murder case. He'd already told her that Strong seemed to be giving him more responsibility in this case, almost letting him lead it, and that could be

213

crucial when it came to his chance for promotion which would be great for both of them. He positioned himself in a corner at the far end of the corridor and dialled the number. His wife answered quickly,

'Hi,' she said before he was able to talk, 'are you on your way?'

'No, look, I'm sorry but something's come up at work, with this murder investigation. I need to be in a meeting with Strong and I'll try and be there but there's a chance I'm not going to be able to make it. I'm really sorry, but you know how it is.'

There was no response.

'Hello, you there?' Campbell spoke, looking at his phone to check the call was still connected.

'So you're not coming?' his wife answered.

'No, I'm sorry, I don't think I can. You know I would if I could. But you know what to say anyway, what to ask. Just like we've been talking about. Ask him what our options are now. What would he advise. You'll be ok,' Campbell replied, hoping his wife understood. After a short pause she replied.

'Looks like I'll have to be…. as usual. I'll see you later then,' she said and the line went dead.

Campbell exhaled loudly and turned to make his way back to Strong's office. He opened the door, forgetting to knock, and sat back down in the same chair as before. Strong was reading a document and the two of them remained sat there, silent, each lost in their own private thoughts. A few minutes later, Dr Collins arrived and she sat down in the chair beside Campbell. Strong quickly welcomed her, took off his glasses and handed her the letter that had been delivered to the Reynolds house. She read through it quickly and passed it back to Strong, explaining she'd also been sent an electronic copy and so had been able to review it and refer back to the notes she'd made on the previous year's accident.

'So did you find anything, any idea why Austin would have sent the letter?' DS Campbell asked eagerly.

Dr Collins looked across to him with a wry smile on her face then turned back to address DI Strong directly.

'What I did find was one interesting piece of the jigsaw which, based on our assumptions that Austin is suffering from post traumatic embitterment disorder, or PTED, could make sense.' Dr Collins paused for a few seconds then carried on.

'As you know several of Austin's family were killed in the accident, but not all at the scene. In fact only his mother died at the roadside, the others survived and were taken to hospital. On reviewing the various medical reports of the other three I found out that the injuries suffered by Austin's father, David Austin, were similar to those detailed in the letter you received from our supposed killer earlier today.'

215

Dr Collins paused and took a sip of water from a white plastic cup.

'So....what are you saying exactly?' asked DS Campbell.

'So, what I'm saying is that Austin, assuming it is him that sent the letter, has told one of the occupants of the car that his father is suffering from the same injuries as Austin's father had before he died. So that guy....Jason Reynolds,' she said looking at her notes, 'he will be feeling exactly the same emotions Austin would have felt when he was told his own father's injuries in the hospital.'

'Jesus Christ!' Campbell exclaimed, getting up from his seat. 'What sort of guy are we dealing with here? He's a bloody lunatic. It's like he's playing a game and enjoying it. So that must mean he's holding this, this Bill Reynolds somewhere....he's smashed him up to be in the same condition his dad was and he wants Jason Reynolds to know that so he can feel the same suffering as he did? The man's crazy.'

'Yes, that's largely correct although we don't know for sure that he has actually injured Bill Reynolds at this point. The key thing is that he wants, no he needs, Jason Reynolds to believe that his father has these injuries. He may not actually be injured. In reality it would be difficult to cause these serious injuries exactly as those suffered by Austin's father.' Dr Collins replied. 'It would appear that one of the specific factors of his particular PTED condition is that he wants to replicate almost exactly

216

what happened to him onto those he sees responsible for that wrong he endured. So as long as Jason Reynolds believes this note,' she said picking it up from Strong's desk, 'then his objective will have been achieved.'

DI Strong leant forward with his elbows on the desk in front of him.

'Okay, what we do know though, if your theory is correct,' he said turning his head to look at Dr Collins, 'is that Austin must be holding Bill Reynolds captive somewhere because he can't kill him yet according to his rules. Austin's father survived for ten days after the accident in hospital before he passed away. So in a few days time, unless we get him before that, Austin is going to kill Bill Reynolds. And if he plays by the rules, his rules, we'll find Bill Reynold's body that same day so that Jason Reynolds finds out about his father in exactly the same timescale as Austin did about his. Do you agree?' he asked, looking directly at Dr Collins.

'Yes, I do, I think that pretty much sums it up' Dr Collins replied.

DS Campbell's mind was racing and he began to walk around the room.

'So far we have two murders which correlate time wise to when the first two victims of Austin's family died. We are assuming he has the third victim holed up somewhere….wasn't there a fourth victim as well?' Campbell asked.

217

'Yes,' replied Dr Collins, 'I had a look at that. The fourth victim was his cousin, Phil Austin. He was also in hospital but died a few days after Austin's dad. His was a bit unfortunate in that it wasn't actually the accident that killed him directly. He died in the operating theatre from heart failure. Apparently it was just one of those things that occasionally happens. No-one could have predicted it. Very sad.'

DS Campbell exhaled loudly, 'Jeez, talk about bad luck. You survive getting run over by a car and then have a heart attack on the operating table. How unlucky is that? So what does that mean for Austin then – is he going to kill one of the guy's cousins too?'

'Well that's a good question,' Dr Collins replied, 'he may do or he may think that it wasn't the accident that killed him and so the four men weren't responsible for his cousin's death.'

'I think he will, the man's a lunatic,' Campbell butted in, 'he won't see the facts, he'll just see that his cousin died because of the accident, directly or indirectly, it won't matter to him either way. Let's face it, he wouldn't have been in the hospital if he hadn't got hit by the car in the first place.'

'I agree,' said DI Strong who had been sitting quietly listening to his two colleagues discussing the case. 'Which means that one of the fourth lad's cousins is at risk.'

218

'I think you're probably right too,' Dr Collins added.

DI Strong had put his reading glasses on and was looking down at his notes. When he'd found what he needed, he looked up again, peering above the glasses.

'Dan Sears is his name,' he said. 'We need to talk to him, find out who his cousins are, where they live. God, I wonder how many he has …. I've got eight!'

One hour later the whole police team were sat in the major incident meeting room and they had just heard the answer to Strong's earlier question.

'Sixteen!' DS Campbell exclaimed loudly, standing up from his chair, 'he's got sixteen bloody cousins. Sixteen potential targets for Austin. How in God's name are we going to be able to protect all of them? We haven't got the resource to do that twenty four by seven. It's impossible.'

'Hang on, it might not be quite that bad,' DI Strong responded. 'If we assume that Austin is trying to replicate his own suffering as much as possible then there might be a way of narrowing this down. We know that Phil Austin, his cousin, was the same age as Andy and they were very close friends. They'd grown up together and were more like brothers than cousins. So I think what we need to find out from our man in the car, Dan Sears, is which, if any, of his cousins best meets that profile. Out of his sixteen cousins which is he closest to? And its probably a male, rather than female but lets

219

not rule that out. If there is one that fits the bill of being more like a brother than a cousin then that's going to be the one. From what we've seen so far Austin's done a lot of preparation for this over the last year so he'll know exactly who he has as his target. Let's get our man Dan Sears in again and see if he can help us narrow it down.'

'Okay, I'll go and find him right away. He actually works for us in this building, in IT. He's one of the techies,' Campbell said and he marched out of the room to go find him.

After a short discussion with Dan Sears in a private office, DS Campbell was confident they had identified the most likely next target that Austin would go for. Dan had told them that there were a few cousins that he didn't really keep in touch with at all and some that they only swapped cards with at Christmas time. However there was one family they were much closer with and they mixed with socially. They'd had family holidays together when they were younger and still met up fairly regularly when it was someone's birthday or some other family occasion. One of the cousins from that family was called Kevin Green and he was a couple of years older than Dan but they had always been very close as they grew up and they still met up quite regularly now. Out of Dan's sixteen cousins the police concluded that Kevin Green would be the most likely target.

DS Campbell quickly tasked one of his team to track down Kevin Green and bring him in for questioning - and also for his own protection.

Chapter 25,
15th December, one year earlier

Dan was sitting in the front passenger seat of Jack's car. He always got to sit in the front as he was the biggest and he'd told them he sometimes got car sick when he sat in the back. Actually he hadn't been car sick since he was ten or eleven but he hadn't added that piece of detail as he liked sitting in the front where there was more space and he could be on his own. His mates Jason and Chris were in the back, messing around as usual. Dan was the quiet one, he didn't say much. He preferred listening to other people and laughing along with them. They were funnier than him and they seemed to get drunk quicker than he did too. Dan never felt that drunk really even when he drank a lot and really wanted to let go. Even then he stayed disappointingly sober and his acting skills weren't good enough for him to even pretend he was drunk.

As usual, they'd all had a good night in the pub and Chris the comedian had chatted up a girl, but then somehow she'd disappeared. Dan didn't really know how to talk to women but he enjoyed watching his mates try. Sometimes he would join in and say something if there was a big group of them and one of the girls was a bit quiet too. He didn't like loud girls, or ones that talked a lot, they scared him.

He looked on his mates like they were family, like brothers or at least he imagined that's what brothers would be like. Dan had grown up as an only child and his dad had left home when he was young, so most of the time it had just been him and his mum. His mum had also been an only child and so it seemed perfectly natural that there was just the two of them. His dad visited occasionally and there was a large family on his side, uncles, aunties and cousins, who they'd sometimes get together with at Christmas, but he didn't really know them all that well. The only one he really got on with was his cousin Kevin who he would meet up with every now and again. In Dan's eyes his family was simply him and his mum and he was happy with that but Jack, Chris and Jason were a close second.

As usual, Dan was squeezed into the front seat, his knees pressed up against the dashboard and his bum hard into the base of the seat forcing him to sit upright. He felt the car go over a bump in the road and his head hit the inside of the roof knocking his glasses to one side. He pushed them back level again.

'Aww poor Chris,' he heard Jason say from behind him, 'that bird used you to buy her drinks, she was never that interested in you.'

'You prat,' Jack shouted back from the driver's seat and Dan looked across at him. He had a beard now and Dan was pleased as it meant they had something in common.

'You never had a chance with her, she was well out of your league,' Jack continued.

Dan smiled and sensed a scuffle in the back of the car and then he heard Chris shout out,

'Give's it back you ginger dick.'

Dan tried to look round to see what was happening but he was restricted by the lack of space he had and he couldn't quite see. He heard a bump as something hit the floor of the car behind him.

'Oi you two settle down, anyone would think you were all pissed!' Jack called out from the front of the car, glancing in his mirror as he did so.

'Chris is,' Jason shouted back, ''he's pissed off because he got mugged off. She just played along to get free drinks and now he's texting his ex for an easy shag,' he said laughing.

Dan felt more movement in the back and he tried to look around again to see what was happening but still he couldn't turn enough. Suddenly he felt the car make an abrupt jolt to the left causing him to fall towards the car door. He glanced sideways towards Jack who had both hands firmly on the steering wheel and was looking straight ahead. Dan sensed that the car was turning

224

to the left, towards the pavement. He looked out the front windscreen and could clearly see a group of people standing in front of the car, getting closer by the second. He wanted to call out but he couldn't. He tried to grab the steering wheel but there wasn't time. He threw his arms up in front of his face in an effort to protect himself as he saw the car about to hit the group. He felt something hit the back of his seat and then a jolt and a bang on the windscreen. After that, he sat there still with his hands in front of his face and noticed a strange silence.

Chapter 26

DS Campbell pushed the door open without knocking and marched briskly into Strong's office, walking straight up to his desk. Strong was sitting in his leather chair and he looked up at his colleague, realising by his swift entrance that he must have something important to tell him.

'We were too bloody slow,' Campbell blurted out, 'Sear's cousin, Kevin Green, he's apparently missing. No-one has seen him since he left work yesterday evening just after six o clock. We're looking at his normal route home, getting CCTV and stuff but I think we have to assume that he's been taken by our man, Andy Austin. He seems to be a step ahead of us.'

DI Strong pushed himself back in his chair, ran his hands through what seemed to be his increasingly greying hair, crossing them behind his head and looked at Campbell.

"Oh shit,' he said. 'So now we have to assume he is holding the two people somewhere, just waiting until the time is right to kill them.'

'Yes and we only have three days to find them or else we will be looking at the body of Bill Reynolds somewhere instead of tucking into our Christmas dinner,' DS Campbell replied.

Strong sat forward again, seeming to have come to a decision.

'We need to find out where he is,' he began. 'If we're right then they'll both still be alive. It can't be easy keeping two grown men prisoner somewhere. He'll need to have some sort of remote premises like an old warehouse or disused factory or something. Get the team to go over all the statements we got from the people that knew him before. See if there's any area he knew or liked to go to. Maybe a holiday place or something. But it can't be far away, maybe a twenty or thirty mile radius from where he's operating. The farther away it is the more difficult it would be for him coming and going and the more risky that something might happen or someone sees something. See if there's any place mentioned by anyone.'

'Ok will do,' said Campbell and he turned to leave the room.

'Hang on,' Strong replied, 'there's something else.'

'Campbell stopped and turned around waiting to hear what his boss had to say.

'The Chief wants us to go on telly, do a piece on the case and see what we can get, see if anyone recognises Austin and knows where he is now,' said DI Strong.

227

'I'll tell you what we'll get,' DS Campbell quickly replied, 'a bunch of weirdos, do-gooders, would be policemen all phoning in with their wacky theories and causing us a load of wasted effort and time.'

'Yes, probably, but who knows we may get something that is useful and to be honest we haven't got much else to go on at the moment. There's two people dead and two more people missing out there who we believe may still be alive but who will be killed as well if we don't track down Andy Austin in the next few days. We have to look at all options.' Strong replied. 'Besides if the Chief says do it, then we have to do it. He's getting increasingly fed up with all the stuff that's being written in the papers, like the rest of us. I don't know how these guys sleep at night. They just seem to feel that they can write anything even when there's no basis for it what so ever. They just make it up now. It didn't used to be like that when you could trust them to work with us and print what we wanted, what we told them to. Somewhere down the line, we lost control of them.'

Strong stopped for a second and looked across the room at his colleague who had been standing listening to his rant.

'By the way I put you forward for it. Here's where you need to be at two pm for the recording, and here's what I'd mostly like you to say' he said handing Campbell a couple of pieces of paper.

'What?!' DS Campbell exploded and despite the seriousness of the situation Strong fell back in his chair in fits of laughter.

'It'll be good exposure for you, get your face known,' Strong said his eyes sparkling as he recovered himself.

'Feel free to change some of the words if you like, but the gist of what you need to say is there. It'll be on TV later tonight and hopefully they might cover it in the news too. Don't worry, it should only take you a couple of minutes maximum and you won't have to take any questions. In fact you'll see that's in there at the start. We need to keep this under our control. We got what looks like a fairly good photo of him from his workplace; it had been taken for his security pass. Surely someone will recognise him and know where he's hiding out. Just relax, you'll enjoy it,' Strong said smiling and biting his lip.

'Thanks a lot,' DS Campbell replied as he turned and left the room, swinging the door shut behind him.

Chapter 27

Lucy had worked through her lunch hour so she could leave the office an hour early. She was Head of Marketing for a small software company in town and they were pretty flexible on timescales but she didn't like to take advantage of that and always made sure she put in the hours. They were a good group of people and she'd got to know them well over the three years she'd been there. Generally she enjoyed the job and it was an interesting company, specialising in software for the medical industry, hospitals and doctors' surgeries mainly. But lately she'd found herself starting to worry that she was getting *too* comfortable and that she should be looking for something bigger. She knew that was partly due to her blossoming relationship with Paul which had given her more self- confidence.

Today though, her mind was on other things. Her recent find of the box in Paul's cabinet had confused her and she couldn't get it out of her head. She hadn't been able to make any sense of it and she hadn't had enough time to really look at the contents when Paul had come home unexpectedly.

All she could remember were a few bits of paper and some newspaper cuttings. She'd tried subtly asking Paul about it a few times but she didn't really know what to ask, or how to ask it without giving the game away. And the yes/no game she'd come up with in the country pub hadn't really helped her at all. It had just made her more confused. Although she had noticed that Paul had looked a bit uncomfortable, especially when she had raised the subject of a road accident with him.

The last thing she wanted was for him to find out she'd been looking at his personal stuff. She knew that was indicative of a lack of trust in a relationship and with everything going so well with them she didn't want to do anything to upset that. But something was nagging at her and she needed to sort it out. Just for her own peace of mind. So she had come up with a plan of action.

She opened the door to her flat and called out,

'Hello…Paul, are you home….Paul?'

There was no reply and the flat was silent and felt empty. She was relieved. She hadn't expected him to be home but you never knew nowadays. His hours working on the book were irregular to say the least. He'd even been out a couple of times in the evening. When she'd left the flat this morning he'd said that he had to go somewhere, something to do with his book and that he would probably not be back till about seven pm. His usual vagueness. But this time it suited Lucy, it

231

would give her two or three hours to do what she needed to do which should be plenty of time, even if he came home unexpectedly early again.

She put her bag down and hung her coat up on the hook in the hallway. She thought about getting changed and then making herself a cup of coffee but decided against it as she was too nervous and needed to get on with the task in hand. She couldn't focus on doing anything else that might delay it. Besides there was always the chance that Paul would come home really early and so it was best to get on with it as soon as possible. She went straight into the bedroom and opened the wardrobe door. Last night she'd noticed that the keys were no longer in the lock of Paul's cabinet and while he was in the bathroom, she'd found them in the pocket of one of his jackets. She reached inside the jacket pocket and was relieved to find they were still there. She took the keys out delicately, smoothing the pocket back down, subconsciously not wanting to leave any trace of what she was doing, and she bent down to unlock the cabinet drawer. All the while she was listening intently for any noise in the flat, any sign of Paul coming home. She was almost frightened to breathe. But the flat remained silent. She opened the cabinet drawer slowly, trying not to make any sound and took out the same small box she had looked at the last time.

Lucy sat down on the bed with the box again resting on her lap. She took the lid off and reached inside gently hooking her fingers underneath the bottom layer of the papers and the notepad below. Very cautiously she lifted them out as one whole bundle before laying it down on the bed beside her. She was desperately keen not to leave any indication to Paul that anyone had been in his cabinet and she didn't know if the order of the various papers meant anything so she was careful to keep them exactly as she'd found them. She placed the empty box and lid on the other side of her, leaning against the pillow, and turned back to look at the contents now lying next to her.

She picked up the top piece of paper and saw that it contained what appeared to be a list of mobile phone numbers. Lucy counted six numbers, all mobile numbers, but there were no names against them, just two or three letters which Lucy guessed were either the person's initials or some other indication of their identity so that Paul would know who they were. She stared at the letters for a few minutes but nothing came to mind. No names that she could think of. Frustrated at not being able to work any of them out she put the piece of paper face down on the bed on the other side of her and picked up the second piece of paper from the pile. It was blank. She turned it over to look at the other side but it was blank too. She quickly put it on top of the first piece and picked up the next one. This was one of the newspaper clippings she had briefly seen the last time. It had been cut out somewhere from the middle of a page so she couldn't tell which newspaper it was from nor the date of the article.

233

She turned it over but all that was on the rear was part of an advert for a cure for back pain. Flicking it back over, she read the article. It wasn't a big piece but it was about a car crash in a place called Moorhill. Lucy paused for a moment and thought she could remember Paul saying he'd once lived in Moorhill. But she wasn't sure, he hadn't talked much about his life prior to their meeting so she couldn't be certain. Maybe it had been someone else. She returned to the article and read it again, this time more slowly, looking for any clues as to why Paul might have kept it in a box in a locked cabinet. It appeared a car had hit a group of people and one of them had been killed, a man. There weren't any other details of anyone involved in the accident. No names or descriptions. No eye witness statements. Not much detail at all. All the article said was that three people had been taken to hospital and the car driver had been taken to the local police station for questioning. She read through it again to see if there was anything she'd missed but she couldn't see anything. There was nothing she could relate to Paul, other than the vague connection that he might have lived in the place where it happened. She sat up again, running her hands through her hair, and tried hard to think what it might mean. If Paul had lived there, maybe he knew the person that died or some of the other people involved? Maybe that's why he had the cutting. But why had he never mentioned it and why keep the cutting locked away in a box? She carefully put the article down and picked up the next one to see if it could give her any further clues. It was another newspaper report about the same accident but somewhat longer with a bit more detail. Again there was no indication of which paper it was from or the date of publication but Lucy surmised it was probably a day or so after the first one due to the additional detail it now had. This second article named both the man who had died and also some brief detail of the driver of the car. The man's name was Steve Austin and he had been twenty five years old and lived in Moorhill. The driver of the car was also said to be a local man, aged twenty three but it did not say what his name was or give any further information on him.

Lucy stared into space, thinking. Her mind was racing. Depending on when this happened, could Paul have been the car driver? What age was he now?.....twenty eight. That would mean it happened five years ago, long before Lucy knew him. Was this something he was keeping from her, his dark secret? He had never talked much about his past. Maybe that was why? Perhaps he liked to keep it all locked away in his mind, locked away in this box? A road accident wasn't the worst thing though was it? Okay someone had died but it was an accident. But Lucy knew if she and Paul were going to have a long term relationship, if it was going to work between them, then they couldn't have any secrets. Somehow she'd need to find out the truth from him, but he'd need to tell her. He had to want to tell her, to share all his secrets with her, even

235

something like this, but at this point she didn't know how that was going to happen.

There were a few more newspaper cuttings about the accident but they were shorter and contained even less detail than the others so they didn't help her in any way. There were also two further newspaper pieces about a court case. Once again these were very short and didn't contain much detail other than the name of the defendant who was said to be called Jack Wilson. From the information given, Lucy worked out that the accident and the court case were related. It appeared that this Jack Wilson had been the driver of the car that had been involved in the crash and he had been charged with careless driving, found guilty and given a year's ban. Not much for killing someone, Lucy thought. Although she had no idea who Jack Wilson was she felt strangely relieved that her earlier fear that Paul had been the car driver had turned out not to be the case. However this still meant that she was no clearer as to why Paul had kept these cuttings and what they meant to him. What was his interest in this accident? Maybe he knew this Jack Wilson, but she'd never heard him mention that name. What was the other name that was mentioned? She looked back at the cutting. Steve Austin. She thought hard – had she heard that name before? It sounded familiar but she couldn't place it. After a few minutes she gave up and carefully put the cutting back in the same place she'd got it from.

The next item she picked up was a white sealed envelope. She turned it over in her hands but there was no name or address on it. She felt all the way around it with her fingers, pressing at various points and concluded that it contained a document, or at least some paper. Maybe a letter? That would certainly make sense, being in an envelope. She held it up to the light and although she could see the outline of the paper inside, that was all. She couldn't make out what it was or whether there was any writing or printing on it. Strange, she thought, and she wished there was some way she could look at the contents but she knew if she opened it Paul would find out. She thought about steaming it open but decided it was too risky. Even if she resealed it, he might see that it had been tampered with and she wouldn't be able to lie to him. Maybe it was a will or some other legal document but it was strange there was nothing on the envelope. Reluctantly she put it back down on top of the other papers until she could think of some way of getting to the contents.

She turned to the last item from the box which was the small notebook she'd felt at the bottom. Lucy realised that she'd subconsciously left this till last as she was frightened of what it might contain. Up till now her relationship with Paul had been great and she didn't want anything to spoil that. In her mind she felt that looking at this small note pad was going to change everything. But she knew she was here now, it was there in her hands,

237

and she had to look. She slowly opened the notebook to the first page.

At the top of the page there was a two word, doubly underlined heading written in blue ink. She read it out aloud,

'The Anniversary.'

She sat back and smiled, of course that was the name of the book Paul was writing, wasn't it? Now that she said it, it seemed right. Yes, it was as she remembered the conversation from the visit to her mum and dads. That damned book that seemed to take up so much of his spare time. This must be his note book for it, for collecting his ideas. And, of course, the newspaper clippings were probably just background examples to help with the plot of his story. She guessed he was probably basing it around a car accident and the subsequent court case similar to that which she'd just read in the newspaper articles.

She smiled widely and chuckled to herself, of course that was it, she thought. All her wild, stupid ideas of what secrets Paul had been keeping disappeared instantly and she felt so relieved. It had all been about his book and he'd already explained to her how he wanted to keep it to himself until it was finished, until he was ready to show it to her. She should have believed him.

Lucy sat for a minute getting her thoughts together. She knew she should just put the box away now and not look at anything more otherwise she would be betraying Paul's trust. But she had come this far and she couldn't resist looking further into his notepad just to get some idea of what the book was actually about. He'd never really told her much and it would be interesting to see, just to get a little insight, just a few clues. She wouldn't mention it to him and she could easily act surprised when he finally told her what it was about. She turned the page and was surprised to see that the second page just contained a list of names in what she recognised was Paul's handwriting. As she flicked through the remainder of the notebook, she was even more surprised to see that it was empty. She skimmed through it a couple of times, turning each page carefully, just to confirm that there was definitely nothing else. It was all just blank lined pages, no writing. No ideas for the book, no plot lines. Nothing. She turned back to the page with list of names again and read them out aloud,

'Jack, Chris, Jason, Dan, Pete, Hilary, Bill, Kevin.'

She read them again but the names didn't mean anything to her. She knew some people with some of these names but not all. She felt very frustrated and wished she had just put the notebook away when she had been going to. She guessed the names were probably those of some of the characters in Paul's book, but it was strange that there were no further notes about either them or the plot of the story. Maybe they were nothing to do with the book but just a list of friends he'd jotted down once. But then why would he have done that

239

here and kept it locked away? It didn't make sense. She'd been hoping that she'd find out a few answers today but now she felt even more confused than ever. She sat back again on the bed, propping up a pillow and leaning against the headboard. After a bit, she decided it *was* probably to do with his book but it did seem strange that there was so little detail there. Didn't writers keep copious notes? Initial drafts of plot lines, scenes, ideas? Why just a list of eight names...what did it mean? Maybe Paul worked differently, Lucy surmised, not all writers worked in the same way and this was his first attempt at it so maybe he was just doing it in the way that worked best for him. He probably kept all the detail on his laptop. Maybe he'd started off with the notebook and then decided he didn't need it any more, using the laptop instead. It'd be much easier, not having to do everything twice. That could be it.

Anyway, she thought, there didn't seem to be anything bad in what she'd found. There was no evidence that Paul had done anything wrong or that this was anything other than workings for the book he was writing. She told herself to stop worrying and not to look for reasons to spoil what she had with him. She decided to put everything back as she'd found it but before doing so one more thing caught her eye and made her think again.

She'd noticed that the names had been written in two columns. Against the first four names, Jack, Chris, Jason and Dan there was a single tick and against the second four names there

240

was a double tick against the names Pete and Hilary and just a single tick against Bill and Kevin.

Lucy stared at the page for a few minutes but had no idea what that meant. Probably nothing, she thought smiling reassuringly to herself.

Chapter 28

Lucy was standing in the kitchen making dinner, singing quietly to herself. After her earlier look through Paul's papers, she'd changed into a white blouse and her favourite blue jeans. Paul had returned home earlier than he'd said he would, but luckily well after she'd put his stuff back in his drawer. Lucy was relieved she hadn't been found out and, as she had time, she had decided to prepare and make a proper dinner for them. Tonight she was making a beef casserole with a nice bit of beef she'd got from the local butchers and lots of different vegetables to mix in with it. She enjoyed cooking but didn't always take the time to do it. Like most of her friends she'd become a victim of the fast food and takeaway society they all now lived in. Everything had to be done as quickly as possible. She remembered when she was a little girl helping her mum out in the kitchen and she had always been fascinated by how her mum would take an apparently random set of ingredients and create a masterpiece out of them. Or maybe she just remembered the ones that turned out well! It was the

242

creative process that Lucy enjoyed most though, taking a bunch of stuff and turning them into something nice and tasty. And she'd also liked when her mum let her lick out the bowl!

Now when Lucy did have time to cook something properly, she got a great sense of achievement and satisfaction when the timer pinged and she took the final product out of the oven. Made by Lucy. She liked cooking for other people too and seeing how they enjoyed something that she had created. She especially liked cooking for Paul though because he seemed to genuinely appreciate almost everything she had made him. That was just another reason she loved him.

Paul was sitting in the lounge reading a magazine, wearing a checked blue shirt and black jeans, his shoes lying by his feet. The television was on in the background but neither of them were really watching it. It had just become a habit to switch it on, like in many other households up and down the country. A bit of comfort noise. It was some sort of quiz show. The whole TV schedule seemed to be full of quiz shows, or cookery programmes or something to do with antiques. No doubt someone would come up with a quiz show about ancient cookery soon. That would obviously be a hit!

Lucy popped the last of the vegetables into a casserole dish, put the lid on and slid it into the oven. She opened the fridge and took out a half full bottle of wine and poured out two glasses. She headed through to the lounge to sit with Paul while the casserole did its magic in the oven.

'Here you are,' she said handing one of the glasses to Paul and bending down to kiss him on the lips.

'Mmm. That's good service,' he said laughing as he wriggled himself upwards and Lucy sat down beside him. ' Something smells nice,' he added motioning his head towards the kitchen.

'What are you reading?' Lucy asked him, moving closer and looking at his magazine, her bare feet tucked up behind her..

'Oh, it's just an article about the Caribbean. Quite interesting, it's all about how they are being affected by the whole global tourism thing. How it's affecting their economy and their environment.'

'Ooh, the Caribbean, that sounds good, are you planning to whisk me off there as a Christmas surprise,' Lucy asked him, giggling and poking him in the side.

'Ah, well, you'll have to wait and see what Santa brings you, otherwise it wouldn't be a surprise, would it?' Paul replied, turning to give her another kiss. In truth Paul wasn't at all sure how Christmas was going to turn out this year and he preferred not to think too much about it. Maybe they could go off somewhere nice for a holiday though? It all depended how the next few weeks turned out. He hadn't thought about going away with Lucy but maybe it would be possible and he could see some advantages in doing that. In fact, at this point in time, he couldn't think of anything else he'd rather do.

'What about Spain?' Lucy said, 'I remember you telling me you'd been to some beautiful places off the beaten track in Spain. Little villages with town squares and cafes that not many tourists knew about. It sounded idyllic. I'd love to go there one day with you.'

Paul just smiled and Lucy snuggled up closer to him on the couch, waiting for the oven to ping. As he burrowed closer, something on the television caught her eye and she turned her head to the side to get a better look. The evening News was now on and they were showing a photograph of a man the police were apparently looking for. It looked quite an old photo, like a mugshot, and the screen cut back to the reporter before Lucy could get a proper look. Something about it niggled in her brain though and she reached for the remote to turn up the volume to see what they were saying. As the volume increased, she heard the reporter say the police were looking to find a man in connection with two recent murders. The police had named him as Andy Austin and although they said he wasn't a suspect they were keen to talk with him to help with their enquiries and were asking the public if anyone knew where he was. As Lucy continued to watch, she became aware that Paul had put his magazine down and was turning towards her.

'Pass the remote will you? I want to see what else is on. Not the boring news,' he said

245

reaching across Lucy to get the remote which she was still holding in her right hand.

'Wait a minute…, I just want to see this,' she said moving the remote further out of Paul's reach. She pressed the volume up a notch and heard the reporter say,

'…..in connection with the murders of sixty one year old Hilary Potts and twenty five year old Peter Wilson, who was the brother of the driver Jack Wilson……'

Lucy's heart began thumping and she could feel the blood draining from her face. Paul had already reached across and grabbed the remote from her turning the channel to one broadcasting a wildlife programme. But it had been too late. Why hadn't she let him take the remote when he asked? She heard it but she didn't want to know it, didn't want to believe it. She wanted to stand up but she was frozen. She couldn't move. It felt like she was tightly strapped into the settee. Almost without realising she dropped her wine glass and it smashed on the floor and she felt tears begin to roll down her cheeks. Although the strangest thing was that she didn't really know why she was crying.

Paul had stood up and he was standing in front of Lucy looking down at her sat on the settee, His face had turned pale too. He didn't know how, but it was obvious that somehow she knew. Somehow she'd made a connection and he knew what had to happen next. He leant forward towards Lucy, who still hadn't moved. It was like she was

246

frozen in time. He put his hands on her neck and the moved them onto her face, wiping away her tears and kissed her lightly on the forehead. Lucy still didn't move. She just sat there with tears running down her cheeks, dripping off her face and turning into two small, wet patches on her white blouse. The oven started pinging from the kitchen telling them the casserole was ready but neither of them moved. The casserole was from another lifetime.

'I'm so sorry,' Paul said and he picked up his shoes, turned and walked out of the room.

A few minutes later he returned. Lucy was still sat there, exactly where he'd left her a few minutes before. Paul stood looking at her. He was carrying a small sports bag.

'What are you doing?' Lucy sobbed, fearing the answer she already knew.

'I'm really sorry,' Paul replied, 'I have to go now' and he leaned forward and kissed her again, this time lightly on her lips. He turned and walked away and Lucy heard the sound of the front door closing behind him. She howled in despair, beating the sofa wildly with her clenched fists.

Chapter 29
15th December, one year earlier

'Stay on the pavement son,' Pat said to Andy.

Andy smiled and stepped back up onto the kerb. It was funny how your mum was always your mum, even when you were grown up. He wondered if he'd be like that when he had kids. Of course he'd have to get a proper girlfriend first. One step at a time, eh? He smiled to himself.

He admired his parents hugely, their relationship, how it had lasted so long and he thought of them almost as two halves of the same person. He hoped he'd find a relationship like that but in truth that thought also scared him. His mum and dad had been married for twenty seven years and their closeness still seemed the same as it had always been – as far as Andy could remember.

It was Friday night and they'd all been to their favourite Italian restaurant, Francescos. They'd been celebrating his dad's birthday, although in truth his actual birthday had been a couple of weeks before and this had been the first day they could all

248

get together. They had discussed it on the phone, his dad not that bothered about celebrating it, but he'd been persuaded.

'Come on don't be so grumpy dad. You have to celebrate your birthday. It's the law!' Andy had told him. 'Besides you're getting old now, you might not have that many more to celebrate.'

'Oi, you cheeky git,' his dad replied, 'I've got a few more years left in me yet son, don't you worry. I'm gonna live long enough for you to have to look after me, you better believe it!'

Andy didn't see his parents as much now since he'd moved out of the family home and got his own place but they still spoke regularly on the phone. Usually it was the same conversation. His mum would ask him about the house, work and his mates and he and his dad would discuss football. He often thought he could have recorded it and just played it once a week to save them money on the phone call. But of course things did change a little over time. Now that he saw his parents less frequently, each time he did, he noticed they were getting just a little bit older. Just small changes. Maybe moving a bit slower, a bit more effort to get out of their chairs, a few more grey hairs or lines on their foreheads. But all in all, for their ages, they seemed pretty fit and well.

After the meal they'd decided to get a taxi back to Andy's parent's house for a coffee or maybe another drink before all going home. However after a few phone calls they found out that with there

249

being five of them in the group, the first big enough taxi was going to be at least forty minutes. They could easily walk back to the house in that time and as the rain had stopped and the skies looked clear they decided to do just that.

Andy's mum and dad were walking in front, side by side and behind them were Andy, his brother Steve and his cousin Phil. Steve was a couple of years younger than Andy but Andy and Phil were the same age and had grown up together as best mates. The boys were all chatting about football, as usual, and who they thought would win the various games due to be played the next day.

'I think Spurs will sneak it past Man U,' said Phil hopefully, 'they're on a good run at the moment.'

'I can't see it,' said Andy, who was an Arsenal fan, 'they haven't got enough up front.'

'Best game will be Liverpool versus Brighton, that's the one to watch if you want to see goals, the way we're playing lately,' Steve, a Liverpool fan, chipped in.

Dave, Andy's dad, was listening in on the conversation and turned his head back towards the boys as he walked,

'They're all soft nowadays, them footballers. Get knocked over by a bit of wind and then roll around as if they've been shot. Wouldn't have happened in my day,' he said and they all laughed.

'Do you men have to talk about football all the time?' Andy's mum asked. 'Look at the lovely Christmas lights – I bet you haven't even noticed them with all your stupid football talk.'

The men all laughed, 'Sorry mum,' said Steve, 'you're right, too much football talk.'

They passed a set of traffic lights and Andy stumbled slightly. Looking down he noticed his shoe lace had become undone. He stopped and knelt down to retie it before standing up again and quickening his pace to catch up with the others who had kept on walking. As he got nearer to them, he heard the sound of a car engine behind him and he looked around as the noise got louder. He saw it just as it mounted the kerb. It was a dark colour. Instinct told him to jump inwards, towards the fence on the inside of the pavement. But he wasn't quick enough and he felt the car catch his left leg and spin him around and through the air. At that point everything seemed to go into slow motion for Andy as he saw the car carry on through and hit his brother and cousin. He saw them both fly through the air, Steve's red jacket and Phil's blue coat crossing over in mid-flight like some sort of strange Red Arrows display. Then he saw his parents disappear from view before he, himself, crashed into the fence head first and landed in a heap on the ground. He lay there for a few seconds, his head throbbing, hoping he was having a nightmare but knowing it was real.

251

Chapter 30

Paul was in a car on his way back to the farm, but his mind wasn't really on driving. He was on autopilot. He had always known this day would come at some point. It had been inevitable, but he had tried to lock that thought away somewhere in the back of his mind. When it did happen, he'd always assumed that he would have been more in control of the timing - but that wasn't to be.

In his mind, in his plans, he'd believed, or at least hoped, that he would end things with Lucy on *his* terms and it would be somehow amicable and they'd stay as friends. Somehow. Thinking about it now though he wasn't sure how that would have been possible, but it didn't matter anymore anyway. It had happened and life had to go on. Somehow his beautiful Lucy had found out who he really was and there was no turning back. He had to complete what he'd started.

He wasn't sure what she knew, or how much and he couldn't really ask her. But her reaction to the news report had been sufficient to convince him that she knew enough to mean that their time together would have to come to an end. He loved her too much to involve her in any way in what he was doing or what he still had to complete. He had briefly thought about confessing all to her and begging her forgiveness but he didn't want to give her the chance to make that choice. She was too good for that and he didn't want to risk making her less than the perfect person she was. It wasn't *her* problem and the last thing he wanted was to drag her into it and the serious implications that could have for her.

He wished he had met Lucy before all this had happened, but then maybe that would have been worse. Perhaps it was better that they had the time together without her knowing. It was the only way their relationship could work even if it meant it was only for a relatively short time.

Paul knew that he had fallen in love with Lucy. He hadn't set out to, but she was so gorgeous and he realised that there are some things you can't plan, some are out of your control. Like love. And the end of love.

He knew Lucy would be devastated and he'd really hoped there would be some way that this could end without her getting hurt, but as he drove along imagining different scenarios, he couldn't come up with any where there was a happy ending. That only happened in fairy tales. Maybe in a different life, once upon another time. But not since the accident. That had changed everything. And now the end had come, at least the end for him and

Lucy as a couple. In reality, he perhaps knew that it was always destined to end in pain for her but he hadn't wanted to think about that and so he'd ignored it as much as he could. He'd known it was always going to be painful for him, but then that was his choice. He hadn't really given Lucy that choice and now he knew he had really wounded her.

But he also felt that, given time, Lucy would survive, her life would go on and she would get over him. That's how life was. Part of him hoped that she would recover quickly but another part also hoped it would take longer as he had really loved her and he knew she had loved him back just as much. They had had something special. Paul knew Lucy was a strong, determined woman though and somehow he believed she'd get through it. He hoped she wouldn't hate him but he knew that was a possibility and whatever she decided to do next could have a major impact on his plans for the next few days. He had known this time would come and he had planned for it but now that it was here he felt both sad and nervous as to what might happen next. He also knew he might have to do things more quickly now and although everything had gone exactly to plan so far, now, for the first time, he was feeling a bit anxious and that he'd lost a bit of control. He could feel his head start to ache.

He turned off the road onto the narrow, bumpy farm track and after a few minutes he pulled to a stop on the gravel drive in front of the main farm house. He got out of the car quickly and went into the house. He put the fire on and sat down on the settee letting himself relax as the room began to warm up. He reached into his bag and took out his bottle of pills, popping two of them from the foil and swallowing them quickly. He needed to compose himself and then decide what to do next. The two men were still locked in separate rooms in one of the old stable buildings and he knew he would need to go and see to them at some point, but not just yet. He wanted to try and work out what Lucy would do next and what impact that might have on his plans. From the television report it was obvious that the police had Andy Austin as their prime suspect. But that wasn't so much of a problem as Andy Austin didn't really exist anymore, he'd made sure of that, and they didn't know the link between Andy Austin and Paul Smith. Not yet anyway. Apart from himself only very few people knew Andy Austin was now Paul Smith and the only one who might tell the police was Lucy. He sat there thinking about the different possibilities of what she might do. Maybe she wouldn't tell anyone, but that was unlikely. It wasn't really something you could imagine she would be able to keep to herself and carry on living as normal. Even if she didn't go straight to the police, she would surely confide in a friend or her mum and they would tell her she had to report it. It was the sensible thing to do. In the short time that Paul had known Lucy he had come to know her as one of the most honest people he had ever met. Now that somehow she'd realised who her

255

boyfriend really was, her mind would be in turmoil. No doubt she would be grieving the sudden end of their relationship but he knew that she would quickly decide what she had to do. And Paul believed that she would feel she had no alternative other than to call the police and tell them what had happened.

However that didn't necessarily mean the end of his mission. Nothing could stop that. The police already knew they were looking for Andy Austin and all that Lucy would be able to tell them was that he had been living with her under the name of Paul Smith. She would be able to give them a recent photograph of Paul Smith but she wouldn't know where to find him. She had no knowledge of this farmhouse which he'd rented under a different name, paying up front with a bank transfer from a false, now closed account. He'd only had to go to the Estate Agents office once to sign the lease document and he was in and out as quick as he could. Everything else had been done over the phone and on-line. Furthermore with a pair of scissors, some make-up and hair dye…. along with a new passport, Paul Smith would soon no longer exist.

He also had an escape plan and was confident that if the police did somehow trace him to this farm he would be gone before they arrived. He'd spent a long time planning this and he wasn't going to fail now.

Having thought through the various possibilities he felt less worried. He guessed Lucy would have to tell the police and he knew they were perhaps one step closer to him but there should still be plenty time for him to finish his plan and do what he had to do.

He went through to the kitchen and picked up two wooden trays and took two sets of sandwiches wrapped in tin foil from the fridge. He opened another cupboard and reached inside for two cartons of fruit juice. He put the whole lot into a plastic carrier bag and went out through the back door of the house. He walked across the gravel courtyard, listening to his feet crunching, the sound echoing as he went, until he arrived at the old stable yard. Taking a large metal key from his pocket, he unlocked the solid wooden door and stepped inside. There was no electric light but there were enough gaps in the roof letting light through to help him see where he was going. The building still smelt strongly of hay and horses although Paul didn't think there had been any horses in here for many years, yet the aroma had hung on.

He walked past a number of gated pens, which would have held horses when the stable was in use, until he got to the end. He then turned to his right and taking another key out he unlocked a solid white door and entered a room which, at some point, had been a kitchen or utility type room. There was still a sink, a work surface and a couple of cupboards but it hadn't been used for many years

257

and was in an advanced state of disrepair. At the far end of the kitchen there were another two solid white doors which had been built as more utility rooms or just large storage cupboards. When Paul had seen the pictures of these in the Estate Agent's on-line advert he'd known they would be ideal for his purpose.

He stopped at the work surface and arranged the sandwiches and drinks on the two trays. Picking the first one up with one hand, he grabbed a metal pole which had been leaning against the sink and walked towards the door on the left. He walked quietly, having learned from his previous mistake although he knew that wouldn't happen again as he'd now taken the extra precaution of chaining both men to the far wall of their respective rooms. Bill had still been unconscious and Kevin was a different character, he just did what he was told.

After all that had happened earlier with Bill though, he didn't want to waste any time and so he quickly opened the first door, placed the tray on the floor and edged it forward with his foot until it was within reach of Kevin Green who was sat on the bench opposite. Kevin looked up, startled, but before he could say anything Paul had already closed and locked the door. He repeated the same process for the other room which housed Bill Reynolds, who, although lying on his bench obviously in some pain did manage to shout a few expletives at him before the door fully closed. For a second Paul wished he could help Bill with the pain from his injuries. He was an old man, but then he remembered what had happened to his own dad that night and his conscience was clear again. His dad had survived the initial hit by the car and although he had multiple injuries he was stable. He was a fighter. But when he came round and they'd had to tell him his wife and son had died he seemed to lose the will to fight on and he'd gradually got weaker and weaker until a week later he too was gone.

Chapter 31

Lucy wasn't sure how long she'd stayed sitting on her sofa after Paul had left. It could have been a few minutes or it could have been a few hours. She'd completely lost track of time and, if truth be told, she'd also lost a bit of reality. Nothing seemed to matter any more. She'd stopped crying or maybe she'd just run out of tears and she could feel the two cold, damp patches on the top of her blouse. All she could hear was the news reporter repeating the same names over and over in her head.

'... the murders of.... Hilary Potts and.... Peter Wilson, the brother of.... Jack Wilson......'

Hilary, Peter, Jack Wilson. Why couldn't they have been different names? Why not Jane, Nathan and Dave Mason? She shook her head and made herself get up off the settee. Her legs felt weak and she stood there for a few seconds just to steady herself. She still wasn't sure what it all meant but she knew it wasn't good. Somehow Paul was involved in these murders and she didn't want to think too much further than that. There had been something about the photo of the suspect they had shown in the report. This Andy Austin guy. She'd only seen him for a second but it was the eyes, or the mouth, there was something. Something familiar. Something she recognised, but didn't want to admit.

She cleared up the broken glass and sponged the wine from the carpet as best she could. Now she stood there and realised she didn't know what to do next. She needed to think but she didn't want to think. She just wanted to blot it out. She wanted to go back to yesterday and start again. Yesterday when everything had been normal. How did the song go again?

"Yesterday, all my troubles seemed so far away,

Now it looks as though they're here to stay
Oh I believe in yesterday."

But she knew that wasn't possible. Yesterday was gone.

Maybe she needed to talk to someone, but who? There was no-one she could think of that she could even start the conversation with.

'I think my boyfriend might have been involved in some murders, what should I do?'

It wasn't a normal conversation, and not one she could imagine having with anyone she knew. Certainly not her mum or any of her girl friends. She knew they'd all tell her right away to go to the police.

261

But this was a once in a lifetime moment. There was only one person who could help her make any sense of this and he was the one person she really couldn't talk to right now. Even if he was still here, she was too fearful of what he might say. If he lied she'd know it and would never be able to forgive him, but if he told her the truth it could be just as bad, or even worse. She wasn't ready to know any more yet. What she did know, and feared, was enough. She needed some time to think, to try and make some sense of it all.

Yet Paul was her soul mate, or had been until today. He was one of the nicest, kindest people she had ever met. He was the one she could talk to about anything. Her hopes and fears, her ambitions. Just a short time ago, she'd been talking about going on holiday with him. Her whole future was all about him. She wished this was all a bad dream and she'd wake up soon. She pinched her arm but she knew it was all real.

Was she just an idiot? Should she have seen this coming? He'd never spoken much about his past – wasn't that an obvious indication that he had a guilty secret? But in her worst dreams she'd never thought of anything remotely like this. Maybe an ex-girlfriend or something. But two people murdered, how could her Paul possibly be involved in that? It was just ludicrous.

She shook her head, trying to rid it of all these bad thoughts going through her mind. She felt she needed to do something and although she couldn't speak to Paul, she decided maybe she could at least text him. Somehow she felt she needed to keep the lines of communication open with him. She needed some answers. If she didn't do it now time would pass and it would be harder to restart what they had. There must be some explanation, something that wasn't as bad as some of the things she was now thinking. These things never were. She picked up her mobile phone and began to type. She looked at what she'd written and deleted it. She started again. A few minutes later she read what she'd put and deleted it again. Finally she decided on a simple message.

"Please call me tonight or tomorrow please. We need to talk x."

She knew that was true. Somehow they needed to talk. She needed Paul to talk, to explain everything. To tell her things were going to be okay. Tell her that it was just all a misunderstanding and everything was going to be all right. When you talked things weren't as bad as they at first seemed – wasn't that what people said? At this point she wasn't convinced by that but she felt if they didn't talk soon then it would just get harder and harder. She hit send.

A few seconds later she heard a familiar noise coming from the bedroom. It was the sound of a phone. More specifically she realised it was the sound of a mobile phone receiving a text. She walked through to the bedroom and saw Paul's phone lit up and lying on the bed. He hadn't taken it with him, why not she thought? Did that mean he was coming back? Maybe he'd just forgotten it. He'd only left with a small sports bag, perhaps he was intending to give Lucy a night on her own to think and then he'd be back in the morning? She picked up the phone and saw her text on the front screen. It was then that she noticed the phone had been lying on top of a white envelope. She picked it up and realised it was the same envelope she'd seen in Paul's secret box earlier that same day. She turned it over and saw that it now had the name Lucy written on it. Her name. It was for her after all. She could have opened it earlier but she hadn't known it was meant for her at that time. He must have got it out and written her name on it before he left.

She sat down on the bed with the envelope in her hands and sighed. She was shaking. She knew she had to open the envelope now and read what was inside but every thought, every feeling in her body was telling her not to do it. She breathed in and out deeply and started to slowly open the envelope, frightened of what she was going to find inside. She pulled the contents out gently and saw that it was three pages of white paper. She carefully unfolded them and spread them out in front of her. She immediately recognised Paul's handwriting and her heart started pounding even faster as she began to read what was written,

My Dearest Lucy,

I hoped that you would never have to read this letter but in my heart I knew that one day you would have to. Before I go any further I want you to know that I love you and although you will see that there were some things I deceived you with, but it was honestly just to protect you. I didn't deceive you with my feelings for you. They were, and still are, completely genuine. I honestly love you.

As I guess you now know, I didn't tell you everything there is to know about me and now that it has come to this point I owe it to you to explain that now. I am sorry I couldn't do it face to face but I don't think I would have been able to. I am sorry for being a coward. I don't expect you to understand or agree with what I have done, but I hope in time you come to terms with it and perhaps in some way understand why. As you may have guessed by now, I am not really an author, I haven't been writing a book, but I do need to tell you my story and then it is up to you what you do. I won't judge you in any way for any action you decide to take. Please just do what you think is right. You are a strong woman and its one of the many things I admire in you. You will always have a special place in my heart and I so wish things could have been different.

Lucy stopped reading, realised she was crying again and wiped her eyes with a tissue. She was really hoping that this was a dream, a nightmare. Anything other than it being real. She

265

breathed deeply, picked up the letter and carried on reading, frightful of what was still to come.

Last year, just before Christmas, I went out with my family for a lovely meal at one of our favourite restaurants to celebrate my dad's birthday. I was with my parents, my brother Steve and my cousin Phil. I am sorry I was never able to tell you about them and you were never able to meet them. They were a great family and you would have loved them as much as I did. And I know they would have loved you too. I wish we could have had a different life where that would have been possible.

We were all walking home from the restaurant when, suddenly, out of nowhere, a car mounted the pavement and hit me and all four of my family. My brother died at the scene and my mum, dad and Phil all died in hospital over the next ten days. Somehow I had managed to dive out of the way of the car and only banged my head as I fell. They said I was lucky but I can honestly say that I have never, ever felt lucky and many times in the following weeks I really wished that I had been killed too so I could be with them all again.

Lucy let the letter rest in her lap for a few seconds trying to take in what she'd just read. It didn't make sense to her. How could Paul have gone through such a horrific thing without her knowing? She felt compelled to read the section again, focusing on every single word so she didn't miss anything. She remembered the newspaper clippings she had seen earlier and realised this was what they

266

were about. The accident and the trial. She then carried on with the next part of the letter.

The next few weeks were a bit of a blur for me. I guess I was ill, depressed, certainly out of it. I don't really know how I functioned, how I got through that time. My friends and work colleagues tried to help but they had their own lives to live and I guess I shut them out a bit too. It wasn't long before I was really on my own. I kept getting flashbacks. I could see it all so vividly. It was horrible. Then a few weeks later it was the trial. Maybe just as I was beginning to think again, to live, it all came back. The car that killed them had been driven by a young lad with three of his mates in the car with him. He pleaded guilty to careless driving and was given a twelve month driving ban. There was no explanation as to why it had happened, why he'd mounted the kerb and killed my family. Because he'd not been drinking and pled guilty, that was it. It was all over in a few minutes and only I really knew the truth. Nothing happened to his mates. I saw them come out of the court, laughing and high fiving and go straight into the nearest pub to celebrate.

I guess it was then that I decided I had to do something to make them understand what it was like to lose your closest family. What they'd done was too much. They needed to understand how I had suffered. They needed to feel the same pain they had inflicted on me. Please believe me it was not an easy

267

decision. But I felt I had to do something for my family.

Lucy stopped reading again and thought about all she had read so far. She still couldn't take it in and was even more frightened about what was still to come. This last piece was worrying and didn't sound like the Paul she knew at all. Not her kind, generous, loving man. She carried on reading.

I don't need to tell you everything I've done and its best you don't know anyway. I don't blame you if you don't think what I did was right and if I was anyone else I may have felt the same. But, for me, I had to do it. I had to make them feel the consequences of what they did. Nothing else mattered. It became the only thing I had to do. I know I became obsessed but there were reasons.

If I had met you before all this happened, or before I started down the path I did, maybe things would have been different. I honestly don't know. The time I have spent with you has been the best and happiest time of my life and I have really loved you.

I am sorry that it has turned out this way and that I have disappointed you. I hope in time you will be able to forget about me, or at least only remember the good times we had together and move on with your life. You truly deserve it.

I will never forget you.

Yours with all my love,
Paul xx

Lucy sat for a few minutes sobbing then read the letter again, stopping on some sentences and re-reading them over and over, trying to make sense of it all. It was clear he hadn't told her everything but she probably didn't want to know that anyway. Maybe she would find out over time but at this point she didn't really care. Finally she put it down, placing it carefully on the dressing table and she lay back on the bed, curling into a foetal position and crying loudly.

Chapter 32

The next day Lucy had woken up early with a surprisingly clear head. Although she couldn't remember exactly when, she'd somehow taken her clothes off and gotten into bed. She'd slept better than she thought she would and she was now focused on what she had to do. She knew that however much she loved Paul, what he was doing was wrong and it was her duty to try and stop it before he did anything more. Other people were suffering, other families, and if she could help then she felt a moral obligation to do so. Maybe then, depending on what he'd really done, they might be able to find a new way forward. Although she couldn't quite see that yet.

She'd got up, got dressed in a simple top and jeans, put on her coat and driven to the nearest police station taking with her, Paul's secret box, the letter and some recent photos of him. Not having had any previous contact with the police she'd had to Google it to find out where the police station actually was. After that the rest of the day had been a bit of a blur. She'd been interviewed by a number

270

of different policemen and policewomen and driven between different police stations and her flat at various times during the day. She had been allowed to pack a bag of her stuff and then her flat had been sealed off and when she left it was swarming with policemen in white overalls literally pulling it apart. She cried again. God knows what her neighbours would think. She'd phoned her mum briefly and given her the minimum of details asking if she could come home for a few days. They both cried and Lucy promised to tell her more later when she got there.

The main interviews had taken place at the police headquarters, which had turned out to be only a few miles from her flat. It was one of those buildings you just walk past without realising what it is. Just another anonymous grey building. The type of place you don't need to know unless there's something wrong.

The two detectives who interviewed her there looked very tired, their shirts a bit creased and dark shadows showing they hadn't shaved recently, but at the same time they seemed excited to be talking with her, especially the one leading the process who every now and then would pace around the room. They also helped her fill in a few of the blanks.

The main detective was a DS Campbell, the pacer, he seemed a nice man, very considerate to Lucy, although he did look like he could be tough when he needed to be. He certainly looked solid

271

enough to handle himself in any physical situation if required which Lucy assumed was a handy skill to have in his job. The other one was called DC Jones and he was much quieter, only randomly chipping in with a question or comment. Lucy began to think he was just there to make up the numbers which she realised was probably a bit unfair but today had been such a strange day for Lucy, her mind was making up all sorts of things and then planting them in her thoughts.

Apparently Paul wasn't even Paul. It wasn't his real name. Up until a year ago he had been known as Andy Austin – the name she'd heard on the TV. She told them about the incident in the restaurant in Harden when someone thought he was called Andy. He had been right and she remembered Paul hadn't been too keen to go there. Now she knew why - it was for that very reason that someone might recognise him as Andy Austin. She'd been living with a man who she thought she knew but now it turned out she didn't even know his name. God, he had made a complete fool of her. They'd also been very interested in the country pub that Paul had taken her to and the conversation they'd had about him looking at a farm. But frustratingly Lucy couldn't remember anything else he'd said about it, if he had done. They'd asked her the same questions over and over until she was worried that she'd start imagining things she might have heard Paul say that hadn't actually happened.

Throughout the day she gradually learned more and more about what Paul, or Andy as the police called him, had done. She couldn't believe what she was hearing and she cried a lot. How could someone as loving as Paul be this monster they were talking about? Someone who could, as they described it, brutally murder, two innocent people. It just didn't fit. Paul was one of the most loving, kindest people she'd ever met.

The police wouldn't, or couldn't, give her any reason as to why Paul might have committed these terrible acts but from reading the letter she knew it was something to do with his family getting killed in the car accident. Some sort of revenge thing, but it still didn't make any sense. He wouldn't do that. They'd asked her a number of times where he might be but she had no idea. She thought herself stupid not knowing. She had explained that she didn't know much about his background yet, which in retrospect was pretty obvious, and so didn't know if he had any friends he might stay with. As she said it, it sounded ridiculous even to her, she was living with this man for God's sake, how could she not know? She wondered if the police thought she was lying, keeping something back, but then she reminded herself that it was she who had voluntarily come to the police station. Surely that proved her innocence?

She told them about his supposed writing – although that had been a lie too so it didn't seem she really knew anything about him at all. Everything

273

she said made her sound more and more foolish. When she left the police station that evening she felt totally empty and completely alone.

She had to tell the police where she was staying as they said it was likely they would have to talk to her again. Lucy couldn't blame them for that, she knew if she'd been sitting on their side of the table she'd have some doubts about how little she apparently knew about this man. She rejected the offer of a lift to her parents' house as she didn't want to embarrass them by turning up in a police patrol car. Instead she drove herself and as soon as she arrived there, her mum was at the door. Without saying anything, she took her hand and pulled her inside, closing the door quickly. Once inside they just stood in the hallway and hugged each other for a long time. Finally they went and sat down in the lounge where she'd been with Paul just a few days before. Her dad gave her a hug and then went to make them all a cup of tea.

Lucy and her mum talked it all over, Lucy explaining what had happened, or at least as much as she knew. Her dad sat in the background listening and regularly providing fresh pots of tea. Her mum tried to continually reassure her that she hadn't done anything wrong but Lucy could see that even she couldn't understand how she hadn't suspected anything about the man she had been living with. Lucy couldn't blame her and when they had done all the talking and there was no more to say, Lucy's mum took her upstairs and helped her into the bed she had slept in when she was a child.

Chapter 33

The police were doing a thorough search of Lucy's flat. They'd emptied all the cupboards, moved all the furniture around, eased up the carpet edges, looked in every conceivable place where something could be hidden. But so far they'd found nothing.

'Looks like he's been pretty careful, according to his girlfriend he didn't bring much when he moved in with her and so he was ready when he needed to make an escape, not leaving anything behind,' Campbell was on the phone to Strong giving him an update.

'Yes, I'm not surprised,' said Strong, 'he knows what he's doing and doesn't want to be caught. Not yet anyway.'

'What?…, hold on a minute,' Campbell interrupted him. 'Let me call you back, one of the guys may have found something.'

He hung up on Strong and walked through to the bathroom where he'd heard the call coming from. There were two policemen standing, poring over the contents of a small silver bin which they'd emptied out onto the bathroom work surface. They were picking through it carefully wearing their blue synthetic gloves.

'What is it?' Campbell asked.

'We're not quite sure,' one of the policemen replied. 'But it doesn't look like this bin's been emptied for sometime, maybe because it's so small and was kind of hidden away in this bathroom. Maybe they forgot about it. Anyway we found some small pieces of paper in it, stuck to the bottom. with some writing on, looks like numbers. We're gradually piecing them back together and it looks like it may be a phone number, look,' he said nodding towards a small white pile on the wooden work surface.

DS Campbell moved closer and stared down at the small scraps of paper. He leant further forward and screwed up his eyes, gradually making out some ink numbers.

'Okay, looks like it could be a phone number,' he nodded. 'When you've finished get it logged and find out who the number belongs to, and let me know as soon as possible. Could be interesting or could be nothing but we haven't got much else to go on at the moment so make this a priority.'

A few hours later the team were all re-assembled in the main meeting room. As Strong had suspected they hadn't found anything at Lucy's flat that could help them identify where Andy Austin might now be and so they were all keen to see what had been found out about the phone number. All eyes looked towards the two policeman who had found it and pieced it back together. One of them looked up.

'Right, okay, what we found was that the phone number belongs to a chain of estate agents. And this one is based in an office just North of town. We checked with the girlfriend and she'd not had any dealings with them and seemingly had no knowledge of the scrap of paper we found in the bin. So we went out to visit them and had a look through their records for the past year. There were quite a few rentals as you might imagine but their systems are pretty good and so we were able to narrow it down to looking at remote locations, farms especially, minimal communication from the renter, anything slightly out of the usual. We found one that ticked all the boxes. It's a place called Milton Farm, just north of town. It's a pretty remote location, the nearest town is just a little village a couple of miles away. Hang on a sec.'

The policeman reached forward and grabbed a cable from the conference room table and plugged it into his laptop. He hit a couple of keys on his keyboard and suddenly a map appeared on the screen in the wall behind Strong and Campbell. They both shifted their chairs round to have a look at it and saw it was a map with Milton Farm shown in the centre. It did indeed look pretty remote with no other obvious buildings nearby. The policeman carried on talking.

'The guy that leased it fits the description of Austin somewhat although they only saw him once when he took out the lease and that had only been briefly. A couple of them remembered him coming into the office but he was wearing a baseball cap. When we showed them the photo of Andy Austin they thought it was him, but couldn't say for definite. Unfortunately they only keep two weeks worth of CCTV so that was no good. We think it could be him though and another unusual thing was that he paid the whole rent upfront. Six months worth. The Estate Agents said that was really unusual but they hadn't thought any more about it at that time, they were just doing business and happy to get the place leased. Apparently they'd had it on their books for some time. They said the guy was pretty quiet on the day and they haven't heard a peep from him since. In their eyes, he was an ideal tenant. They're supposed to go and check on the place every now and again but none of them have.'

The policeman stopped speaking and the room fell silent. Heads turned towards the top of the table looking for guidance. Strong nodded his head and leant forward.

'Okay, that's good work guys,' he began. 'There's definitely enough there for us to pay a visit to this…Milton Farm,' he said, looking down at the notes he'd made.

He glanced at his watch.

'We need to do this properly so that if he is

279

there we don't give him the chance to escape or do any further damage. That's assuming he's got the two other guys held prisoner there too.' He turned towards DS Campbell.

'Get a team together as quickly as possible. You know the drill. Make sure you cover all routes in and out, looking at that map it looks like there's only one way in. Take any firearms you need, I'll sign it off. This guy is dangerous. Don't take any chances. Best time to hit him will be just as its starting to get dark, so let's say…,' he glanced at his watch again, 'two hours from now – that's about four thirty. Should give us enough time. Let's get moving.'

There was a murmur of excited voices around the room as DI Strong picked up his papers and walked out through the door, heading back to his office, relieved that at last he had some real news to tell the Chief Constable.

<u>Chapter 34</u>

Wayne punched in the code and returned to his desk in the IT department. He looked across at Dan sat at the desk opposite him.

'Jeez it's all kicking off out there,' he said.

'Where? In the incident room?' Dan asked, looking towards the door.

'Yep, well I assume so, they ask for all the latest technology and then when they get it and try to use it they don't have a clue. I had to show one of them in the office how to project from his laptop to the screen. He said no-one had explained Windows 10 to him. I said didn't you do the on-line training but he just looked at me blankly. He didn't seem to know anything about it. I don't know why we bother sometimes although maybe he is busy on other stuff, trying to solve murders and that, but it ain't rocket science is it?'

'What are they doing, did you hear anything?' Dan asked standing up from his chair.

'Yep from what they were talking about it looks like they think they've found out where that Andy Austin bloke is hiding. They were all getting ready to go into a meeting and this guy had the map of the place on his screen but didn't know how to project it. Lucky for him, good old IT came along and saved the day, solved the murder for them. But will we get any thanks for it? No way Jose,' he said laughing at his own joke. Dan didn't laugh.

'What was the name of the place – did you see?' Dan asked leaning across towards his colleague.

'I think it's called Milton Farm, on the other side of New Bankhead,' Wayne replied.

'Do they think he's definitely there?' Dan asked.

'Looks that way, they seemed pretty excited about it,' Wayne replied.

Dan looked at his watch, he still had an hour to do before he could leave work, but he knew this could be interesting and maybe an opportunity for him to be the first to tell his mates about what he'd found out about the man who was going around killing their families. He knew there was nothing they could really do but just knowing what was going on seemed something at least. He guessed it would take the police a couple of hours to get their act together and make it to the farm so at least they'd be ahead of the game.

He had a wild thought that maybe they could get to him first and teach him a lesson, he deserved it. Any repercussions would be worth it although he felt the police probably wouldn't press any charges anyhow. They'd just be glad they'd got him. However he knew that wasn't sensible and Dan, if anything, was a sensible guy.

However this was too important just to sit on. He decided he needed to do something so he made up a story to his boss that he'd just had a call from his mum and she sounded upset. He asked if he could nip out for a few minutes to make a call, check she was okay. His boss said it would be fine and so five minutes later he was out the door and making his way to the car park. He sat in his car and called Jack's number.

'Come on, Jack, pick up...' Suddenly the phoned clicked,

'Hello,' he recognised Jack's voice.

'Thank god. They've got him. They know where he is. I know. I....'

'Hold on, slow down,' Jack interrupted, 'start again, but slower this time.'

Dan took a deep breath in and told Jack what he had found out from his colleague Wayne.

'So you think it'll be another couple of hours before the police get there?' Jack asked.

'I think so, they need time to prepare, get warrants, all that sort of stuff,' said Dan. 'Why what are you planning to do?'

'I'm not sure yet, but I may need to borrow your car. I'll be there in five minutes, meet me in your works car park.' And before Dan could say anymore, Jack hung up the phone.

Chapter 35

DI Strong turned into the Wood Street public car park and drove all the way up to the sixth level. There were only a couple of cars parked here, all day stayers probably awaiting their owners to return from work. He drove to the far corner and parked in one of the empty bays. He looked in his mirror and adjusted it slightly so that he could see any other cars as they came up the ramp onto level six. He sat still for a minute looking and then, satisfied that no-one was coming; he reached across to the passenger side and picked up his briefcase. He opened it up on his lap and fished around inside, moving documents about until he felt what he was searching for. He hooked his fingers around, and eased out, a small cloth pouch with a drawstring at one end. He checked his mirror again and seeing nothing he undid the pouch and took out it's contents – a small, folding mobile phone. He opened it up and looked at it as he held it in his lap. He checked the mirror once more and then pressed the power button. A few seconds later the display lit up, reflecting in his face as he stared at it. He pressed the phone icon and the screen changed to show the list of numbers he'd previously called. But in fact there was only one number. He pressed the icon to call that number and at the same time pressed the loudspeaker button keeping the phone out of sight in his lap. He glanced at his mirror again and saw nothing. The phone rang three times and then a voice answered.

'Hello,' the voice said.

Strong bent his head down slightly towards the phone and spoke.

'It's me. It's over,' he said simply.

'How long have I got?' the voice replied.

'A couple of hours at the most. You should go now. Give yourself a head start, after that it's gloves off,' Strong replied.

'Okay, one thing. I assume this has come from Lucy. Go easy on her please. She didn't know anything and what I've put her through is bad enough. I didn't mean for her to be involved, it just….happened. She doesn't need any more shit.'

'I know,' Strong replied, 'I'll see she's looked after.'

'Thanks and one other thing,' the voice at the other end of the phone said.

'What?' Strong replied, glancing again at his mirror.

'You're wrong. It's not over,' the voice said.

'Really? Don't you think you've done more than enough already? You didn't say you were going to murder people, innocent people. You've

285

got your revenge. They've suffered. You've achieved what you set out to do. Stop now, quit while you're ahead,' Strong replied forcefully.

'Not quite, there's more to do yet,' the voice carried on. 'I haven't finished what we agreed at the start....'

'Hold on,' Strong interrupted, 'I didn't agree to this. There's no way I wanted two people killed. I didn't know what you were planning to do but I didn't think it would be this, this was just you.'

'Maybe so, but don't try and stop me. Remember I can bring you down too,' the voice replied.

Are you threatening me?' Strong said, raising his voice. He was getting angry at the way this conversation was going. 'Because if you are...'

'Calm down,' the voice replied. 'If you think we're all even now, you should look a bit further into the accident.'

'Go on,' said Strong intrigued by this comment.

'Well after we'd met and I was planning all of this, obviously I had to look more deeply into each of the four men's families so I could identify who best to target. While I was doing that I found out something which took me by surprise, I must admit, but after a bit it made sense. It would seem that the accident might not have been an accident after all. Maybe, the driver, Jack Wilson, actually knew what he was doing.'

'What do you mean?' Strong asked, taken aback by this change of direction.

Strong listened for a few minutes longer as the man continued to speak and then he hung up. He sat in his car thinking for some time, regularly glancing in his mirror. What he had just been told changed things somewhat and he needed to work out what best to do now. Eventually he switched the phone off, undid the back and took out the sim card. Reaching into his briefcase he took out a small pair of scissors and snipped the sim card into four tiny pieces which he carefully placed in his jacket pocket. He put the phone in the other pocket, returned his briefcase back into the seat-well, re-adjusted his mirror and drove off. Coming out of the car park, he turned the corner into a quiet side street and pulled over to the opposite side, stopping by the kerb. He opened the car door slightly and dropped one of the sim pieces into a drain at the edge of the road. He looked around, there was no-one there, then he closed the car door and drove off.

A few miles away Paul Smith was also in the process of dismantling a mobile phone, throwing it bit by bit into the log fire in the room he was sat in. The fire crackled and sparked yellow flames as it burnt. He'd already been out to the outbuildings and made sure the police would get his message when they did arrive. After he was sure the phone was burnt beyond recognition he took a pile of documents from his bag and arranged them into two piles on the coffee table in front of him. Each stack of documents was similar, both having a passport, a driving licence and some other personal documentation.

He picked up the documents from the pile nearest to him and briefly glanced through them before cutting each item into small pieces and throwing them into the now blazing fire. He watched carefully as each piece curled up and turned from brown to black and then finally grey ash. He turned to the second batch of documents and picked up the passport, flicking it open to the page with the photo. It was a photo of him.

'Goodbye Paul Smith and hello James Gilmour,' he said as he placed the second pile of documents back into the briefcase by his feet.

Chapter 36

When DI Strong had first met Andy Austin in the police station following the terrible accident a year earlier, he immediately felt a certain sympathy for him and couldn't help but draw parallels with his own situation. Eighteen years prior to that, Strong's parents had been killed by a hit and run driver as they walked home along a narrow country lane. They had also been out at a restaurant near where they lived and were making their way home. The police estimated the car had been doing between sixty and seventy miles per hour and his parents would have had no chance of surviving the impact. They both died at the scene, alone on the road, and lay there for at least thirty minutes until they were found by another passing driver. The hit and run driver was never found.

Back then, Strong was just a young Police Constable and the world was a different place. He'd always wanted to be a policeman, to do the right thing, make the world a better place. He really believed in all of that and he loved doing the job. In fact he couldn't imagine himself doing anything else. He wanted to help people and see justice being done. The bad guy getting caught and having to pay the penalty for what he'd done. The victims getting some sense of fairness, some closure to help them carry on with their lives.

He remembered the very first case he'd ever worked on. It had been a burglary at a house in Talbot Gardens, not far from the station where he was first based, where he'd started his career. The householder was an old lady who lived on her own, her husband having died a few years before. Someone had broken in through her kitchen door one night while she was asleep upstairs and stolen some money and jewellery she'd left in a kitchen cabinet drawer. It wasn't a lot of money and the jewellery hadn't been that valuable but one of the items had been an inscribed bracelet her late husband had given her on their Golden wedding anniversary. She'd worn it every day since and only took it off when she did the washing up and when she went to bed. Strong remembered how distraught she'd been at losing it, it was as if it was her fault and she'd somehow let her husband down. Luckily they'd caught the burglar quite quickly, he was a well-known local petty thief, and he still had all the jewellery he'd taken from her hidden in a sock in a drawer in his bedroom.

Strong could still remember the look on the old ladies' face when he returned the bracelet to her – he'd never seen anyone look so happy. That was justice. That was why he'd joined the police force, for moments like that when he could help make things right again.

After those initial days learning his trade, he'd worked hard and progressed through the ranks working on a variety of cases. A lot of drugs related crime, plenty of domestic violence and alcohol induced fights. Over the years he'd begun to realise that things weren't always as straightforward as that first case he'd worked on. They didn't always find the burglar or the assailant; they didn't always satisfy the victim as much as he would have wanted to. The rules he thought were right didn't always work.

As time went by, he began to take note of how some of his senior colleagues operated. He'd see how they sometimes bent the rules, maybe turned a blind eye, or perhaps suggested a particular scenario to a witness. Nothing as obvious as planting evidence or seeking a conviction for someone who wasn't obviously guilty but he began to understand how to make the system work best for the police, and the victims. Just a little tweak here or there, making sure no-one could come back on it. You had to be careful, once or twice he'd seen some clever defence lawyer uncover something not done completely by the rule book and immediately the case was lost. He began to learn how the best detectives were able to play the game and achieve a successful conviction. Over time he started doing the same himself. He knew that sometimes it was the only way of getting justice and fairness for those

291

that had suffered. That was the reason he'd joined the police force in the first place.

When Strong's parents had been killed he hadn't been in the police force for long and he'd still believed that they'd find the hit and run driver and justice would be served. As time moved forward, and no-one was charged, he realised that wasn't going to happen and slowly his attitude had begun to change. Now Strong often thought that if he found that hit and run driver he would have had no hesitation in making sure he paid a severe price. He now knew enough people who, with a quick phone call, would carry out a physical retribution for him. It was all he deserved for taking away two lovely human beings. They were two of the most important people in Strong's life and he knew his life would never be the same again. It was like a piece of him, a piece of his heart, had been cut away never to be replaced. To get real justice, Strong knew, you sometimes had to do things differently. And Strong's view had hardened to one where real justice was paramount, however it was delivered.

The trial following the Andy Austin accident wasn't one of Strong's cases, it was handled by the traffic police, but he had taken a close personal, if private, interest in it. He knew the outcome wouldn't be a satisfactory one. The police had only been able to get the prosecutor to agree to a charge of careless driving which meant at worst the driver would only get a fine and a ban. A fine and a ban for killing four people, where was the justice in that?

Strong had been in the courthouse on the day of the verdict and that's exactly what had happened. Jack Wilson and his three friends all walked out of court as free men and Andy Austin left through the same door but he was still imprisoned in his own world of despair.

Strong had walked away from the court house to a pub a few streets away. One that he knew well having gone there after many a previous case. He liked it because it was tucked away in a back street a little way behind the courthouse and he was able to sit there quietly and reflect on whatever case he had just been involved in. At this stage he usually wanted to be alone. He didn't like celebrating cases he won, he didn't see that there were any particular winners. Sure, he was satisfied if someone he knew was guilty was properly convicted but he always had some regret that it had come to this. Everyone had been born the same, they all started off the same as human beings and he found it sad that some people ended up in these situations, sometimes through no fault of their own.

That day, as he entered the pub, he saw there was a man standing at the bar on his own and as he approached the bar he recognised that it was Andy Austin. He was leaning on the bar, bent slightly with his chin cupped in his hand. He looked older than he was. Strong stood a few metres from him at the bar and nodded as Austin looked his way.

Austin recognised him as one of the policemen who had interviewed him after the accident but he couldn't remember his name. Strong looked at Austin and imagined the disappointment he must have been feeling. He couldn't help but feel sorry for him.

'Can I get you a drink?' Strong asked, looking at Austin's nearly empty pint.

Austin hesitated for a second, thinking, then said,

'Okay, go on, why not, thanks.'

They took their drinks and sat at a small wooden table in the corner of the pub. It was mid-afternoon and the pub was almost empty, although Strong had never actually seen it busy at any time he'd been in before. He sometimes wondered how it kept going. It was like a pub from a bygone age, no food, no music, nothing. Just a place where you could quietly sit and have a drink. An escape from the outside world and all the troubles it brought.

Strong and Austin sat and chatted about life in general, everyday things, initially avoiding anything to do with the trial but gradually, inevitably, the discussion drifted onto what had happened. Strong felt almost obliged to offer some sort of "official" apology to Austin for the weak outcome, but of course it wasn't official and never could be. Sometimes justice was not really justice. And sometimes the system just wasn't good enough.

As they chatted, Austin confessed he had mixed emotions about it all. He'd done his research

294

and knew the driver wouldn't get a custodial sentence so the outcome of the trial hadn't been a surprise to him. But he still wanted more. How could the driver and the three other men just walk out of the court as free men when they'd ruined his life. They'd killed four of his family. Four of the most special people to him and he would have to live without them for the rest of his days, with only memories. All this while they, the four in the car, went back to their normal, everyday lives as if nothing had happened. All with a future. It just wasn't right.

Strong couldn't help but sympathise with him and after a while he told Austin about what had happened to his parents. When he had finished, Austin looked straight at him and said,

'So how can you still be a policeman when that's happened to you? Surely you must see how futile it is. People getting away with murder?'

'Sometimes shit happens,' he replied shrugging, but he knew it wasn't much of a response and he knew he didn't believe it himself.

In truth Strong didn't have an answer for him, he'd thought the same himself many times. He, and his team, would work for weeks to identify and catch a criminal and then watch as the system made a mockery of all their hard work. A form not signed properly. A suspect not given his full rights. A smart lawyer picking a hole in a witness's testimony, bullying him into a mistake. The DPP insisting on a lesser charge. It was like a game to some of them. It

295

all happened, and too frequently for Strong. And all of that that was only when they actually caught the offender. There had been too many times, like that which had happened to Strong's parents, where no-one was ever caught and charged. Over the years Strong had learnt to live with it, how to adapt his expectations and where and when he could bend the rules to his advantage.

When they left the pub that day, Strong had given Austin his number telling him to call if he ever wanted to talk. In truth he'd just done it as a friendly gesture and hadn't expected to hear from him again, so he was surprised when Austin called him the following week and suggested they meet for another drink. Having made the offer, Strong didn't feel it would be right to turn him down and so they had met again one evening in a small country pub on the outskirts of town.

They got on well, the conversation flowed and they found they had similar views about many things. Over the following few weeks they'd met up more regularly. It was at some point during one of these first few meetings that a plan for justice began to be hatched. It had started off almost like a game, something they could play around with, to satisfy their mutual sense of injustice. As if they could. Then, in later meetings, it developed and became the main focus of their discussion, both Strong and Austin coming up with ideas of ways they could get some sort of fairness for what had happened to each of them. Gradually these ideas became more solid, the discussion became more serious and more focused on the recent accident and trial that Andy Austin had endured. The questions began to move from 'what if' to 'how'. They both agreed that the justice system had failed them and they needed to do something in recompense. Why shouldn't they? It was hard to say who first came up with the plan, but they had developed it together with Strong contributing his knowledge of police investigative procedures and how Austin might be able to beat the system. Strong had told him how a person could change their identity and 'disappear.' What they needed to do, who could help them, people he'd met that owed him a favour. People he could trust. He knew where the weaknesses in the system were so that a person wouldn't be easily caught through normal police procedures. Strong knew he was on dangerous ground but as the plan developed, the thought of what someone like Austin could do was giving him some sense of satisfaction, some hope that justice could be got after all. It was too late now for his parents but maybe he could get some element of satisfaction by helping Austin get justice for his. Over the weeks of meeting Austin, Strong had grown to like him and he gradually convinced himself it was the right thing to do and if he was careful, which he always was, he was certain no-one would ever discover there having been any involvement on his part.

After a few weeks of discussion they were happy that they could do no more. Andy Austin had

297

listened to what Strong had told him about police procedures and felt that he now had the framework of a reasonable plan. They'd agreed that as Austin was preparing to put it into action, they should have no further contact except in the event of an imminent arrest, when Strong would let him know to help him avoid capture. That had seemed sensible as it would negate their sense of justice if he were caught and convicted. The whole point of it was that he would somehow deliver the justice that he was owed.

However, to protect Strong as a policeman, he had also insisted that he would treat this largely as he would any other case and, with his team, try and stop Andy as he would any other criminal but without using the obvious fact (to Strong) that he already knew who the main suspect was. Strong only knew Austin's general plan to get some retribution for his loss without any specifics of how or when he was going to carry it out. Both men decided that the less Strong knew the better.

'As soon as you start, the police will be treating this like any other investigation working on any clues they uncover as part of the process.' Strong had told him. 'If it's something that comes under me, which hopefully it won't be, then I'll let my DS lead the investigation but anything he or the team find, I will back them one hundred percent. We will run the process as diligently as always and I have some clever people working for me so if you make any mistakes or leave any clues I have to warn you that its highly probable that we'll find you. If you've listened to what I've told you these past few weeks, which I know you have, then I'm sure that will at least buy you some time.'

Strong knew that if it did become an investigation for his team, then it wouldn't be a trivial offence as he headed up the Serious Crime squad. He also knew from some of the ideas they'd discussed, and maybe from some of the things Austin had suggested, that could be the case but in reality he doubted it would go that far. That had just been them getting over zealous after a few beers. Although that possibility had worried Strong slightly at times, he still believed in the over-riding principle of helping Austin get some justice and convinced himself that whatever Austin did, so be it. It wouldn't be too bad.

At their final meeting, they shook hands and wished each other good luck. A few days later Andy Austin began the process of disappearing and then reappearing elsewhere - under the new name of Paul Smith.

DI Strong had returned to his day job and no-one knew anything about his meetings with Andy Austin. Now it had all started and two people were dead. Austin had also told him about Jack Wilson and that he wasn't finished. Strong was feeling worried. He'd feared that would be Austin's stance, especially after what Dr Collins had suggested to him. It seemed she had been correct about the PTED diagnosis. He'd run through this over and over in his head these past few hours. Austin had never actually told Strong what he had planned to do and Strong had preferred it that way. The less he knew the better, he'd thought at the time. All Strong had done was to give him a few tips and provide him with a few contact names on how best to not get caught and stay hidden. He knew Austin was looking to exact some revenge, to get some fairness, for the suffering he'd gone through but he'd thought at worst it might just be that Jack Wilson would be the victim. Maybe beat him up a bit. He'd never envisaged that Austin's goal would be to kill four people and by the time he realised what was going on it was too late to stop him. He'd thought often about anything he could do to stop him but there was no simple answer. If he'd steered the team towards Austin as a suspect earlier in the investigation, Campbell and others in the team would have been asking why – it seemed such a tenuous link. That would have been too risky for him as if they got Austin and the truth came out he'd be seen as an accessory to murder. And even if he had been able to help in some way, he doubted whether that would have helped them track Austin down any more quickly. That had really been down to Lucy coming forward and the scrap of paper they'd found following that. Good old fashioned solid police work. Now that he knew what he knew, if Strong had known Austin's plans at the start he realised he wouldn't have helped him. Like Austin, he'd wanted some justice but this was way over the top. Thinking back he couldn't help but conclude that Austin had used him all along and now he was in an impossible position. If only he hadn't gone to the pub that day after the trial. If only he hadn't felt sorry for Andy Austin and bought him that first pint.

Chapter 37

Jack was driving Dan's car. He knew he shouldn't be but he'd insisted. Now that he didn't have one of his own he had to and he knew he could persuade Dan to let him take his. Dan would always do what you asked him, especially if you insisted; he didn't like conflict and was always the first to back down. When Jack had arrived at Dan's work, there had been an awkward moment in the car park when Dan had brought up the night of the accident.

'You know when we had the accident,' Dan said, looking down towards the ground.

'Yes, I do kind of remember that,' Jack replied sarcastically.

'Mmm, well you know I was sitting in the front as usual,' Dan carried on, tugging the bottom of his beard.

'Yes,' said Jack, 'you're always in the front, what's your point?' Jack replied, eager to get going. What was Dan up to, he didn't usually talk this much Jack thought and he desperately wanted to get to Austin before the police.

'Well,' Dan replied, kicking a loose stone across the car park, 'the thing is, I've never said this before, not to anyone, and I wouldn't, never,' he said raising his head and looking at Jack seriously. His glasses had slipped a bit and he pushed them back up his nose.

'What is it mate?' Jack replied, wondering what Dan was going to say. This was not like his quiet, shy friend at all.

'Well, just before the accident. Just before we hit the people, I thought you seemed to turn the steering wheel. I tried to grab it and shout to you but it was too late. We hit them,' Dan replied, immediately diverting his eyes down to the ground again.

'Mate, what are you saying that I did it deliberately?' Jack asked in a surprised voice. 'You think I meant to run them down? Why would I do that? Where's all this coming from?'

Dan shuffled his feet before replying.

'I don't know, its just, it, it... looked like you drove towards them. I know its daft and I wouldn't say it to anyone else but it just...., you know?'

Jack looked at his friend and took hold of his upper arms.

'Look at me mate,' he said and Dan raised his head, his glasses slipped forward again. 'You know what happened, they said it at the trial, the car hit a bump and then it hit the kerb. It was an accident. There was nothing I could have done, it

303

was just one of those things, you know that, don't you?' Jack said looking Dan straight in the eye. Dan was looking back at him and noticed Jack's beard had got thicker, more like his. After a few seconds, he nodded his head and spoke.

'Yes, of course, sorry I don't know why I said that. It was just in my head with all this going on, you know?'

'Of course mate, it's hard for us all. The sooner this is all over the better,' Jack replied smiling. 'So, we're all good, yeah?'

'Yeah, of course,' Dan replied, relieved that he'd got it off his chest and Jack hadn't taken it badly.

It had been a strange conversation but Jack was glad that they'd had it as he knew that now Dan had got it out, he wouldn't bring it up again. After that Dan had agreed to let Jack borrow his car. In Jack's mind, this was too personal and he wanted to be in control. He needed to be in the lead. He had his mobile phone plugged into the dashboard holder and he was looking at the map which was guiding him towards the red circle that pinpointed Milton Farm. The farm where he knew that bastard Andy Austin was hiding. As soon as Dan had told him on the phone, Jack knew he just had to go. There was no second thought and he knew that he'd need to get there quickly before the police arrived. Dan had been worried about telling him and also more concerned about what Jack might do when he got there but Jack had convinced him that he just wanted to talk to Andy Austin and that there would be no way that it would be traced back to Dan. Reluctantly Dan had let him go but, sitting back at his desk, he was still wondering whether he'd done the right thing. Maybe the police would get there first and then everything would be okay. He hoped Jack wouldn't do anything stupid. Ending up in jail would be a terrible outcome and he'd blame himself if that happened.

Jack was driving as quickly as he could but also taking care to make sure he wasn't speeding. The last thing he wanted to happen was that he got stopped by the police for some minor traffic offence before he got there and then getting found out for driving without a licence. His ban was almost over now and he was really looking forward to being able to get behind the wheel of a car, legally. In fact this was the first time he'd driven a car in over six months. Although Dan's car wasn't the punchiest car on the market, it only had an 1100cc engine, it still felt good to Jack to be driving again.

He still wasn't certain what he was going to do when he got to the farm. At first he'd had no doubt that he was going to beat this Andy Austin guy to a pulp. He didn't care how badly he hurt him, he would deserve every punch, every kick Jack gave him. At that point, he realised he was wearing a pair of trainers and thought maybe he should have put on his black boots, or a pair of shoes at least.

As he drove, he began to think about what he was doing. He knew he was taking a big risk just

305

going on his own. This guy had already murdered two people, including his brother, and so presumably would have no qualms about killing Jack who was really the one who had caused him all this trouble in the first place. He still didn't know why Austin hadn't picked on him, maybe that was still to come. He took a deep breath, and focused his thoughts on the phone and the road ahead. He could see he was getting closer and should be there soon. He needed to make a plan. He really wanted to hurt this guy, make him pay for all that he'd done but he couldn't just walk in blindly and attack him, that would be stupid and would probably end up being worse for Jack. Before he did anything he wanted to hear from Austin the reasons why he had done what he had done so far. Jack needed to understand. His thoughts began to drift back to the previous evening.

Jack had been sitting on his bed, his pillow propped up, alone in his bedroom. It felt safe and cosy. The day had been cold and bright but the snow had now moved in and looking out his bedroom window, he could now see it falling heavily outside. It had been one of those days where you could wrap yourself up in a coat, scarf and gloves and convince yourself that it was a beautiful winter's day. But the cold would eventually get to you, especially around your face.

This had been the most depressing Christmas ever for Jack and his family. It was even worse than when they'd lost Sarah. Now Peter was gone too and Jack had started to feel very lonely and exposed. He couldn't imagine how bad it must be for his mum and dad but he could see that they were both broken. And he didn't know if they would ever be mended again.

Jack had been spending more and more time alone in his room these last few days. He felt guilty about shutting himself away but the truth was he couldn't face sitting downstairs with his family. The atmosphere was just too bad, too depressing, and he didn't know how to make it better. None of them seemed to know what to say to each other anymore and his mum was in tears half the time. They'd have the television on but no-one was really watching it. It was all Christmas shows and they were supposed to be funny but none of his family was laughing. There were unopened presents for Peter still sat under the Christmas tree and on the mantelpiece stood photos of all the family, including both Sarah and Peter – a constant reminder of what they had lost. It was like a dark cloud had positioned itself above their house and was refusing to move.

But for Jack, by far the worst thing was that he knew that what had happened was probably all his fault. He hadn't *meant* for any of it to happen - but it had and now there was no way back.

He stood up from his bed and reached up to retrieve a blue and white box from the top of his wardrobe. It was an old shoe box and he could remember his dad buying him the Adidas trainers that had been in it. God how he had loved those trainers. For his fourteen year old self they had been

307

such an important possession. He'd proudly shown them off to all his mates at school but now he had grown up, and with what had happened lately, a pair of trainers seemed so trivial. If only he could turn back the clock and be fourteen again.

There weren't any trainers in the box now though, they were long gone. They'd been worn out by endless games of football and teenage adventures with his mates. He lifted the lid off the box and took out its current contents which were a few photos and some scraps of paper. He picked up one of the photos and stared at it as tears started to roll down his cheeks. It was a photo of his sister Sarah. She had been about seventeen at the time and it had been taken when they were on holiday in Portugal. She was standing on a beach with the sea in the background, her long blond hair wet against her forehead and tumbling down either side of her beautiful face. She was laughing, her mouth wide open, and he remembered her laugh. It was so infectious you couldn't help but laugh along with her. Sarah and Jack had the same sense of humour and when the two of them were together they'd play off each other and often end up in hysterics with everyone else wondering what was so funny. She was such a beautiful person.

He'd adored Sarah and she had adored Jack, her big brother. She was more than just a sister to him, they had been best friends since they were little children. Always looking out for each other. They would share secrets, things they wouldn't dare tell anyone else. Sarah was very popular at school with a lot of friends and on the outside she seemed to be very confident and secure but Jack knew that at times she was also vulnerable and often had mood swings. She largely managed to keep these hidden though and only confided in her brother when something had upset her or she was just feeling down. Although she was growing into a lovely young woman Jack knew that at times she could still be just like a child, just like she had been when she was his little five year old sister.

As they grew up, the two of them became very close and would spend a lot of time together just talking about anything and everything. Most of the time it was just nonsense and they played a game where they would try and make each other laugh, the first one to break being the loser and having to do a forfeit. During their teenage years the discussion often became about boyfriends and girlfriends, both of them advising each other on the suitability or otherwise of people that they had met. Although they didn't always take each other's advice, in retrospect, it often turned out that the one giving the advice had been correct.

'I told you he was a waste of space,' Jack said quietly, smiling to himself at the memory.

He put the photograph back down on his bed and a break in the snow outside let in a beam of moonlight which lit up another of the photos lying there beside him on the bed. It was another photo of Sarah, but this time she was with a man and they

309

were both pulling a funny face at the camera. He remembered when Sarah had told him about this one. She'd really fallen heavily for him but he was a few years older than her and he'd wanted to keep their relationship secret for a bit. The man had told Sarah that he'd had a couple of bad experiences in the past and just wanted to be sure before they became more public with their relationship.

Knowing how men's minds worked this had set a few alarm bells ringing in Jack's head and he'd warned Sarah that she should be careful and not get too deeply involved or she might get hurt.

'I'm not sure about this one,' he'd told her. 'He seems to have too many secrets for my liking. You should be careful.'

Sarah tried to reassure him that she knew what she was doing and that this one was different, but Jack still felt uneasy. He could see that Sarah was fully committed and that there would be no persuading her otherwise at this point. He just hoped she would cool off a bit.

She'd fallen big time though and it was the man who had in fact cooled off first. After making excuses for not being able to meet a few times, he eventually stopped returning her messages. Sarah was devastated. She'd split up with boyfriends before but Jack could see that this was different. As usual she kept her feelings hidden from everyone else but when they were alone she opened up to Jack. She'd really thought that this man was different. Maybe that he was the one for her and she'd let herself believe that he'd felt the same about her. She'd sat in Jack's room for hours, crying her heart out and asking questions that he found impossible to answer. Why would anyone do this to someone as genuine and beautiful as his little sister Sarah? Try as he might, Jack couldn't think of anything to say to her and so he just listened and hoped that given time she would get over him.

The night before she died she'd made Jack promise never to tell anyone about her relationship with this man and he had kept that promise.

The next day she was gone. She'd said goodnight to Jack, as they always did, gone to sleep and never woke up. It wasn't clear how she'd died. Unknown to everyone else except Jack, she'd been taking sleeping tablets and there was the possibility that she'd just taken too many in a short space of time. The doctor said that her heart had just stopped and she'd died peacefully in her sleep. It was one of those unexplained deaths that unfortunately sometimes just happened. Jack wanted to believe that but only he knew the heartbreak she had been going through the previous couple of weeks. Had that caused it or had that made her take an overdose, accidental or otherwise? He'd never know for sure but he did know that if this man hadn't dumped his little sister there was more chance she'd still be around today. Jack had lost his soul mate.

The night of the car accident had been a spur of the moment thing. Some sort of unconscious action, he hadn't realised what he was doing and there hadn't been any time to think through the repercussions. If only he had been driving down that road a minute earlier or a minute later then none of this would have happened.

He just saw him as he'd approached the traffic lights. He'd looked straight at him. It was definitely him. Although they'd never met, he recognised him straight away, the red light illuminating his grinning face as he looked back at Jack. When the lights had changed and Jack had driven away and saw him separate from the group, crouched down, tying his shoelace something just happened. Something in Jack's head. It was instantaneous, he wasn't sure what he was doing. Maybe he could just give him a fright, make him jump, maybe knock him a bit at worst, but then the car had hit the kerb and he had lost control and it all went disastrously wrong.

Jack's thoughts were suddenly interrupted by the satnav on his phone telling him to take the next right onto Bridge Road and as he turned he could see in the corner of the screen that he was now only ten minutes away from his destination, Milton Farm. As he accelerated into the clear stretch of road ahead, he could feel his heart beating that bit quicker. After a few more turns into what seemed to be increasingly narrow roads, he found himself in a remote part of the countryside with no houses to be seen. The road he was now on was a single track and he was driving slowly, looking for a sign that would hopefully say Milton Farm.

'You have arrived at your destination,' the satnav voice helpfully informed him but he seemed to be in the middle of nowhere. He still couldn't see any farm or even anything resembling a farm, no buildings, nothing. Just fields and hedges and trees. He slowed right down and strained his eyes ahead trying to cover both sides of the road. Suddenly he saw an old wooden post. It was leaning at an angle in the grass verge on his left by the entrance to what looked like a narrow dirt track. The signpost was partly obscured by some overgrown bushes and he had to stop and get out of the car to have a proper look at it. He moved some of the branches aside and saw that it had some words on it, written in faded white paint.

'Milton Farm,' he read out aloud and he looked up the muddy track and saw some buildings in the distance maybe about a couple of hundred metres away. This was it. Now he really needed to think. He couldn't just drive up to the farm, he'd easily be seen as he approached. But he also knew he had to get there quickly before the police turned up. Dan had told him that they'd probably get organised and then move rapidly and so he knew he only had a short window of opportunity to confront Austin. This would be his one chance to hear what Austin had to say before he made him pay for what he'd done. Damn the consequences. He went back to the car and moved it up onto the verge, parking beside a tree, a few metres before the track entrance. He got out and checked he wasn't blocking the road

313

and, satisfied there was room to pass and with no-one in sight, he opened the car boot. After rummaging around for a few minutes he took out the wheel brace and then locked the car. The tool felt nice and solid in his hand. After another quick look around, he started part walking, part jogging up the side of the track towards the farm. He tried to stay crouched down, as low as possible under the shade of the trees, so that he wouldn't be visible. He soon reached the end of the track and stopped to survey the scene ahead. There was a gravel driveway which also extended around the side and presumably the back of the main house too. To the left of the house there were a number of other buildings which Jack guessed were a mixture of barns and storage sheds. It was starting to get dark and focusing on the house he could see there was a light coming from the window to the right of the front door. There also appeared to be a thin trail of whitish-grey smoke rising vertically out of the chimney before merging and disappearing into the murky sky above.

He started walking forward again, slowly, keeping to the left side of the driveway and trying to place his feet softly on the gravel although his every footstep still seemed to be very loud. He kept expecting a security light to come on but nothing happened and he soon reached the left hand corner of the house. He stopped for a minute, stretching himself, before crouching down and making his way across the front of the house, under a window until

314

he arrived at the step up to the front door. His hands were sweating and he felt himself tighten his grip on the wheel brace. Everything was still quiet.

He moved up onto the front door step, still crouching, and pressed his ear to the door. He could feel his heart racing. He couldn't hear anything from inside. He stood for a few seconds wondering what to do next. I should have planned this better, he thought, I don't really know what's going to happen. He listened at the door again but it was still silent. In fact he noticed the whole place was silent. There was no sound coming from anywhere. No birds in the trees. Nothing. Just a deathly silence.

Jack thought about edging along to the window with the light on to see if he could look inside but he decided that would be too risky. If Austin saw him he'd completely lose any element of surprise and who knows what would happen then. He turned his attention back to the front door. It looked pretty solid. There was no window or any glass in it at all. It was made of some sort of thick wood with a brass letterbox, knocker and doorknob. He reached forward with his free hand and placed it on the doorknob. It felt very cold and he immediately pulled his hand away. He clasped the doorknob once more and carefully tried to turn it to the left. It began to move, silently. He stopped then started again, this time pushing forward on the doorknob as it turned. A thin line of light appeared between the door and the frame as he felt the door slowly open inwards.

The door kept moving slowly and Jack was gradually able to see into the hallway inside. There was still no noise. He kept pushing until the door was open far enough for him to step up and get inside the farmhouse. He stood in the hallway, rigid, still holding the doorknob with one hand, the other firmly gripping the wheelbrace. He listened. Nothing. He carefully pushed the door back towards the gap without closing it completely and finally let go of the knob. He looked around.

He was standing in a lit, carpeted hallway. There were two doors to his right, two to his left and another at the far end of the hallway. The only door that was open was the first one on his right. Jack worked out that must be the room where he'd seen the light coming from. He slowly edged forward, staying close to the wall until he was at the frame of the door with the door opposite him, opened into the room. The house was still silent and for the first time he began to think that perhaps there was no-one here. Up till then he had been convinced that he'd find Andy Austin in the house but now he wasn't so sure and the thought made him annoyed but slightly relieved at the same time. He moved his head forward cautiously to get a first look inside the room.

The first thing he was aware of was the smell of the fire and he saw it glowing in the fireplace in the middle of the far wall. It was a distractingly homely aroma. The second thing he saw was a man sitting in an armchair. He appeared

316

to be staring at the fire. It was Andy Austin. He looked different to how Jack remembered him, he was clean shaven and his hair was shorter and darker but it was definitely him. Jack froze, not knowing what to do next. He felt his heart pumping even faster. This was it. The moment of truth. It was what he'd wanted, wasn't it? He pulled his head away from the door and looked down towards the floor, his knuckles had turned white with the tool grasped so tightly in his hand. He rubbed his face, took a deep breath and stepped into the room. Austin suddenly became aware that he was no longer alone. He turned in his chair to look at Jack and began to stand up.

'Sit down,' Jack said more loudly than he'd intended, but it had the desired effect. Austin looked at him for a second then sat back down in the chair.

'What are you going to do with that?' Austin asked him, motioning his head towards the tool Jack was holding by his side. 'You know the police are on their way?' he added.

'You'll just have to wait and see,' Jack sneered back, not really knowing the answer himself. He so wanted to just hit him but something was holding him back. He hadn't been in a fight since he was eleven years old and he'd certainly never attacked anyone before. Austin looked slightly taller than him and pretty fit. Now he was here, and the moment had come, it didn't seem so easy. It didn't seem right, no matter how much Austin might deserve it.

'What do you want?' Austin asked him. 'Have you come to finish me off? Let's face it you've only killed four of my family so far. Why not a fifth? Make it the full set.'

'I didn't kill them it was an accident. You're the killer. You're the one that's going around murdering people,' Jack replied defensively. He hadn't expected this, he thought he would be the one in control, the one asking the questions but somehow Austin had taken the initiative.

'We both know it wasn't an accident Jack,' Austin continued emphasising his name, 'you knew what you were doing that night. You deliberately mowed us down without a care in the world. What does it feel like to lose your brother Jack? Horrible, isn't it? Imagine losing all your family. How do you think that feels Jack? How would it feel to see them all killed in front of you because that's what happened to me one year ago. One year ago Jack and you did it. You killed them. Why did you do it Jack? Was it because of your sister? Some sort of revenge? Was that it Jack?'

Jack stood there, his mouth open. He'd been caught off guard. He hadn't expected it to be like this. Austin's words had struck home and every time he had emphasised Jack's name it had cut into him. How did he know? How long had he known? Suddenly it seemed that something so trivial, a broken romance, had somehow exploded out of all proportion. He didn't know what to say but again he felt he had to defend himself.

318

'That's not it,' he blurted out. 'It…, its not like that. That's not what happened. It was an accident, I didn't mean to…You don't understand. It was Sarah. She was just a kid. She was just my little sister. She was just beautiful. You really hurt her, She didn't deserve that,' Jack said and he could feel his eyes stinging.

Austin looked up at Jack and began to speak softly, staring into space as he did.

'I didn't mean to hurt Sarah, Jack. She was a lovely kid, we had a laugh for a few weeks, that's all it was. But she was too young for me. It was never serious for me. Believe me I never led her on. I couldn't help how she felt. She thought it was more, but it never was. She got too much. Kept calling me, texting me. I tried to let her down gently, I really liked her but we were never going to be more than friends. Good friends. But she wouldn't listen and in the end I had to cut her off. When I heard what had happened to her I was shocked, of course I was. But it really wasn't my fault Jack. She just wouldn't accept that me and her had just been a bit of fun.'

Jack was still standing in the middle of the room. His grip on the wheelbrace had loosened and he felt like he needed to sit down. He knew what Andy Austin had said was probably all true but he didn't want to admit it. Sarah had always been very sensitive, or even over sensitive, with some dramatic mood swings. But Jack had loved her more than anything. She was his precious little sister and

319

he'd always seen it as his role to look after her. To protect her. And he'd failed. And because he'd failed, he wanted someone to blame and that someone had been Andy Austin. Now he had to admit it wasn't Andy who was to blame for all that had happened since, or at least not wholly to blame, part of it was down to him. He sat down on the nearest chair running this through his head. Austin was right about Sarah, but Jack hadn't meant to kill Austin's family. That had been an accident. He'd only meant to give Austin a bit of a fright and just lost control of the car when it hit the kerb. That didn't justify Austin going around murdering all his friends. He stood up again, consciously gripping the wheelbrace a bit tighter.

'You killed my brother. I can't let you get away with that,' he said shaking his head.

'You killed my brother,' Austin replied calmly.

'Its not the same. I didn't mean to,' Jack said.

'It feels the same, though doesn't it?' Austin replied.

'What about the others? Why did you murder an old woman, what good did that do? She hadn't done anything wrong. She didn't deserve to die,' Jack said.

'My mum hadn't done anything wrong, she didn't deserve to die,' Austin replied.

'But it was Chris's mum – I don't understand, why kill her?' Jack asked.

'You were all in the car. You all played a part in what happened. You all got off. I saw you all laughing at the end of the trial. None of you understood what you'd done. You needed to know what it *felt* like,' Austin said looking determinedly at Jack.

'But murdering innocent people, really? Are you sick in the head? That's just not normal,' Jack replied, then suddenly remembering, 'what have you done with Jason's dad…have you murdered him too?' he asked angrily, leaning forwards.

'No he's still alive,' Austin replied, glancing over Jack's shoulder at a clock on the far wall.

'Where is he?' Jack said stepping forward and raising the wheelbrace.

'Don't worry, he's safe,' Austin replied.

'WHERE IS HE?' Jack shouted.

'Calm down, I told you he's safe. He's in one of the barns. I'll get the key,' he said standing up and walking towards the room door. 'Its in the kitchen,' he explained as he left the room with Jack still standing there, the wheelbrace in his right hand hanging down by his side. He was still in a state of shock and before he could move he heard a door slam shut from somewhere else in the house, from the direction Austin had just gone.

'Shit,' he exclaimed and ran out the room along the hallway to the door at the end. He opened it quickly and found himself in the kitchen. He looked around but Austin was nowhere to be seen.

321

He ran to the back door and pulled down on the handle but it didn't move. It was locked.

'Shit,' he repeated and looked around for a key but couldn't see one. He heard a car engine kick into life and he looked out the window in time to see a dark coloured car moving across the gravel. He turned around and quickly ran back down the hallway and back out through the front door. He turned right and ran across the stony driveway, this time not bothering about any noise he made, until he got to the end of the house. He kept running around the side until he got to the back corner. He turned the corner and stopped. The courtyard was empty. All he could see was a set of tyre tracks in the gravel. Austin had gone.

'Shit,' he said again and sunk down on his haunches, his head in his hands.

'Why didn't I just hit him when I had the chance,' he said to no-one. 'Why?' he repeated and he let the wheelbrace fall to the ground.

A few hundred metres away, the man now calling himself James Gilmour, turned off the narrow dirt track onto the main road and headed south.

Chapter 38

Later that day, DI Strong and DS Campbell were sitting in Strong's office, both slouched back in their chairs, either side of Strong's wooden desk which was littered with papers. Both men had their sleeves rolled up and were drinking coffee from brown, plastic vending machine cups.

'So looks like he's fled the country, do you think?' Campbell asked, trying to stifle a yawn.

'Yes, the tiny bits of burnt passport forensics found would suggest that he's changed his identity again and I'd think he'll be lying low somewhere abroad for a bit,' Strong replied. 'We've got checks going on at all the main airports and ferry ports but we don't know what name he's using now and so I don't think we'll get anything from that. No doubt he will have changed his appearance too.'

'But the message, "see you next year", looks like he's intent on coming back to do some more damage. Cocky bastard. Like the psychologist said he might. At least we know when to expect him, I suppose' Campbell frowned and continued, 'but I don't know how we're going to catch him.'

'Yes, I know. I'm going to get Dr Collins back in and see what she makes of that,' Strong replied. 'She's been pretty accurate up till now so we'll see what she says. If we don't get him, we may have to think about what it means for the two guys he had prisoner. Maybe he'll come back for them.'

'What does the big boss think?' he asked Strong.

'He's not happy,' Strong replied, 'but he'll get over it. It'll soon be yesterday's news and that's all he's worried about. We'll keep looking for Austin. At least we know for now he's not a danger. I'm sure he'll pop up somewhere and we'll nab him. Europol and all the other main police forces have been alerted and have his details. He can't stay hidden forever.'

'But what I don't get,' Campbell replied, 'it was like he was a step ahead of us all the time. How did he know we were onto him at the farm? He left the place pretty clean – it looked like he'd had time to prepare his escape. Somehow he knew we were coming and got out before we got there,' Campbell surmised aloud to his boss.

'Yes,' replied Strong, 'it could have just been because Jack Wilson had found him I suppose. But how did Wilson know where to go, has he said anything?' he asked Campbell.

324

'No, he's staying quiet and he knows we don't have anything on him. He hasn't broken any law as far as we can see apart from the likelihood that he drove there while he was still banned,' Campbell replied. 'There's still something nagging me though that Austin knew we were coming today. Like, when did he write that message? The paint was still pretty fresh. It must have been today.'

DI Strong was looking down at some papers in front of him.

'Mmmm.. this Dan Sears, one of the four lads. You said he works here, an IT technician. Could he have accessed the systems, or just overheard something? They're in and out of the main office pretty regularly aren't they, maybe he overhead some of the team talking when we were getting ready to go to the farm?'

'Yeh, there are strict rules about when they can come through but now you mention it I've a feeling I did see one of them in earlier on, before we had the meeting.' Campbell replied sighing and scratching his chin. 'Could have been him, I suppose. He might have picked up what we were planning, the address of the farm or something. That could explain how Jack Wilson got there before us, but they wouldn't have warned Austin they were coming, would they?'

'No, I reckon he was just well prepared,' Strong replied, 'he'd be ready to move at short notice, to get away. He'd need to be. He's been pretty professional all along. He would have had an escape plan ready. He probably saw Wilson coming, thought it might be the police and escaped out the back way. There was that dirt track that led out the back through the woods, it wasn't on any map, or certainly not on the map we had. He probably got out that way. We'll see what the forensics boys come back with on tyre tracks and that but I guess he's well gone now. He chose the farm well, there's no CCTV for miles in any direction so guessing which is his car when it does get in range of a camera would be impossible. I suppose him leaving so quickly after Wilson turned up would also explain why he didn't finish off the other two he had locked up in his outbuilding.'

'Yeh, I suppose,' Campbell replied, 'although if he was planning it in the way Dr Collins suggested then it wasn't time for them to die yet, lucky for them. At least they were both relatively okay, considering. That Bill Reynolds seems a tough nut, especially for an old bloke, he was ex-army I read. Austin had beaten him about a bit but from what he said it was apparently after he tried to escape. At least he didn't have the injuries that were detailed on that fake medical report Austin sent to the Reynolds' house.'

'Yes, I heard that, which I suppose is something positive,' Strong replied.

'That Jack Wilson is a stupid bastard, we ought to throw the book at him. If it hadn't been for him stumbling in and alerting Austin, we probably would have got him,' Campbell added.

'Yeh leave him to me,' Strong replied, 'Remember the poor kid has probably suffered with his brother getting murdered. It can make you do strange things. I'll have a word with him and our man Sears too. I'll put a rocket up his backside and make sure he doesn't do anything like that again if he wants to keep his job.'

'Okay, so what do you want me to do now? Do you want me in the meet with Collins?' Campbell asked.

'No, I think now would be a good time for you to take a few days off. Its been pretty hectic these last few days and you look like you could do with a rest. Go away and recharge yourself and then come back next week,' Strong replied. 'Nothing much is likely to happen in the next few days. We'll get the report back from the farm but I don't expect there'll be much from that. We know who he is and what he has done. I don't think there will be anything more that tells us where he's gone. It'll hit the news and papers tomorrow but I don't think there'll be anything useful will come from that either. He's been too clever. I'm sure he's in a bolt hole abroad somewhere – probably living in a remote farmhouse somewhere in the middle of France peddling his same story that he's writing a book, if anyone asks him.'

DS Campbell nodded.

'Okay thanks guv,' he said, 'a few days break would be useful, I have some stuff I need to sort out at home. Give me a call if anything comes up or you need me though.' Strong nodded and Campbell got up and left the room.

Although he wasn't quite convinced that they'd tied up all the loose ends yet and he'd have liked to ask a few more questions, he couldn't disagree with Strong's suggestion. A few days off might not be a bad idea. It would give him some time to sort things out with his wife. She was still a bit funny with him about him missing the last hospital appointment and it had all blown up again the previous night, after he'd got home. She'd accused him of constantly putting his job before her and asked him if he really wanted to make their marriage work. He told her of course he did but that his work was also important to him. She should know that.

'I don't see that one has to be more important than the other,' he'd said. 'It's not a competition.'

'Well that's not how I see it,' she'd replied. 'It seems that every time the job takes priority over your marriage, over me. I think it would be best if I go and stay with my mum for a few days. It looks like we both need to think about what we really want from this marriage and some time apart might do us good.'

That had been the last thing Campbell wanted and after a while he managed to talk her out of doing that. However he had slept in the spare room that night and he'd left early in the morning for a hard session at the gym, taking care not to wake her. Now that he had a few days off, maybe they could go away to a nice hotel somewhere and just find some time to talk. Yes, a few days together, just the two of them, somewhere quiet, that would be good, he thought as he locked his papers away in his desk drawer and set off for home.

Immediately DS Campbell had left his boss's office, Strong's mobile rang. Strong picked it up, looked at the number on the screen and answered without saying hello.

'I need the names on the passports you gave him,' he said immediately.

He waited a few minutes and then wrote down four names in a notebook in front of him and ended the call. Tearing the page from his notebook, he walked out into the main office and headed to a desk in the far corner of the room.

'Marsha,' he said bending down towards a middle-aged woman sitting at the desk, 'A favour please. I need you to look up these names.'

He handed her the piece of paper, carefully checking that no-one else was looking in their direction. Marsha took the note from him, looking away quickly and glanced at the four names written on the paper.

'Keep this between you and me,' he said quietly, smiling. 'One of my hunches, you know,' he said winking at her. 'I need to know if any of them leave the country today or in the next couple of days. If they have, where they've gone and where they're staying. Can you do that?'

329

'Sure, I'll get on to it and let you know if anything comes up.' Marsha replied, still not looking at Strong but sitting upright, getting ready to start typing in the names on her computer.

'Okay, come and tell me as soon as you find out anything and remember this is just between us okay? No-one else needs to know at this point.' Strong said, emphasising his point by leaning in closer and looking directly at Marsha, and she nodded obligingly.

Marsha had worked for the police for over twenty years and for the last ten of those she had been working in various roles in the Serious Crime squad. She admired Strong and had seen him progress through the levels until he became a DI and the head of the team. She'd worked very closely with Strong at times over that period, providing him with information as he needed. Strong had done this sort of "secret request" thing with her a few times before and she found it quite exciting. It felt personal, like he trusted her more than anyone else and it definitely beat the routine of her normal daily police work. Marsha thought of it as their secret and it made her feel special.

Chapter 39

Doctor Collins had been pleasantly surprised to get the call from DI Strong. From what she'd heard of him previously she'd thought he would be pretty sceptical about how much she could help him. To be truthful most policemen were. But she felt she'd done a good job on this one, she'd certainly put the effort in, and so to get another call from him requesting a follow up meeting was very rewarding. She'd also enjoyed the previous meeting they'd had, despite her fears, she'd found Strong a likeable detective, unlike some of the others she'd had to deal with previously. And for his age, he wasn't too bad looking which was an added bonus!

Collins was sat comfortably with her legs crossed on one of the chairs in Strong's office, just the two of them this time. She assumed DS Campbell was busy writing up reports on the day's events. DI Strong was explaining what happened at the farm. Apparently the police turned up there and made their way to the main farm house, surrounding it on all sides, but when they'd made their assault on the house instead of finding

Andy Austin inside, they'd surprisingly found Jack Wilson.

Wilson hadn't said much but claimed that he'd found out himself that Austin was at the farm but he wouldn't or couldn't explain how he knew that. He'd said that as soon as Austin had seen him coming towards the front door, he'd made a run for it out the back and driven off in a car. Unfortunately Wilson hadn't seen much of the car and could only say it was a dark coloured 4x4. Just like thousands of other cars on the road.

The police had done a complete search of the farm and had found both Bill Reynolds and Kevin Green alive, locked in two separate rooms in one of the farm outbuildings. Reynolds looked a bit beaten up, with a number of obvious injuries and so he was immediately taken to hospital but the latest news was that he seemed to be stable and the doctors were confident he'd soon be able to go home. Kevin Green hadn't been harmed and so they'd been able to interview him immediately. However, although both of the men had confirmed it had been Andy Austin holding them hostage, neither had been able to tell them anything more that was of any particular use.

A thorough search of the farm hadn't uncovered anything else either. It looked like anything personal that Austin might have taken to the farm, he'd also driven away with, when he made the escape in his car.

'So it was like he was already prepared to leave, if what Jack Wilson is saying is correct?' Collins asked. She looked down at the notes she'd been scribbling as Strong had been talking. 'Wilson said Austin must have seen him approaching the front of the house and he fled out the back door, Collins read from her notes, 'so he either already had any stuff in his car or he took it with him then. Either way he was obviously prepared for a quick escape.'

'It would seem so,' Strong nodded. 'He's been pretty clever all along and I think we must assume that he was ready to leave at any point if anything went wrong. We assume he saw Wilson coming up the driveway and it gave him a couple of minutes to grab his things and escape out the back door. There's another track leads away from the back of the house through some woods to the main road. It looks like there's some fresh tyre tracks on that. We're checking them to see if we can identify the tyres and maybe from that, the make of car.'

'Mmm…you're probably right. The only other explanation would be that somehow he knew the police were coming but I cant see how,' Collins said. She was really enjoying this, pleased that Strong was sharing all of the information with him, that didn't happen very often. Usually she was called in for one meeting to give them a psychological profile and then never asked back. Often, the only time she heard any more detail was when the case hit the newspapers.

333

'No, me neither, the logical explanation is that Wilson messed it up for us. He'll get a severe reprimand but there's not much else we can do. He hasn't actually broken any law, or at least not anything that's worth the bother of processing,' Strong replied. 'What I need from you now though,' he carried on, 'is your thoughts on where this leaves us. What do you think he'll do next? You've been pretty good at predicting what he'd do up to now so I'd be interested to get your thoughts.'

Dr Collins could feel herself blushing slightly at the complement she'd just received. That was highly unusual and to come from someone as senior as DI Strong meant a lot to her.

'Ok, let me think,' she started, 'obviously the message he left, the "See You Next Year" in red paint on the wall of the outbuilding was pretty clear. It would seem, as we suggested, that the date is key to him so my guess is that he won't do anything now until the same time next year. I think that's a pretty safe bet. So I would assume he's gone into hiding somewhere, just lying low, presumably under a new identity. What he'll do after that though is not as obvious. I think we have to assume that he is still thinking of doing something similar to exact his revenge. In his eyes, the job's not finished. Remember the PTED causes this obsessive behaviour. But its open to debate who he might pick on. It could be the same two again or he could start afresh and go for some of the men's other relatives, or even friends.'

'Yes that's what we thought,' DI Strong replied, 'but with your knowledge of this PTED condition and what he's done so far what would be your best bet. That Bill Reynolds is a tough guy, even though he's getting on a bit. Maybe Austin would want to avoid him second time around. From what I hear old Bill is keen to have another crack at him,' Strong laughed. 'What would you say though, if you had to stake your house on it?'

Doctor Collins thought for a few seconds before replying.

'If I had to call it, I'd say he'll do exactly the same next year. He's been pretty specific up to now in his choice of victims to exactly mirror his family so I think he'll do the same again.'

'So Bill Reynolds and Kevin Green will be his targets again in a year's time?' Strong asked.

'That would be my educated guess,' Dr Collins replied. 'On the anniversary.'

Chapter 40

When DS Campbell had returned to the Serious Crime Squad office the following week it seemed that everything had almost returned to normal. If there ever was a "normal" in police work. Every day brought something different. Something you couldn't make up. But at least the office seemed much the same as it had been before *"The Anniversary Killer"*, as the press had dubbed him, had arrived on the scene.

The newspapers, especially the tabloids, had had a field day with the story, which hadn't pleased the Chief Constable. It had been front page headlines for three days in a row before eventually being overtaken by a story about an international footballer apparently snorting cocaine. Unfortunately, despite all the publicity, Andy Austin's whereabouts were still unknown.

The investigation had been massively scaled back which to all intents and purposes meant that no-one was actually working on it. The case now sat in the category they called "Reactive Mode" which meant if any new information came in then they would act on it and allocate a resource if required. However in practice what this meant was a file full of call reports from cranks, or would be detectives, claiming to have seen Andy Austin or knowing where he was now hiding. Campbell had glanced through the file, reading a couple of the reports, wondering why people thought it acceptable to waste police time in this way.

"I think he lives next door. He always has his curtains shut."

"I think if you did a police stake out over a few nights, like they do in CSI, you'd catch him."

"He looks well dodgy and he lives on his own. I wouldn't trust him"

Surely even these people knew that what they were reporting wasn't going to lead anywhere? Maybe somehow it made them feel important, even for a short time.

'*I told the police about that bloke that moved in upstairs that looks like The Anniversary Killer. I haven't seen them go up there yet but they're probably going to surprise him with a dawn raid or something. That's usually how they do it. The one I spoke to said he'd have to discuss it with his Sergeant and that. I expect they've got him under surveillance. I wonder if I'll get a reward. You think there would be.*'

From a practical perspective the incident room had been turned back into a normal conference room and all of the staff had been reallocated onto other cases or back onto general administrative duties. It was certainly a lot quieter, which Campbell realised he should be thinking was a good thing, no major murder enquiry ongoing, but he did miss the buzz. He'd got himself sorted, catching up on emails, but it didn't seem anything else had happened on the case. He'd wander along to DI Strong's office later and see how the land lay.

He was feeling refreshed after his time off. He'd needed it, more than he realised at the time. Luckily he'd managed to find a nice little hotel down the coast that had been as good as the previous customer feedback had promised when he'd browsed it on the internet. It had been perfect for him and his wife and they'd spent the whole time with each other, just walking and talking, eating and drinking. It had got easier and easier as the time had gone by as they relaxed into each other's company again. It had reminded them how much they loved each other and why they had got together in the first place. They'd just needed some time away from everything else to rediscover that and the last few days had been perfect.

Towards the end of the break, they'd sat down and agreed to make more time for each other at home and Campbell had acknowledged that he needed to switch off from his police work when they were together. They had also decided to give the "Date Night" idea a try making sure they had at least one night out together, just the two of them. All in all, they'd both returned from the break in a much more positive frame of mind and determined to carry that forward and Campbell was glad that Strong had given him the time off to do that.

A little while later, Campbell was sat, uncomfortably as usual, in DI Strong's office. Strong had filled him in on everything that had happened while he'd been off, which, as Campbell thought, hadn't been much.

'So Austin is hiding out somewhere, but could be anywhere,' Campbell concluded. 'I reckon he's probably abroad, under a different name, different appearance. But what do we do now? If what Dr Collins says is right he'll be back same time next Christmas ready to strike again. Do we just wait for him? Maybe we can take Green and Reynolds into protective custody or something and see what he does then?'

Strong pushed his chair back and stretched his legs out in front of him.

'I think we have to find him before that,' he replied. 'We can't take the chance that he puts on a repeat show next year, it'll make us all look fools. We need to keep his profile in the public domain, someone is bound to see him in the next twelve months, or somehow he'll make a mistake. We've got quite a lot of information on him now, medical records, dental records, we even got his fingerprints and DNA from the farmhouse. He won't know that and he just needs to make one little mistake, maybe a driving offence or something and we'll have him. I'm confident we'll get him before its time for him to strike again.'

339

DS Campbell felt inspired by Strong's confidence, although he didn't know quite how they'd catch him, his boss had often proved him wrong in the past and so Campbell really hoped that he was right again this time.

Chapter 41

'Come on, get your coat, I'm taking you out. You need to get out of this flat and get some fresh air. And more importantly you need to have a few drinks. And so do I! They've redone the Anchor and it's really nice now. We'll go there. And I'm not taking no for an answer.'

Lucy looked at her friend Jane standing there on her doorstep, sounding all jolly and positive. She'd gone blonde now, her hair shoulder length and it suited her Lucy thought. She was the same age as Lucy and had always been very attractive. Lucy knew she worked hard on her appearance and she had never been short of male admirers. It was nice to see her friend, but Lucy really didn't want to go out. She hadn't been out socially since everything that had happened with Paul or Andy. She didn't even know how to refer to him now. How crazy was that? She'd always known him as Paul. A couple of months ago she was thinking of maybe getting married to him, now she didn't even know his proper name. As much as she loved Jane, she was thinking about how she could put her off. She just didn't feel like going out yet.

'Come on,' Jane repeated, 'don't try and come up with some excuse, I know you too well' and she reached past Lucy, grabbing a jacket from the coat hook in the hallway behind her.

'This one will do,' she said taking Lucy's hand and pulling her forward.

'Wait, wait,' said Lucy smiling. Jane was a good friend and very persistent. Lucy had already put her off a couple of times over the phone, but she knew now that Jane had turned up on her doorstep that she'd probably have to give in.

'Can't we just stay in? I think I've got some wine in or we get can get some more from the off-licence,' she made once last appeal, 'Besides, I haven't got any make-up on and look,' she said motioning at the sweatshirt and jeans she was wearing, 'I can't go out like this.'

'Five minutes then, I'll give you that to get ready and then we are going. No excuses,' Jane smiled, flashing her perfect set of white teeth and stepped into the house, giving Lucy a hug.

Thirty minutes later they were sat at a quiet table in the corner of the Anchor pub, both with a cold glass of Sauvignon Blanc resting on the table in front of them. Lucy was wearing a blue top and white trousers, her hair and make-up done as best she could in the time Jane had allowed her. She felt plain at best, next to Jane but at least there didn't seem to be anyone else she knew in the bar. She took a couple of sips of her wine and reluctantly admitted to herself that she was glad that Jane had come around and forced her out. It was nice to have a change of scenery. Her mum had tried to get her out a few times too but she'd put her off. But it had been hard sitting in the house on her own the past few nights and the distraction of the television hadn't been enough to stop her thinking about Paul. She knew she'd have to get out sometime and there was no way that Jane had been going to take no for an answer. Jane usually got her own way and despite everything Lucy knew that life has to go on.

Lucy and Jane had known each other since they were kids. Although they'd gone to different schools, they'd both attended the same Brownie group and had got to know each other there. They'd stayed in touch ever since and Lucy felt guilty that she hadn't seen her since she'd started going out with Paul. Over the last few nights she'd realised that she'd lost touch with a few friends as her relationship with Paul had developed. Paul had never really wanted to go on nights out, or to parties with her friends and although she didn't worry about it too much at the time because she just loved being with him, she realised now it was probably because he was frightened someone might have recognised him. Just like what had happened at the restaurant that evening.

Her friend Jane worked in a high street travel agents and as they drank their wine, she was entertaining Lucy with stories of holidays that had

343

gone wrong and customers that didn't know what they were doing. Lucy was beginning to feel relaxed for the first time in a while and was content to just sit there, sipping her wine and letting Jane do the talking. It was good to think about something else other than Paul and what he had done.

'Last week I had a couple in who said they wanted to go to Spain and I said is there anywhere in particular you'd like to go? There's a lot of nice places so I was hoping we could narrow it down a bit. And the woman said she quite fancied Rio. Rio de Janiero?, I said, you mean in Brazil? No she said, just Rio, in Spain where they have the bulls and the Olympics and carnivals and stuff. That would be fun, she said looking at her husband who looked like he never had much fun. And isn't there some big statue of Jesus? We could do that one day, couldn't we? She said to him and I swear I thought he was going to cry. By this time I was trying my hardest not to laugh and I'd crossed my legs really tightly under the table. Yes but Rio's actually in Brazil though, I said. Oh, the woman said. Are you sure? Isn't it in Spain? It sounds Spanish, doesn't it? Her husband nodded and they both looked up at me expectantly. Oh fuck it I thought, and you know what I did?'

'No, what?' Lucy replied, engrossed with her friend's story.

'I booked it for them.'

'What…., what did you book?' Lucy asked eagerly.

The Anniversary

'A holiday in Rio,' Jane replied. 'That's what they wanted and so that's what they got. It's a lovely place anyhow. Or at least it looks it on-line, I've never been there myself. Ten out of ten for me for customer service though don't you think? I told them they were right. My mistake, Rio *was* actually in Spain, one of the parts that was a bit further away and took a bit longer to get to but they'd enjoy it when they got there. So they left happy and I was happy. Nice bit of commission. Couldn't be better!'

Lucy's mouth was wide open and she shrieked with laughter, and for a few seconds she just couldn't stop. This was just what she needed, this and the wine she thought as she took another sip and felt it warmly trickle down the back of her throat and down through her abdomen. After a few more of Jane's stories and a few more glasses of wine, Lucy was feeling much better than she had for a while. She realised that she'd hardly thought about Paul at all this evening and that was surely a good thing. Time is a great healer and it was beginning to work its magic. That and the alcohol.

'How's your love life going anyway?' Lucy asked her. 'You're not still seeing that married bloke are you?'

'God no,' Jane replied, 'that finished ages ago. His wife found out and came into the shop looking for me. Luckily I was through the back office doing the foreign currencies and Deborah told her I didn't work there anymore. Somehow she didn't clock the empty desk she was standing next

345

to with my nameplate on it. Anyway that seemed to do the trick cause she never came back and I never heard from him again either. She probably killed him and buried him under the patio.'

Jane looked at Lucy and suddenly realised what she'd just said.

'Oh, I'm sorry….I didn't mean to….' she pleaded.

'Hey, don't worry.' Lucy replied, 'I know you didn't mean anything and anyway I don't want you treading on eggshells, what happened was nothing to do with you and I don't want you to worry about that.'

She reached over and squeezed her friend's hand and smiled at her.

'So are you currently single again?' Lucy asked.

'Yes, I'm young, free and single,' Jane replied laughing, realising she'd said it a little too loudly and several people were looking her way. They both giggled and quickly took a drink of their wine.

Lucy knew that they'd been consciously avoiding mentioning Paul but she also knew that they'd have to talk about it at some stage and with a few glasses of wine inside them, now was probably going to be as good a time as any. As soon as she started talking about him, it was like a floodgate had opened and it felt good to get a lot of it out in the open and off her mind. She'd talked a bit with her mum, but it had all been a bit raw and emotional.

346

Talking with Jane was easier as she was on the outside and it helped her reflect on a few things that she'd just assumed were normal when she'd been with Paul, or at least Paul had come up with some sort of logical justification.

Even the simple things like her not having met any of his friends – he'd said that not many of them lived nearby and he had never been one who liked going to dinners or parties. He preferred just being with Lucy, he said. And when she'd tried to organise nights out with her friends, there had always been some reason Paul hadn't been able to make it and it kept getting put back. Even Jane had never met him which was a shame as she knew they would have got on well, at least before…. Then of course there had been the story that he'd told her that he was writing a book, which she now knew was a complete lie and just a cover for his….his crimes. She still found it difficult to say that out loud or even admit it to herself in her inner thoughts. How could someone as nice as Paul be a murderer? How could she be living with someone like that and not know. It just didn't add up.

She told Jane about everything that happened and also what the police had explained to her. Apparently he was on a mission of revenge for the accident that had killed his family a year before. The police psychiatrist had said he may have developed some sort of brain disorder from a head injury he had got in the accident, but there was no actual medical evidence to prove that. She could tell

347

that the other police detectives didn't really believe it, or couldn't accept it as any sort of excuse. The way they saw it was that he had killed two innocent people and there could be no justification for that. Lucy did want there to be some sort of logical reason for him acting in such an extreme way though, but she tended to agree with the detectives.

Now, the police believed that Paul, or Andy as they referred to him, had escaped somewhere abroad but they were confident that they would track him down. He wouldn't be able to stay hidden for ever was how they put it. But it didn't seem they had any real idea where he was and neither did Lucy.

Jane had sat listening, allowing Lucy to talk, realising that this was a good thing for her, getting it all out, and she was pleased that she was doing that with her. Lucy had always been one of her best friends and she didn't like to see her hurt. She was glad she could help in some small way. Occasionally she asked Lucy a question and then made sure she agreed with Lucy on all her conclusions. Now was not the time to raise further questions in Lucy's mind, she just needed someone to understand her and that was the role Jane was happy to play. When Lucy had finished, Jane nodded and spoke decisively.

'Men are all a waste of space and time,' she proclaimed. 'Who needs them, they're only ever after one thing and most of them are not even very good at that. Cheers to being female and single,' she said raising her glass and touching it against Lucy's a little too forcefully making some of the wine spill over the top of Lucy's glass.

'Oops,' Jane said and they both burst into another fit of giggles.

'Another bottle?' Jane asked and without waiting for a reply she'd signalled to the waiter to bring one over.

A few more drinks later and the discussion had regressed to their time together many years ago in the Brownies.

'Do you remember that group leader we had for a short while when Mrs Adams was away having a baby?' Lucy asked.

'You mean Mrs Brown?' Jane replied.

'Yes,' Lucy laughed then in unison they both chanted.

'Mrs Brown went to town and one day her pants fell down!'

'Oh my god, how do we remember that?' Jane shrieked.

'I don't think I'll ever forget it!' Lucy replied laughing. 'Do you remember the day we were all sitting, cross legged in the hall, and she was standing out front talking to us about something or other and we could all see her skirt slowly slipping down. It was just moving a little bit at a time but it was definitely going and we were all just sat there waiting for it to finally plummet past her knees..' Lucy was laughing so much she had to stop to catch her breath.

349

'…and then teachers pet Julie Robertson stuck her hand up and said, Excuse me Mrs Brown but I think your skirts falling down! And the rest of us just broke into fits of laughter. That was the best Brownies day ever.'

'Yes, it was,' Jane replied, 'that and the camps we went on they were great too. We used to have so much fun when we went away together.'

Jane suddenly stopped talking and looked straight at Lucy.

'Oh my god,' she said.

'What?', Lucy replied, wondering what was wrong.

'We should do that now. That's what we *need* to do.' Jane said.

'What, go on a Brownie camp – surely were a bit too old for that now?' Lucy replied laughing at her friend.

'No, you idiot,' Jane replied, 'we should go on holiday together. Here's me, a travel agent, of course that's what we should do. Why didn't I think of that before? I could get something sorted quickly and cheaply too!'

'Cheaply, I like the sound of that,' Lucy replied. 'Let's do it!' and they clinked their glasses together as if to seal the deal they'd just made. Afterwards, looking back, Lucy could pinpoint that moment as the first time since Paul left that she realised she was probably going to be okay.

Chapter 42

The man walked quickly through the revolving door, his head down, focused on the tiled floor in front of him. People passed by on his left and on his right. The green and white sign up above the door looked brilliant in the strong sunlight and proudly proclaimed 'Clinic Barcelona, Hospital Universitari.'

He'd been here before, a few months previously, and so he knew exactly where he was headed. He walked quickly along the corridor until he reached the lift and took it to the fourth floor. As it arrived, the doors slid open and he stepped out turning quickly to the right and walking along the corridor until he came to an opening on the left with a white sign above it stating 'Departamento de Neurología'. He stopped for a few seconds taking a few breaths. Looking around he saw he was on his own and he turned to his left and walked up to the reception desk. He gave his name to the receptionist and sat down in the waiting area, checking his watch as he did so. There was a television monitor on the wall showing a news channel. The sound was muted

351

but it was apparently reporting on an earthquake somewhere in Japan. It kept showing the same clip of a building collapsing, over and over again, interspersed with what appeared to be an excitable Japanese TV reporter. He stared at it without really taking in what was happening. A few minutes later he heard his name being called and he stood up and followed a white coated nurse along a narrow corridor to the left of the reception desk. After a minute they stopped outside a light brown wooden door with the one word 'Privado' attached to it on a metal plate. The nurse knocked twice on the door and pushed it open, stepping aside to let the man pass her and enter the room. She pulled the door closed and remained outside leaving the man on his own.

It was a small room, painted white with one narrow window, shielded with grey vertical blinds keeping out the day's bright sunlight. In front of the window, on the far side of the room, opposite to the door, a man in a white coat was sitting behind a desk with a computer terminal to one side and some papers in front of him. He looked away from his computer and stood up as the man approached, holding out his hand.

'Welcome Senor Samuel,' he said with a part Spanish, part American accent. The other man shook his hand.

'Please, sit down,' he continued, indicating the plastic chair on the other side of his desk. The man sat down.

'So, please tell me, how are you? How have you been? It's been some time since you were last here, no?'

The man shifted in his chair, making himself comfortable.

'I've been okay doctor,' he replied, 'a few headaches now and again but the tablets you prescribed have helped.'

'Mmm,' the doctor replied, 'so tell me the headaches, have they been getting worse, more frequent?'

'A bit, but not too bad,' the man replied. 'If I take the tablets in time it's generally okay. After a bit of rest they usually go away.'

'Any problems with your vision? Any blurriness or double vision?'

'Once or twice, maybe, but only for a few minutes,' the man replied frowning.

The doctor jotted down a few notes on the pad in front of him as the man spoke. He then leaned back in his chair, twirling his pen between his fingers.

'What about your general wellbeing? Have you had any mood swings, any temper, anything like that?'

'No, not really,' the man replied, 'nothing unusual I don't think.'

'Not really?' the doctor replied, raising his eyebrows as he spoke.

'Well what I mean is not any more than anyone else. I mean everyone loses their temper

353

sometimes don't they? But I think I manage to keep it pretty much under control. I'm always pretty focused on what I'm doing.'

'Mmm…,' the doctor replied, writing down some more notes on the paper in front of him before looking up at his patient sat directly across from him.

'Okay, that's good. So now I have the results of your latest scan,' the doctor said, reaching to his right and opening a buff file of papers in front of him. He flicked through the contents to remind himself and also to give him a few moments to prepare for what he was about to say. He looked up and faced the man opposite him directly.

'I'm afraid the tumour has grown since the last scan, quite a bit in fact. But as we discussed last time that's not to be unexpected. However we are now fast approaching the stage where we have to make a decision on what best to do next. In fact, in my opinion, if we delay any more there won't be any decision to make. In a few months, or perhaps even weeks, the tumour will have become inoperable.'

He stopped talking, still looking directly at the man sat across from him, wondering what he was thinking. This mysterious Englishman who, although he had now met twice, he felt he didn't really know anything about him other than the basic essentials. Normally he would get to know his patients, learn a bit about their lives, their families and that often helped somehow normalise the situation on both sides. After all they were all human beings. But this man, this Mr Samuel, sat across from him was different. He was still like a complete stranger. All he knew was that he was originally from the UK but was now living in Spain. He hadn't said anything about any family, or even friends. The doctor had noticed that he didn't appear to wear a wedding ring and so he guessed he wasn't married, but that was all it was, just a guess.

As was often the case, the man had remained silent, so the doctor continued.

'As we have discussed before I would strongly recommend the operation to remove the tumour, or at least part of it. As you know it is a high risk procedure with no guarantee of a successful outcome but the alternative is gradual deterioration and ultimately you will die. Do you understand?'

The man sat forward in his seat and spoke.

'How long?' he said.

'As I said the tumour will soon become inoperable. After that life expectancy will maybe be a year, perhaps a bit longer, but it could also be less, it's not an exact science, everyone is different. But that would be my best guess at this point. If you come back in three months I could maybe have a better idea but that would be too long. If we're going to operate, we need to do it now.'

He looked at his screen and then smiled back at the man sat opposite.

'I could fit you in to my clinic next week.

We could do the operation and then, assuming all has gone well, you'd be back out in a few weeks or so, maybe a month.'

The man looked straight at him.

'It's my decision, yes?'

'Of course,' the doctor replied, 'I can only advise you on what I think is best for you as a medical professional.'

The man sat forward in his seat, gripping the sides with both hands.

'I don't want the operation,' he said flatly. 'I've got something to do, something to finish off. Ideally I need another few months, till the end of the year. Give me some more tablets to get me through that and then my job will be done.'

The doctor looked him straight in the eye.

'Are you sure, you've understood what I've told you? There's no way back from this. Have you discussed it with your family?'

The man held the doctor's gaze and answered firmly.

'I'm sure. Once this is over, then I'll see my family again.'

A few hundred miles away, Strong was sitting alone in his office, thinking about packing up and going home. It had been another long day but thankfully since Austin had disappeared he was able to get home at a sensible hour most nights again. As he locked his desk drawer, there was a knock at his door.

'Yes,' he called.

The door opened and a woman entered the room, carefully closing it behind her. It was Marsha and she was holding a single sheet of paper.

'I've got something for you,' she said smiling, and she approached Strong's desk, handing over the piece of paper.

'Thanks Marsha,' Strong replied, 'I owe you one. No-one else knows? Only me and you?' he said smiling at her.

'No sir, of course and I'm only doing my job,' she replied, blushing slightly and with a nod she turned and left Strong's office, closing the door quietly as she left. All done in a few seconds, it was as if she'd never been there.

Strong was already reading the text on the paper, he memorised the key parts he needed to know before turning around and feeding it into his personal shredder sat on the floor behind his chair. He spent a few minutes more printing out a couple of sheets of paper from his PC before switching off and putting the paper in a plain brown envelope which he then placed inside his briefcase. He looked at his watch and then got up and left his office to head for home.

Chapter 43

Lucy woke up and stretched out across the bed, enjoying the sensation of feeling her body come alive right through to the tips of her fingers and toes. There was something about holiday beds, they always seemed big and the mattresses were just right, not too firm, not too soft. She had slept well again, although the amount of wine she'd drank last night had probably been a factor too.

This holiday was definitely helping her. Just getting away from her normal life, her usual places, everything that had some memory or connection with Paul was doing her good. She was glad that Jane had persuaded, or more accurately insisted, that they go away for a week. Somewhere quiet where she could relax and start to recover from all that had happened over the last few weeks. Jane had found a perfect place. It was a small villa with a private pool hidden in the Spanish countryside. "In the middle of nowhere" as Jane had correctly described it to her friend.

After Jane had dragged her out to The Anchor, what seemed like a lifetime ago, but was in fact only a couple of weeks, she'd wasted no time in booking them a holiday. In fact she'd done it the very next day when she'd been at her work. She'd phoned Lucy later that day to tell her the news.

'You know we were talking about going away on holiday last night?' she'd asked.

'Yes, I seem to remember something about that although events of last night are still a bit hazy,' Lucy had replied.

'Ah, well you agreed we should go on holiday, so I've booked it. We leave in ten days time for a week at a villa in the Spanish countryside,' Jane had informed her.

'What?' Lucy had exclaimed.

'Get your passport ready girl. We're going to have some total R and R. Nothing to worry about and especially no men,' Jane had added.

And so it had been, so far perfect, thought Lucy as she showered and then pulled on a pair of white shorts and a pink t-shirt. She shook her hair gave it a quick brush. She was so glad she'd got it cut short and dyed blonde. It had been a big change for her but it was ideal for the holiday and she liked it. It was the new Lucy. She walked down the stone steps, cool and refreshing on the soles of her feet and came into the kitchen. Jane was sat on a stool at the kitchen island, looking pretty as always. She was sipping from a mug of coffee, the aroma hitting Lucy's senses as she approached.

'Morning, sleep well? Fancy a coffee?' Jane asked.

'Mmm, like a baby,' Lucy answered, 'and yes please to the coffee,' she added.

'What do you fancy doing today?' Jane asked as she poured her friend a mug of hot coffee and handed it to her. 'Another day by the pool or she we be a bit more adventurous and have a drive around some of the countryside and see what we can find?'

'Yes, that sounds good,' Lucy replied, taking her first sip of the coffee and sighing as the sensations of both smell and taste filled her head.

'Great,' Jane replied, 'I've been looking at this map,' and Lucy noticed for the first time that there was a map spread out on the worktop in front of Jane, 'and I think we should be able to drive through this valley,' she said indicating with her perfectly manicured finger, 'and end up at this little village or town maybe in time for a spot of lunch. Assuming it has somewhere we can eat.'

'What's it called?' Lucy asked, reaching for her phone.

'Emm,' Jane looked for it again, tracing with her finger along the map, 'Rupit,' she said. 'Want me to spell it?'

'No, its fine, I've got it here,' Lucy replied, staring at her phone. 'Yes, Rupit. It looks nice. It says it's a small market town and there's an old church and a town square. Looks very pretty,' she added, showing Jane the images of Rupit on her phone.

'Let's just check Google maps,' Lucy added. 'Here we go, looks like it's about twenty kilometres from here, should be a nice easy drive.'

Half an hour later they were in their hire car, one from the small economy range, but perfectly adequate for them. It only had two doors but it had air conditioning which was a bonus. Jane was driving and Lucy was sat in the passenger seat studying a map in the guide book Jane had found in the villa.

'I'm not very good at navigating but I think we're going the right way,' Lucy said, looking up from the map. 'According to this we should come to a crossroads soon and we take a left turn there and then second right, I think.'

She picked up her phone but it still had no signal. Ten minutes later they hadn't reached any crossroads and Lucy wasn't sure where they were.

'I'm not sure where we are,' she said, staring at the map.

'Look there's a village coming up ahead,' said Jane, 'let's see if we can stop there, grab a coffee and maybe ask someone for directions. I don't think that map's very good,' she added in support of her friend.

'Ha-ha yes, maybe the map or more likely it's the map reader that's not very good,' Lucy replied laughing. 'Maybe we'll pick up some wi-fi connection in the village, you never know,' she added hopefully.

They entered the village and soon found a lovely cobbled square in the centre where they parked up and sat down outside a café under a shaded parasol. They ordered two white coffees and when the waiter returned they asked him for directions to Rupit and were pleasantly surprised to find that it was only about ten minutes further up the road they were on and they had actually been heading in the right direction.

'See your map reading skills aren't that bad after all,' Jane said. 'You'd get a badge for that now if we were still in the Brownies.'

Jane took a final sip of her coffee and looked at her friend. She was pleased to see Lucy smiling back at her. The holiday had definitely helped her and she looked more like her old self again, albeit with a different hairstyle.

'Maybe we'll find a nice bar in Rupit with a couple of gorgeous, young, fit Spanish waiters who'll show us all the sights and more....' Jane said, laughing.

'I thought we were here to forget all about men!' Lucy replied, feigning outrage.

'We've done that now, that was the first three days. Now it's time we moved on,' Jane replied and she leant forward across the table towards Lucy, her long blonde hair falling in front of her.

'What about him over there?' she whispered, moving her head slightly in the direction of a man sitting at a table outside a café across the street.

Lucy had seen him ten minutes before, just after they'd arrived. She hadn't been sure at first. He had a tan and stubbled beard and his hair was cut short, a slightly different shade of brown with wisps of grey showing at the sides. Then she'd caught his eye and he'd smiled at her. A small, almost imperceptible, wry smile. But it was one she recognised. One she knew. He wanted to tell her how good she looked, how he loved her new hairstyle, but he knew he couldn't. She'd smiled back shyly and looked away. It was then, that smile, that told them both that Lucy was going to be okay. Despite what she'd been through she was going to be fine.

'Nah, he's not my type,' Lucy replied, gathering her stuff and standing up. 'As you said it's time to move on, let's see what Rupit has to offer.'

Chapter 44

Jack had been very surprised to get the call from the detective, DI Strong. He'd only met him a couple of times before, once in the house and the other time at Pete's funeral. Jack had just started to move on with his life again and had just about stopped constantly thinking about the accident or Andy Austin and the murders. Perhaps it was normal police protocol to have some sort of follow up meeting but it wasn't anything he had heard of before. And why him and no-one else?

He'd also been intrigued by the nature of Strong's call. He'd been very cagey, not telling Jack anything other than he had some interesting information for him and they should meet up. He had also been very insistent that Jack shouldn't tell anyone about the call or them meeting.

'Let's just keep this to ourselves,' he'd said. 'Let's just say it'll be to your benefit to do that.'

Another strange thing was that Strong had suggested they meet at a quiet country pub a few miles out of town. It wasn't one that Jack had been to before and he had to Google it to see exactly where it was. It certainly didn't sound like normal police procedure to Jack but he felt compelled to go to see what it was all about.

Jack arrived a few minutes late and as he entered the bar he looked around noticing that it was very quiet. He couldn't see DI Strong or anyone else that looked like a policeman so he ordered a drink for himself and sat down at one of the empty tables by the window. He put his coat over the back of his seat and took out his phone to see if he had any messages. A few minutes later he saw a car arriving and DI Strong get out of it, carrying a brown leather briefcase. He looked a bit older than Jack remembered, maybe a bit greyer but still tall and slim, almost lanky, Jack thought. He was on his own. Jack watched him enter the bar and as he made his way across, Jack put his phone away and shook DI Strong's outstretched hand as the policeman sat down at the table directly opposite him, laying his briefcase by his feet.

After a bit of general chit chat, Strong brought Jack up to speed on where the police were with their investigations into Pete's murder. He confirmed, as Jack already knew, that Andy Austin was the only suspect and that they believed he was suffering from some sort of post traumatic stress disorder following the car collision which was a contributory reason for his recent violent actions.

'So you're saying it was the accident, the bump he got, that's causing him to go around murdering people?' Jack asked.

365

'Well yes, we can't say for definite but it's a strong possibility. So you can see what that means Jack. It is likely that you hitting him with your car was the catalyst that set off this tragic chain of events,' Strong replied, looking straight in Jack's eyes.

Jack could feel himself going red and he looked down at the table as he spoke, clasping his hands and trying to avoid Strong's stare.

'But there's nothing I can do about that. It was an accident. I wasn't to know the bloke was going to go mental was I? Why are you saying that? I don't get it,' Jack blurted out.

DI Strong maintained his gaze on Jack.

'Well the thing is Jack, because things have escalated so much and the situation has become so serious, what with two murders, a couple of abductions and other stuff, it's caused us to have to look at things afresh, from a different perspective. Its standard police protocol, I'm sure you understand. We need to consider these things from a number of angles,' Strong replied, smiling as he spoke. He paused and Jack felt compelled to speak.

'I guess you have to investigate everything yes,' Jack said, 'but I don't understand what that means for me. Why are you telling me this now?' Jack was feeling uncomfortable and not sure where this meeting was going. Although he hadn't known what to expect from Strong, it certainly wasn't this.

'Hang on,' Strong replied, 'I'm just going to grab a drink, do you want another one?' he asked Jack.

'What, no, no thanks,' Jack replied.

DI Strong got up and walked slowly over to the bar. He could see Jack was getting anxious and so he wanted to let him sit there for a bit on his own to worry a bit more. He took his time in ordering a drink and then took a couple of sips before turning around and walking slowly back to re-join Jack at the table. He sat down, stretched out his legs, took another sip of his drink and looked out of the window.

'Nice day, isn't it' Strong said calmly, 'hopefully the worst of the winter is past now.'

Jack was confused and keen to restart their previous conversation.

'Look it's been good to get an update on where you are with the case and I really hope you catch Austin soon,' Jack started, 'but I'm a bit confused as to why you wanted to meet to tell me that, and why we're meeting here in some pub in the middle of nowhere and not at the station or even my house?'

'Okay, let me explain Jack,' DI Strong replied, smiling. 'Some new evidence has come to light which could potentially change things.'

'What… new evidence?' Jack asked anxiously, rubbing his beard and fearing what might come next.

'Well it's still confidential and I probably shouldn't be telling you this, which is why I asked you to meet me here, but I like you Jack and I want to give you the benefit of the doubt,' Strong replied.

'Benefit of the doubt, what doubt, what do you mean?' Jack responded, pushing his chair back slightly.

'Well, and this must stay between me and you Jack, but it appears there may have been a connection between Austin and one of your family prior to the, emm… accident,' Strong replied.

Jack felt himself slump down in his seat. All his weight seemed to be sinking to the floor and it was an effort to pull himself up again. Shit, he thought, shit he knows. Somehow he knows about Austin and Sarah and he's put two and two together and thinks I deliberately mowed down Austin and his family in revenge. But how could Strong know?

Shit, they must have found a photo of Austin and Sarah together or maybe some of the texts or emails she'd sent him, Jack guessed. When Austin had run from Jack at the farm he must have left his phone or laptop and the police will have gone through it. That's how they would have found out about Austin and Sarah. What was it Strong had said before, at Pete's funeral, something about not believing in coincidences. That was it. So when he'd found the connection between Sarah and Austin and then all that had happened since, he'd concluded that Jack's accident wasn't really an accident.

Jack just sat there, his heart racing, not knowing what to say or do now. The tall policeman sat across from him watching.

'So the thing is Jack,' Strong spoke, filling in the silence, 'Austin isn't going to stop now. He's on a mission, whether it's because of the bump on his head or something else, we know he is going to come back and finish the job. Which isn't good news for you or your mates. Somehow he needs to be stopped.'

'But surely you'll catch him at some point, won't you? You always said you would,' Jack asked hopefully, glad that the detective seemed to have forgotten about the accident for now.

'Yes, I believe we will,' Strong replied, 'but what then Jack, if we do? No doubt the whole story will come out then and the police will be obliged to look into the full circumstances including the original accident and what might have led up to that. I've no doubt Austin will be happy to fill in the detail.'

Jack's mind was racing, trying to play catch up and make some sense of everything that had happened over the last few minutes. What was Strong saying exactly and why was he telling him all this now? If they had suspicions that it wasn't really an accident why weren't they questioning him about it in the police station? None of this made any sense to Jack. He realised Strong had begun talking again and he refocused his attention back on the detective.

'So that's our dilemma Jack,' he was saying, 'we either catch Austin and that opens up a whole can of worms which I'm sure you wouldn't want to happen. Or, we don't catch him and he comes back at some point and carries on killing you and your mates' families. Neither of these, I'm sure you will agree, are a pleasant outcome.'

Once again Jack just sat staring at the detective not able to think of anything to say. He felt like he was tightly bound to the seat, his whole body was heavy and he didn't think he could move. As Strong had just said, it looked like whatever happened it was going to be disastrous for Jack. Prison or more killings, what a choice!

Strong had sat back in his chair, letting Jack consume everything he'd just told him. Letting him chase it around in his mind and knowing he'd be feeling desperate. He waited a few seconds more and then spoke again.

'Having said that Jack, there may be another option. But I don't know if it would work.'

'What do you mean, another option, what?' Jack replied; keen to hear something different to what he was now thinking.

'Well, we've discussed the police catching him, or not catching him, neither of which turn out well for you,' Strong said. 'But what if someone else finds him, not the police, and persuades him to stop? That could be a better outcome.'

Jack thought for a second then replied.

'But what, what, … persuades him, what do you mean?' Jack asked, confused by the detective and this new turn of events.

'Look Jack, let me make it clear for you. Austin is a killer, he has already murdered twice. He killed your brother Jack, slit his throat, and he is going to kill again, unless someone stops him. You must know that. Why did you go to the farm that day, Jack, what were you planning to do? What would you have done if you'd caught him? Had a chat with him….or taught him a lesson, given him a taste of his own medicine?'

'I, I , I don't know. I thought about it but…' Jack replied remembering how he'd had the chance to stop Austin that day, but he'd blown it. Maybe he should have just hit him and ended it all then but it hadn't felt right.

While Jack was mulling this around in his head, Strong reached down to his briefcase and took out a plain brown envelope. He placed it on the table between himself and Jack, before slowly sliding it across in Jack's direction.

'Here's some information you may find useful,' the detective said.

Jack looked at the envelope, not quite sure what to do until Strong nodded towards it which he took as a sign that he should open it. He picked it up and took out two sheets of paper. The first sheet was a photocopy of a passport photo. The image looked similar to that of Andy Austin but instead the name beside it read Timothy Samuel.

Jack put it down and looked at the second sheet. He scanned it quickly and saw that it was a print-out from the holiday rental site, Airbnb. It showed the address of a house in Spain and underneath the address there were directions detailing how to get there from Barcelona Airport. He put it down on top of the other sheet and looked across at DI Strong. The detective was staring at him intently.

'Austin needs to be stopped Jack. There's only one way. You know what I mean,' Strong said. Then leaning forward, Strong added quietly but clearly.

'This time you need to finish the job,' and he stood up and walked out the pub.

Jack stayed sitting, not moving and not sure what to do next. He didn't want to look out the window but he saw Strong drive off out of the corner of his eye. A few minutes after that Jack was back out in the car park and he'd never been more happy to leave a pub in his life. When he'd got the call from Strong he'd never imagined in his wildest dreams that this was how it would turn out. He could feel his shirt sticking to his back with sweat as he got in his car. He sat down with a big sigh and gripped his steering wheel tightly. He put the envelope and his jacket down on the passenger seat and took his mobile phone from his jacket pocket. He looked at the screen and then pressed the big red button to stop the recording.

He hadn't been sure why Strong had wanted to meet with him but now he knew the reason and he was really glad he'd got every word of it on his phone. Jack knew he couldn't kill Austin, it wasn't in his bones to kill anyone, even someone like Austin. He'd realised that when they'd met at the farm. The car accident had truly been an accident, Jack had convinced himself of that.

If DI Strong knew where Austin was then Jack knew, when Strong realised he wasn't going to do what he wanted, that Strong and the police would have to arrest Austin themselves. Then, at that point, when the time was right, when he needed it, if and when DI Strong came knocking again, he knew this recording would be his safety net.

<u>Chapter 45</u>

'This is the main living area, it's all very modern looking. The owner recently refurbished the whole apartment but I think you can see he spent a lot of time on making this area as good as he possibly could.' There was no response and so the estate agent led his client through to the kitchen.

'As you can see the kitchen is all newly done too with a built in dishwasher and washing machine,' he indicated with an outstretched hand, 'all mod cons.' Again, no reply.

'Out the back, you can see the garden, very quiet and private and the workshop is down the bottom, just behind the trees. Do you want to have a look?' he asked his client who had been very quiet so far and unusually hadn't asked any questions. Usually people renting a place had all sorts of questions, normally about who would fix things if they went wrong, but this guy seemed almost disinterested. Weird.

'No, its fine, I saw it on-line, can I move in straight away?' the man finally spoke.

'Erm yes, just let me check,' the estate agent replied, shuffling through his papers. 'We'll need to do a few bits of admin first but I think its ready to go. The landlord is looking for £750 a month with a month's deposit in advance but I think he'd be willing to move on that a bit if you wanted to make an offer.'

'£750 is fine,' the man replied, pushing up his sunglasses, his head pounding, 'I'll pay six months up front in cash, or at least I mean by direct transfer, just to get it all out of the way.'

He wanted to get rid of the estate agent as quickly as possible. His headaches were getting worse and more frequent and right now he desperately needed to take some more pills and just sit down somewhere quiet.

'Ah, ok, that's great then. I'll let him know. I'm sure he'll be pleased. I just need to get some proof of identification from you. Do you have your passport with you?' the estate agent asked.

The man opened the leather briefcase he was carrying and took out a passport, handing it over to the estate agent.

When DI Strong had given him a contact number for the man he knew who could arrange forged documents he'd also used that network to find another forger prepared to do the same. He knew he might need a second option as part of a back-up plan. Although DI Strong had been incredibly helpful to him, he realised early on in their discussions that Strong wouldn't have been

375

expecting him to have gone as far as he did so he'd not told Strong of the full detail of his plans for revenge on Jack Wilson and his mates. If the detective had known then he'd probably not have agreed and now it had happened, he felt sure that the big detective might now be trying to stop him going any further. He had known all along that he'd have to stay one step ahead of Strong just in case that happened. This was always going to be down to him and him alone. He'd known he couldn't totally rely on anyone else to let him see it through to the end. And he wasn't at the end yet. They all needed to suffer in the way that he had suffered - and he was running out of time.

'That's excellent that you're paying it all up front, Mr Craig' the estate agent laughed, 'Its always easier for us if we have the money straightaway.' Not to mention my commission, he was thinking as he spoke.

'It also cuts down on all the admin and having to chase people for the rent. You wouldn't believe some of the excuses we hear. When they sign the lease you think butter wouldn't melt, but a couple of months later they're coming up with all sorts of reasons for not paying. You just don't know who you can trust.'

The man had gone quiet again and didn't say anything in response. In truth, he was being as awkward as he could, hoping the estate agent would take the hint and just go. However the estate agent wasn't quite finished yet.

'Ok, Mr Craig, all that's left to do is just for you to sign this document….here,' he said handing the man a silver pen and pointing at the document on the kitchen work surface, '….and then here. I'll send you a copy back through the post. I really hope you enjoy your six months living here,' he said, pocketing his pen and handing the man a set of keys.

The estate agent finally started to make his way to the door. As he reached it, he turned back to face the man again.

'It'll be Christmas soon, do you have any plans for it?' he asked.

'Yes there are a couple of things I plan to do,' the man replied, closing the door before the estate agent could ask anything more.

The Anniversary

Also by Ian Anderson:

Jack's Lottery Plan

This is the funny and moving story of Jack Burns, just a normal bloke with a simple dream to get a flat with his girlfriend, Hannah, and help her become the great actress he knows she really is. One day he finds out that a friend has secretly won the lottery and is going to share the winnings with his ten best friends. Jack embarks on a clandestine plan to become one of those ten so that he can get the money to help achieve his, and Hannah's, dreams. But his plan goes hopelessly wrong impacting Jack and his friends in ways he would never have imagined.

For further information please visit the author website below:

www.ianandersonhome.wixsite.com/ianandersonauthor

Printed in Great Britain
by Amazon

86853890R00222